BURNED BY THE MAFIA KING

MAFIA KINGS
BOOK FIVE

BELLA MOONDRAGON

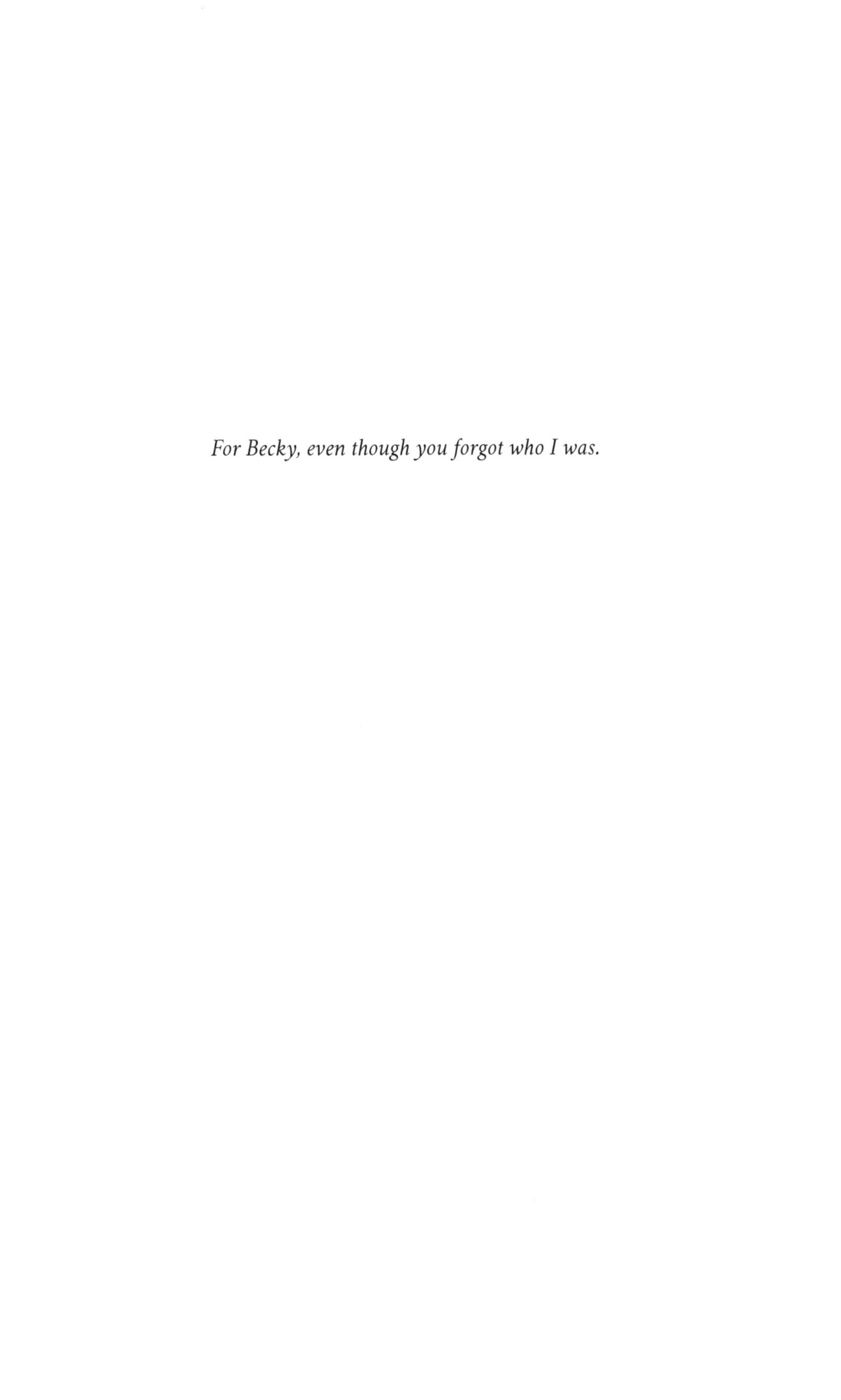

For Becky, even though you forgot who I was.

CONTENTS

1

BURNING HISTORY

HEIDI

ORGANIZING BOOKS HAS ALWAYS BEEN ONE OF MY FAVORITE THINGS TO do in the bookstore ever since I started working with my grandparents. This is where I feel most comfortable, pretending life doesn't exist outside of these walls.

This store has been in my family for decades–*generations*. My grandfather passed his passion for books, and his love for this store, onto me. And as soon as I was old enough to work, I started helping him. Just a few stories above the bookstore, my grandparents have a shabby little railroad style apartment that they've lived in for over forty years. My mom was raised there, and when she passed away, I moved in with my grandparents, learning the tricks of my grandfather's trade.

I'm a very lonely person, but I don't say that in a negative way. I have my grandparents, but other than that, books have always been my only friends. I've never made real friends in school or college, so I spend most of my time with fictional characters instead.

The best time of my day is when the shop closes and the

customers leave, so I have the place all to myself. I always put on some classical music so I can hum to it while I gather the books spread across the store and put them back on their respective shelves.

Tonight is an exceedingly cold Christmas Eve in New York City, and I'm glad I decided to put on a fluffy sweater before I left home this morning. My grandparents are upstate at a Christmas party tonight, and it's already dark, and even though this is my favorite place in the entire world to be, there always seems to be something trying to steal my peace.

This happens practically every night because of the stupid bar across the street. It's always noisy, their customers and workers often deciding to go out on the sidewalk to drink, smoke, and chat loudly as if the whole city doesn't mind hearing them.

That would be the only thing I would change in my daily life if I could change anything at all. I know New York City is not exactly what anyone would call a calm and peaceful place, especially not during Christmastime, but still, inside my store I manage to get the peace I need... if it wasn't for those sulky, sullen drunks across the street.

I don't even understand why anyone would choose to go to that particular bar in the first place. It's not like there's anything special about it. In fact, every single person I've ever seen over there is scary. And suspicious. I would never exchange a night surrounded by my books and a good cup of hot chocolate to hang out in that kind of establishment.

Tonight, in particular, they are unbelievably loud.

What the hell is going on over there?

I peek through the front window, a pile of books in my hands, and narrow my eyes at the dimly lit sidewalk. There seems to be a commotion happening on the other side of the street, or maybe the group of men standing around are just having an exciting night. I can't really tell from here.

That's when I notice that one of them seems to be staring at the store, or better yet, at me.

I don't recall seeing him before, or maybe I have. They all look the same to me from a distance, always wearing dark clothes and sunglasses during the day, as if they're celebrities. At night, there's not enough light to tell them apart from here, even without their sunglasses.

I've never really paid much attention to them, if I'm being honest. I do my best to ignore their presence and focus only on my store, hoping they won't disturb my clients, or *me*. If we stay out of each other's ways, I can pretend they are nothing more than a rock in my shoe.

There seems to be something different about this guy, though. His gaze is so intense, even from across the street, his build so masculine, suddenly my thoughts go somewhere they shouldn't.

I'm probably just reading too many steamy romances lately.

I shake my head, shoving away those thoughts, adjusting my glasses, and preparing to go back to my task. But something catches my attention before I get back to work.

A car comes flying down the street, its tires screeching on the asphalt as it comes to a halt in front of the bar. Everything happens so fast that I can't even make sense of what's going on until it's all over.

I hear noises–gunshots–then another car shows up. A man's hand shoots out of the tinted window and drops something, then a loud blast shakes the entire block.

Broken glass explodes around me. I hit the ground, throwing the books I'm holding onto the floor and using my arms to protect my head. My ears ring, and I smell something burning, but it takes me several seconds to react.

When I look up, my eyes widen with terror as I see the shelves close to what used to be the front window entirely on fire.

"No, no, no!" I gasp, my voice barely audible over the screams from the people outside.

I'm shocked, paralyzed, unable to make myself move. I have no idea who caused this, or whether my store was the target or the bar,, but I can't think of what to do next. My brain yells at me to run away, to get out of this place before it crashes down on me, but my heart is aching for the books, the memories, the history about to be lost….

This is my family's life's work. It will shatter my grandfather to know it was destroyed in the blink of an eye.

How can I do nothing and leave it all behind to burn to the ground?

But then, what can I possibly do to stop it?

I look around, watching as the fire licks the pages of hundreds of stories. My favorite novels begin to be swallowed up by flames. I see the children's book section catching next and imagine all those colorful illustrations melting on the pages.

A loud crash close to the front door pulls me out of my spiraling moment, and I snap my head in that direction, wondering if something hit us again. But then I notice that part of the ceiling has fallen in, blocking my closest exit.

"This can't be happening," I cry to myself, my heart beating so fast that I feel it against my rib cage.

What do I do now?

I head for the backdoor, forcing my legs to obey my commands, and when I get there, I realize that it is also blocked by a toppled shelf that must've fallen over when the ground shook from the explosion.

"Shit," I mumble, frantically looking around for a way to escape this nightmare. Frantically, I run back to the main part of the store.

My eyes land on the broken window. It might be the only way for me to save myself, but there's so much smoke and fire that I can't be sure if it is safe.

What if I try to escape that way and catch myself on fire?

Panicking, I stop in the middle of the store, tears pricking my eyes. It's getting harder and harder to breathe by the second, and my throat feels like I just swallowed a handful of glass. I cough, pulling my elbow up to block my nose from inhaling the thick smoke.

But it's already too late. I can feel it.

My vision is starting to blur, and my hearing is fading away as if I'm drowning in a deep, gray ocean.

All by myself.

There's no one to save me.

I'm all alone.

This is how I'm going to die? Not even knowing who killed me? At twenty-five years old?

I have so many things I still wanted to do! I have no friends, no boyfriend, nothing to call my own.

What kind of life is that?

What about my grandparents? Who will take care of them if I'm not around anymore? I'm the only family they have left. Will they be able to move on without me?

My knees buckle under me, and I fall to the floor, falling into the abyss…

Then, I catch a quick movement out of the corner of my eye. A large form appears through the smoke. At first, I think it must be an angel, even though he looks nothing like the ones I've read about in books.

Am I dead already?

Or maybe this is nothing more than a nightmare. It's nice to think I might actually be safe at home in my bed.

But everything feels so real right now….

The silhouette of the man rushes in my direction, and even though I can't see his face, I know now that he is not an angel. Not in the literal sense of the word.

Could it be a firefighter? Maybe someone on the street saw the store burning down and called for help?

Strong arms pull me up like I weigh nothing. I barely understand what's happening, my eyes and body are too heavy for me to think clearly, but I do manage to murmur something that I hope sounds like "Thank you."

I know I'm being carried out, or maybe this really is an angel taking me to whatever afterlife awaits me, but at this point, the smoke won't allow my eyes to focus, and I'm falling in and out of consciousness.

The only thing I'm aware of before blacking out completely is a deep, hoarse voice saying, "Don't thank me yet, sweetheart."

And then everything goes pitch black.

2

HOLIDAY ATTACK

FIVE MINUTES EARLIER...

CAL

"COME ON, BOSS. LET'S GO OUTSIDE. I NEED TO HAVE A SMOKE," SAM grumbles as he brushes past me. "People are fucking crazy tonight. I can't deal with this sober."

I actually agree with him. The bar is fucking crowded tonight, and truthfully, I could use a smoke too. I need to breathe some fresh air besides the smell of alcohol and sweat for a change.

It doesn't usually bother me, but some days it's hard to run this sort of business. Christmas Eve is one of them.

I follow Sam outside, pulling my pack of cigarettes out of my pocket and lightning one up, offering it to light Sam's next. I shouldn't be smoking. I quit a long time ago, but with all the cartel bullshit we've been dealing with this year... I'm back to old habits.

"I don't know why they have to be so loud all the fucking time," he continues to complain.

"They're just lonely, sad people who have too much shit to deal with during the holidays," I explain darkly. "It's just easier to drown themselves in alcohol and drugs, isn't it?"

Sam shrugs, taking a puff from his cigarette. "I don't know, Boss. I can think of thousands of things I'd rather be doing. Camping, road trips, going 'cross the pond to visit my ma… even just staying in my own bed the whole day…." He trails off.

"For someone who likes it quiet and peaceful, you chose the worst line of work to pursue, don't you think?" I tease with a grin on my face.

We both lean against the side of the building near our motorcycles parked by the sidewalk, watching as the cars pass by on the street. The night is fucking cold, and the streets are bustling with people walking in and out of stores to buy their last minute Christmas gifts.

I've always loved this side of New York City. There's always something going on. The city never sleeps.

My eyes dart toward the bookstore across the street, noticing the lights are still on despite the 'Closed' sign on the door. I take a puff of my cigarette, my gaze never leaving the woman inside while she moves piles of books from one shelf to another, making sure everything is in the right place.

I've lost count of how many times I've watched her do this. I've become mesmerized by the way she looks, the way she moves, the way she scrunches her nose whenever something happens that she doesn't like, and how she seems to be in her own little world whenever she's left alone inside the shop.

She is so painfully *beautiful*. Her long, light brown hair falls down to her hips making me wonder what it'd feel like to tangle my fingers in it. She has these ocean blue eyes that make me want to be the subject of their attention for a change.

I don't even have a thing for bookworms, but I constantly find myself attracted to her tortoise shell plastic framed glasses that insists on sliding down her nose whenever she looks down.

I've only seen her up close once, when I finally grew the balls I needed to step into her cozy little bookstore two weeks ago and pretend like I was doing some Christmas shopping. She barely looked me in the eye when I slapped a stack of random cookbooks on the counter. I noticed that she has a small scar on her right cheek that makes me desperate to know more about her life. I want to know what happened to give her that unique blemish on her beautiful porcelain skin.

"Careful not to drool, Boss," Sam teases beside me, and I snap my head to look at him, narrowing my eyes in a threatening way.

He raises his hands in surrender, but the grin on his lips still makes me want to punch it off his stupid face.

"Sorry, Boss. You're just making it too obvious," he adds.

"About what?" I growl, puffing smoke into the cold night air

"You wanting to fuck the book girl," he explains, gesturing at the store.

"What I really want is to beat you into a pulp and teach you how to mind your own fucking business," I retort, biting back a smile when I see him flinch.

It's clear to me he doesn't really think I'd do that, but he should know that he overstepped. However, it's not the first time I have one of my closest men teasing me about something, and I'm sure as hell it won't be the last.

I'm annoyed because he's right.

I don't know what it is about that girl that makes me so obsessed with her without even knowing her name, but ever since I laid eyes on her, I can't force myself to look away whenever she's around.

Women were never a problem for me. If anything, I don't think I ever had one of them refuse to give me the attention I wanted or needed, but with this girl, it's different. I don't think she even knows I exist.

She comes and goes, making sure she pretends my bar isn't even here.

Shaking my head, I shift my attention somewhere else. My eyes roam along the street, watching couples walking together, tourists taking pictures of the Christmas decorations, families having fun with the thin snowflakes falling from the sky.

Then something makes my stomach turn.

I spot a black car with tinted windows speeding down the street. It wouldn't be uncommon in New York to see crazy drivers, especially during the holidays, but I know this isn't one of those buzzed lunatics leaving an office Christmas party.

The tires screeching make my skin crawl as I watch the vehicle coming to a halt in front of the bar, the back window rolling down.

Before I have time to process what's going on, gunshots fire. It takes me a split second to realize the men inside the car are firing at the bar, at us. Letting my cigarette fall to the ground, I grab my gun from the holster in my belt and aim at whoever's inside that damn vehicle while hiding behind a car parked right on the curb.

Screams from passersby ring through my ears, and I clench my jaw, pissed that whoever came for us is being so reckless as to start shooting in an open space, with innocent people so close and unable to protect themselves.

"Keep your heads down!" I yell at my men who come running out of the bar like cockroaches fleeing from a sewer as soon as they hear the gunshots.

From my peripheral vision, I see some of them shouting at the scared onlookers, guiding them inside nearby stores. I'm glad they didn't think of taking them inside our bar. At first, it might seem like a good idea, but I have no clue who is aiming at us and what they intend to do next.

I fire back when a bullet misses my ear by an inch, unsure of where it came from. Another car stops behind the one already parked in front of my establishment, and more men start firing at us.

"These motherfuckers are cowards," Hunter growls as he drops to the ground next to me. He's one of my best shooters.

"Is everything okay inside?" I ask, not taking my eyes off our enemies. The bastards really are fucking cowards, since they are attacking us from inside a bulletproof car.

"Yeah, we took everyone to the basement," he tells me.

Good, at least none of my customers were hit or injured. Yet.

My mind spirals as I try to think of the best way to end the chaos and prevent innocents from getting involved in a mafia war that I have no idea who just started. I can't say I have a lot of enemies, but I also can't say I have just one.

I don't know who's attacking us. They have their faces covered, so I don't recognize a single one of them, nor their cars.

I look over the parked car, and that's when I notice one of the assholes sticking his arm out of the car window, holding a fucking Molotov cocktail.

"Watch out!" I warn, but it's in vain.

Hunter has already seen the guy and shoots him in the arm as he winds back to throw, making the cocktail fall on the opposite side of the vehicle away from us. It's rolling toward the other side of the street.

In the direction of the bookstore.

"Fuck!" is all I have time to hiss before a loud explosion momentarily blinds and deafens me.

The entire front window of the bookstore shatters, and the books on display instantly catch on fire. In just one second, the glass transforms into a curtain of flames preventing me from seeing what's happening inside.

I can't see the girl anymore.

Was she hit? Is she okay? Is she….

I can't finish the sentence in my head. The idea of it makes me sick to my stomach.

"Boss, are you all right?" Sam calls from behind a bullet ridden trash can, squatting down to protect himself. He has blood running down his forehead, but I'm glad to see it's not from a bullet. It's probably a scrape from shattered glass.

I nod, swallowing the lump in my throat, too worried to think about anything else. I snap my head to the bookstore again, just in time to see the cars vanishing from my sight, speeding down the street as if they were never here in the first place. The sound of sirens splits the air.

"I'm going to check on the girl in the bookstore," I inform Hunter and Sam, who are the closest to me at the moment. "Get the hell out of here. Now" I order before darting across the street, not thinking twice about approaching the huge flames threatening to engulf me.

3

DAMAGE CONTROL

NORMALLY, I'D HESITATE BEFORE JUMPING THROUGH A CURTAIN OF flames. Even to save someone's life. If it was one of my men in there, what would I do? I wouldn't think twice before trying to save them.

Why am I seriously considering letting that pretty girl die by herself, a victim of something she shouldn't even be involved with in the first place?

That thought seems to renew my determination, and finding a breach in the fire, I climb through the broken window and step inside the store, immediately covering my nose with my arm.

The place is a fucking mess already, thick black smoke covering the tall shelves of books.

I look around, frantically searching for the woman who was in this exact spot a few minutes ago.

Did she manage to escape before the explosion? Did she even see it coming?

The front door and the back door seem to be blocked, so I don't see how she could've escaped in time to avoid the fire.

I wish I knew her name so I could call for her, but when I was in here a few days ago, I didn't ask, and she wasn't wearing a name tag.

Through the noises of paper and wood burning, I hear a faint cough, and my head snaps in that direction, desperate to find its source.

It's getting harder to breathe in here, and the last thing I need is to also become a victim who needs to be rescued—or worse.

I toss aside some barriers in my way–chairs, tables, and even a couple of burning bookshelves–and that's when I spot her, a few feet away from me, surrounded by fire. I can't see her clearly, but by the way she's sucking in air, I can only imagine she is about to pass out. Or maybe she's hurt. Either way, there's no way in hell either of us are making it out unless I act now.

She doesn't seem to notice me when I approach. Or, maybe she does, but her eyes aren't able to focus on me. I have no time to ask how she's feeling or if she's injured because the next thing I know, she's falling to the floor, barely conscious.

I launch forward, reaching for her, my arms scooping up her tiny frame off the floor. I lift her, noticing she weighs next to nothing, and turn back. I need to get her out of here before this place fucking collapses on both of us. She mutters something that sounds like, "Thank you."

All I can think to say in response is, "Don't thank me yet, sweetheart."

The only way out is back where I came in–the front window. Both doors are blocked, and I don't have time to try and find another escape route. Sirens wail; flashing lights begin to cut through the smoke. Any second now, the fire department is going to swarm this place, blasting us with water to try to save the levels upon levels of businesses and apartments above the bookstore. I have to get her out. I have to get myself out and far away from any cops.

Climbing out of the window with her in my arms while diverting the flames proves to be a bit harder than I anticipated, but luckily, I manage to do just that. As soon as my feet touch the sidewalk, I sprint around the corner of the building, away from the approaching sirens.

That's when I hear another crash behind me, and looking through the windows on the side of the shop, I notice that part of the ceiling fell just where we were a couple of seconds ago.

I inhale sharply, taking in all the fresh air I can get. I look down, searching for any sign of her breathing. Her chest goes up and down, although so slowly that I fear her situation can get worse soon.

"Get the fuck out of here!," I yell at Hunter and Sam who are both watching from the alley across the street.

I change my mind about trying to get out the back since half my men are still milling around. Instead, I rush to the bar, cutting back through the alley and across the street under the shadows cast by the fire trucks swarming the street. With the young woman in my arms, I storm inside so I can lay her down and assess the damage.

She groans in my arms, and that is enough to spike my hope that she's okay. "Hey, I need you to stay here with me," I urge, seeing her struggle to open her eyes. "You'll be fine. We'll get you to the hospital in no time," I tell her, although I doubt she can hear me or make sense of what I'm saying.

The commotion inside the bar is overwhelming, and now that my men have allowed the customers to finally leave, after guaranteeing that it's no longer dangerous outside, people dart out of the bar, screaming and bumping into each other on their way out.

Hunter comes inside with his phone in hand. "Your car's running. We gotta get out of here, now," he informs me.

The girl groans in my arms again, and my heart shrinks, imagining she might be in pain. I try to look for injuries again, now with the dim light of the bar making it a bit easier to study her. But she's wearing a thick sweater and jeans, so I can't tell if she's wounded or if we only need to worry about smoke inhalation.

"Are you okay? Were you hit? Or burned?" I ask, but to no avail. She doesn't answer me, her eyes rolling to the back of her head.

"Who did this?" I turn to Hunter, trying to keep desperation out of my tone now that she's fainted.

He shrugs. "Some of the lads went after them. But we haven't heard from them yet," he explains.

Before I have the chance to ask Hunter for more details, a trio of ambulances skid to a stop right outside the bar, paramedics darting into the darkened, smoke-filled street.

My brain rewires itself, pushing past my normal aversion to cops–feds in general–and I rush to the sidewalk with the girl still in my arms.

I scream at one of the paramedics to get his attention. He whirls, looking at me, then the soot-covered woman limp in my arms. He motions me over, but whatever he's shouting at me is blurred by the sirens and the violent spray of water as the fire department drenches her book shop.

I lay her down on a stretcher next to him, making sure I'm as gentle as possible so as not to hurt her even more. She's still unconscious, but I can see her chest moving, so I'm holding onto that.

The paramedics rush to her side to assist her with first aid, and I turn away from the ambulance, finding a police officer and a paramedic waiting for me. Another set of police officers are interviewing Sam and Hunter a few feet away from us, and I prepare myself for the questions I might not have answers to. I shoot them a glare that screams, *"Watch your fucking mouths!"*

We have some cops in our pockets, but nothing like the Saints. My guys know to be weary, however. Right now, we're the victims, and we have to let these guys do their jobs… while we plot how to do ours and clean up this mess our way.

"Were you the one who rescued the woman?" the paramedic asks. "Can you provide us with some details of what happened? Was she hit by something?"

I shake my head. "I don't know. I went–I went inside. She was in the bookshop. By the time I got in, she was surrounded by fire. I imagine she inhaled a lot of smoke, but I don't know if she was hit by anything. She–she was near the front window when the explosion happened."

The paramedic nods, having already gotten what he needs from me and rushing to the ambulance so they can leave for the hospital.

The officer keeps staring at me, though, as if he's waiting for more information.

"We were attacked by a gang or maybe an angry customer, I can't really tell," I add before he asks, being as careful as possible so as not to lie but to also not give away too much information about my line of business. I don't need the police snooping around my establishment any more than they have to.

"Did they attack the bookstore as well?" the officer presses, narrowing his eyes at me suspiciously.

"No. Not intentionally, I mean. They were trying to hit my bar with the explosive, but somehow it fell on the other side of the vehicle, hitting the bookstore instead." I leave out the information that one of my men was responsible for hitting the enemy's arm with a bullet, making him toss the Molotov cocktail in the wrong direction.

The officer doesn't seem to believe me, but I simply shrug, resolute.

"Is there anything else you can tell us to help us investigate this matter further?"

I don't like to be cornered like this, and I guess it's partially my fault for not finding out this attack was going to happen before it went down so we didn't catch this much attention, but right now, the only thing I can do is damage control.

I will deal with investigating who the enemies are later.

"Unfortunately, no. Everything happened too fast. I'm sure my employees already told you what they saw, which is pretty much the same as I did," I reply.

"I'd still like to hear your version of it, though," the officer presses.

I clench my jaw, a bit annoyed with this interrogation. But it's not like I can refuse to answer. That would only make him more eager to find out more about me and who attacked my bar.

So, taking a deep breath, I recount what happened.

He doesn't seem to be willing to believe everything I say, pressing for specific answers here and there, and I ponder demanding him to call his boss, who I know is on my payroll, but I don't want to make his life harder. I know he is only doing his job, and there is no way he can find out who attacked us with just the little information we've provided him with.

"Do you have a reason to believe a gang would attack you?" he asks, folding his arms across his chest.

He's testing me. Seeing if I'll slip. This fucker already knows who I am and who owns this bar. But I've been in this business for far too long to fall for his cheap tricks.

"I don't know," I answer with a shrug. "Lots of people come to my bar daily. Someone might have believed they weren't treated as nicely as they'd like and decided to pay us back. Who knows? People are so sensitive these days."

"Right...." The officer trails off, pulling out his notebook and writing something down.

I can't read what it is, but this seems to be enough of an interrogation for him, finally, because he looks up at me and nods, turning to meet his colleagues to move aside and discuss their findings as a group.

It seems we are all free to go, so we step back inside of the bar. "Do we have any clue who fucking did this yet?" I snarl under my breath, making sure no one else can hear us. I glance at the bookshop, at the furious flames still licking through the store.

The place looks like a fucking mess, and I can't help but imagine how distraught the book girl will be when she sees this.

If she survives, that is.

4

———

CHANGE OF PLANS

I OPEN MY EYES, STRUGGLING TO ADJUST TO THE BRIGHT, WHITE WALLS and ceiling surrounding me. I have a major headache, my eyes sting, and I feel a tightness in my chest that makes it hard to breathe.

I inhale sharply, and that makes me cough. A lot.

My throat burns, and when I think I can't handle it anymore, someone walks into my room, offering me a glass of water.

There's some sort of oxygen mask in the way, so I move it aside a bit and take the glass, gulping down the liquid, instantly feeling relief.

"How are you feeling?" the kind nurse asks in a sweet voice.

I cough a few more times and return the glass to her. She sets it on the table next to my bed.

"My chest feels heavy, and I have this awful headache. My throat is also bothering me, but other than that, I feel okay," I tell her.

"That's expected since you inhaled a lot of smoke. The doctor said you should recover soon, but you will need to spend the night in observation," the nurse explains.

That's when my memory starts to return, and I can picture every-

19

thing that happened—the store catching on fire, everything my family built gone in the blink of an eye…. Then I remember the angel who saved me from dying a terrible death.

Did he bring me to the hospital? Did anyone else get hurt?

I try to get up from the bed, but the nurse kindly pushes me back against the pillow.

"Take it easy. You might still be short of breath, so try not to exert yourself. You must get your rest," she advises. "I'll call the doctor in to see you. Your grandparents are also outside waiting to speak to you. I'll tell them that you're awake."

That makes me slightly calmer. Although, if they're here, I suppose they already know what happened. I don't know if I have the strength to face them. I can't see the look of sadness in my grandfather's eyes. I don't think I can handle it.

"Thank you," is all I manage to say before the nurse disappears out the door.

While I wait for the doctor to show up, I force my brain to remember details of what happened. My mind is a bit foggy, and my head hurts as if someone is pounding my skull from inside, but I remember the commotion at the bar in front of the store, then cars coming to attack the men leaning against the front entrance, and after that, the explosion.

I don't understand exactly what caused the explosion, but considering the bar frequently has suspicious customers, I guess there might have been a gang fight or something like that. Maybe someone had a disagreement with a person who works at the bar and went back to get revenge?

Who knows?

The only thing I know for sure, even though I can't prove it, is that the bar owners have something to do with this. I feel it in my gut. And even if they're the victims in this case, I will make sure they pay for the loss they made me and my family suffer.

The doctor arrives to check on me, interrupting my thoughts, but I can barely focus on what he's saying because there's too much going on in my own head. I picture different ways to approach those sulky men I assume own the joint once I'm released from the hospital.

Only my grandmother is able to pull me out of my own head when she shoots into the room as soon as the doctor leaves, her eyes filled with unshed tears.

"Oh, Heidi, honey," she cries as she comes to my side, grabbing my hand and squeezing it tight. "I'm so glad you're safe. You scared us to death!"

"I'm sorry, Granny," I reply with a hoarse voice. My throat still hurts, but I don't want to freak her out even more. I do feel better anyway, so I guess the worst has passed. "I'm so glad you and Grandpa weren't at home. I can't even imagine…."

I shiver just thinking about it. I barely made it out. I wouldn't have been able to get them out by myself if they had been there at the time of the explosion. The whole building was evacuated, from what I heard, and several of the upper apartments sustained damage. Thank God they were upstate.

Which reminds me…

"Is it Christmas already?" I ask, looking at the window. Thick curtains cover it, preventing me from seeing the city outside, so I don't know if it's night or day. "How long have I been out?"

"It doesn't matter. The only thing that matters is that you're alive," Grandma assures me, patting my hand.

"Where's Grandpa? The nurse said you were both waiting for me."

"He's speaking with the insurance company on the phone. He'll be here in a minute," she answers, pulling up a chair to sit beside me.

"Did they manage to save anything?" I don't want to hear the answer to that, but I can't lay here not knowing what happened.

She looks down at our clasped hands and shakes her head. "We lost everything. Even the apartment upstairs. It could be months before we can go back after all the smoke damage."

I swallow hard, fighting back the tears that sting my eyes. I won't cry in front of her. I don't want her to see how distraught I am. Or how guilty I feel, even though none of this was my fault.

I just can't bear the thought of them losing what they spent their entire lives building. I know they would hate to see me like that. I need to be strong for them, but the thought of losing our store, everything we ever owned, is overwhelming.

"I'm sorry you have to spend your Christmas in a hospital room with me," I say instead, an emotionless tone to my voice. I try to shoot her a soft smile to reassure her though.

"Oh, don't be silly, sweetheart. I'm just glad you're okay. And it's not like you'll spend the entire day here. The doctor said you'll be released in the morning, so we will still have time to have lunch together as a family," she retorts, leaning back in the chair and pulling her phone out of her purse. "I'll call your grandfather and tell him to come before visitor's hours are over."

He shows up ten minutes later, saying the insurance company is going to investigate the fire and let him know what will be covered and what won't be. I bite back a retort, not wanting to stress them even more. Grandpa seems irritated enough already.

"Your Aunt Janet has an extra bedroom at her apartment on the East Side," Granny says softly, her eyes full of pity. "I think you should stay there for the time being–at least while the old apartment is being cleaned out and the store is–the store is being salvaged." I can tell by the look on her face that there's nothing salvageable, but she continues, swallowing hard, "Remember how Grandpa and I were discussing moving upstate to that nice, little retirement community where our friends live? A spot opened up. We were going to decline, but… this feels like fate, now. I think it's time we move out of the city."

"But, what about the book shop?"

"Honey," she says gently, shaking her head. "It's a total loss. Even if the insurance company covers what we lost, I'm not sure we can rebuild in the same location… Not with all the bureaucracy with the city, and the owners of the building."

"So, that's it?"

"Maybe," she replies sadly. "Grandpa's doing what he can, trying to get a timeline in the event he can reopen the shop but he's old, Honey.

He–he hoped to pass the shop down to you, and he's still fighting for that."

"Then I'll stay. I'll stay and clean up this mess myself."

"Or, you could come with us, rest and recover in the clean air of upstate New York?"

"That won't be necessary, Granny. I appreciate the offer, but I'll do everything in my power to get our apartment and our store restored as soon as possible," I interrupt her kindly.

"You still need a place to stay until we figure out what to do," Grandpa intervenes, entering the room. "And it's not like you have money to restore the entire place by yourself. We will have to wait and see what the insurance company says about it. Darling, did you mention her Aunt Janet's open room?"

I hate feeling like my hands are tied. He's right. There's nothing I can do by myself. I don't have the money, I don't have the connections… I have nothing. I only have them. I only had the store.

"I hate to say it, but this feels like a fresh start, for all of us. Heidi, you've been taking care of us for far too long. Now you need to take care of yourself, live a little. Young women your age would have been out at parties on Christmas Eve instead of working their tails off–"

Grandpa's phone rings. He checks, mumbling something about how he needs to take it, and leaves the room.

I swallow past the obvious burns in my throat and turn my gaze to Granny. "I'm not giving up on the shop."

"I know," she whispers, patting my leg. "Once your grandpa figures out the insurance, it'll go… to you. We don't need it, and we have some money set aside to help you into your own place. It's not a lot, but while we love your old Aunt Janet, living with her… There's better out there."

"I can fix all of this, Granny. You and Grandpa won't have to go to the retirement home–not yet. We'll just–find a place to stay, together, and rebuild the shop–"

"We know that. And we really appreciate it. But you should live your life and not have to worry about us," she argues.

"Yes, I will always worry about you," I disagree. "If not me, then who? You'd do the same for me."

Granny grabs my hand, her eyes filled with love but also something else I can't quite name. "We'll feel much better knowing you're well on your own. We won't be here for much longer, and knowing you'll be fine by yourself is the best thing you can do for us right now," she explains.

I bite my lower lip, not wanting to cry and not wanting to imagine a world without them in it.

"Also, the retirement community we chose is outstanding. It has everything we could ever wish for. I guess it was a good idea to start saving money when we did so now we can afford something like this," Granny muses, smiling widely at me. "All of our friends are there, and it was time, Honey. Now it's time for you to move on, too."

I gulp, looking away from her. I can't look at her right now.

I hate that I can't give them a better life. I hate that I can't do anything to help. And I hate even more that I can't provide for them the way they have provided for me my entire life.

With renewed determination, I promise myself that, as soon as I'm out of this hospital, I'll do whatever I can to find whoever is responsible for the situation we're in and make them pay for this.

5

FIRST MEETING

CAL

*C*AL — no.

IT'S BEEN ALMOST A WEEK SINCE THE FIRE, AND EVERY DAY I'VE BEEN coming and going to the bar, sitting in the same chair in the corner, just across from the window where I can watch the bookstore that is now just a pile of ashes and burned wood on the other side of the street.

The police surrounded the place with yellow tape, which in my opinion serves no purpose; it only attracts more attention than the burnt out building already did by itself.

New Year's is around the corner, and ever since I saved that woman on Christmas Eve, I can't make myself relax or move past the explosion. To say I'm pissed would be an understatement.

My men still haven't figured out who attacked us, and even though I have my own suspicions, I can't act on instinct. I need proof to make a move. I can't afford to make more enemies by blindly attacking in the name of revenge.

Ever since that day, I haven't heard from *"Book girl"*. Hell, I don't even know if she survived. She hasn't come to check on the shop yet.

The day after Christmas, two women who looked like assessors from an insurance company stopped by the bookstore, but I didn't feel like they would know or want to tell me anything about their client's health if I asked.

I'm going crazy not knowing about her. I need some information–anything at all–about her well-being. I'm also worried that someone will come and mess with her shop, especially during this time of the year, so that's why I'm using my free time to keep an eye on things.

Or, at least, that's the excuse I've been telling myself so I don't feel more pathetic than I already do.

On that same day, two older people also showed up, but they barely spent two minutes on the sidewalk before leaving. I recognized them, but I never got to learn what connection they all have. If I could make a guess, I'd say they are the girl's grandparents and the owners of the bookshop.

That thought alone makes me feel even more guilt. Even though I've been trying to convince myself that none of this is my fault, I know better. I might not be directly responsible; I might not have been the one who caused their store to explode, but the fact that anything happened at all is because of *my* businesses.

Or the people who come after me *because* of it.

I have enemies, of course, like every businessman. However, my line of work makes the list longer and more dangerous than a regular bar owner would have.

And that's what makes me hate this situation even more.

"No signs of her yet, Boss?" my barkeep, Ian, asks from behind the counter where he wipes a glass with a white towel.

He, like all my other men, already knows I'm eager to see the woman I rescued. It's not really a secret that she interests me, but they also know I'm riddled with guilt about what happened.

She was the only victim of the attack on our side of the deal. Thankfully, no one else was injured, and that is a big relief. But the fact that someone innocent got hurt makes my skin crawl with anger.

I shake my head and clench my fist, not bothering to voice my answer.

"You think she survived? Maybe the lads could go to the closest hospitals and ask around?" Ian suggests.

We've all been keeping an eye on the store ever since the incident, taking shifts to make sure she doesn't come by the shop, and we miss her. I need to see her and talk to her. That will be the only way I'll be able to sleep better at night.

I've thought about searching for her at the hospitals, but I don't want to draw any more attention to myself or the situation. My men went to a lot of trouble to cover up the scandal online and on the news. I don't need people knowing my men went to the hospital looking for a victim.

Before I answer Ian, a yellow cab stops on the other side of the street, and a woman steps out. Her long, light brown hair whooshes behind her as she pauses by what used to be the front window, taking in the inside of the establishment.

She has her back turned to me, but I'd recognize her anywhere.

My heart skips a beat when I realize she's in one piece. She has a long black coat on, black boots, and a green scarf. When she turns to face the bar, I realize her soft cheeks are pink from the cold weather outside.

She also looks slightly different without her glasses on, and I have to admit, hotter than ever.

"Oh, there she is. And, well… if I had to guess, I'd say she's ready to kill someone," Ian points out from his spot behind the corner, and only then do I realize what he is talking about.

Bookgirl darts toward the bar with a deadly look on her face. Before I say anything, or even move out of my chair, she throws the front door open, letting it slam against the wall, and heads for the counter, her eyes focused on Ian.

"I want to talk to your boss right now," she snarls, pointing a finger at his chest.

He looks slightly amused at her approach, and I can't blame him. I've never seen so much emotion in her.

I can't deny that I like her feistiness.

I find myself stunned and positively surprised as I watch their interaction, and I wait to see if she notices my presence.

However, she seems too angry at the situation to even realize there's anyone else in the room, other than herself and the bartender.

"I'm sorry, lass. May I ask who's looking for him?" Ian replies, the corner of his lip ticking up as he watches her getting even more wound up by his answer.

"Just tell him he owes me a fucking new store. I don't care what he says, I'm not leaving this place until I see him," she retorts, folding her arms across her chest in a defying pose.

Ian's shoulders move slightly as he chuckles, and then his eyes dart to me.

I close my eyes and take a deep breath, chugging down the rest of the whiskey that's been in my glass untouched for more than an hour. Then, I finally stand, sauntering over to the counter to face the feisty woman for the first time in my life.

I've imagined this moment in my head before, more times than I'd like to admit, but nothing has prepared me for the way her intense eyes take me in as I approach her.

I've always known she had ocean blue eyes, even though I've always seen them through her glasses before now. But seeing them widen slightly as she notices I've been here the entire time does something to me that I can't explain.

My entire being stiffens as I get close to her. I'm so close that I notice the little freckles across her cheeks and nose for the first time.

Dark circles under her eyes make it evident that she's tired, but I can't blame her. She hasn't had it easy for the past few days.

It took me a couple of days to get my breathing back to normal, and I only stayed inside the shop for a couple of minutes while I rescued her.

The scar on her right cheek is a bit more evident from where I'm standing, and I have to force myself to look into her eyes instead. I'm so desperate to know how she got that scar, and I'm so angry with whoever or whatever caused it that I barely recognize myself.

"Anything I can help you with, *sweetheart*?" I ask by way of greeting.

This last word seems to spark something within her, and she creases her brow at me as if she recognizes me or something. I don't think she knows I'm the person who rescued her from the fire, and I'm not willing to provide that information to her either.

"Are you the owner?" she asks instead, her tone bitter and cold.

"I can be," I reply with a shrug. "If you calm down and explain to me what you need, I might be the person you're looking for."

"I'm not in the mood for riddles. Are you the owner of this place or not?" she insists, her jaw clenching as she struggles with her impatience.

It makes me want to laugh at how cute she is, but I fight against it. That would only work her up even more. As much as I enjoy the sight of her like this, I don't want her to storm out of the bar. Not yet.

"Yes, I am. Cal Duncan," I introduce myself. "Now, tell me your name and what I can do for you, lass."

6

SOMEONE TO BLAME

I WASN'T PLANNING ON BARGING THROUGH THE BAR DOOR ACROSS THE street when I left my aunt's apartment this morning. My initial goal was to stop by the bookstore and see if there was anything I could do to make the insurance company just give us the money faster so we can start rebuilding it as soon as possible, or at the very least, relocate.

They are taking so long to get back to us, to let us know what can and will be done to help us rebuild the store. I don't even know if they will pay us or not. I know that the end of the year is slow and bad to get things done, and no one is really making an effort to solve things quickly. Not to mention that getting someone to rebuild an entire establishment during the holidays won't be easy. If possible at all.

That's why I'm getting so worked up and anxious.

Other than the fact that I lost everything.

That's why, as soon as my eyes fell on what used to be my grandfather's biggest achievement in life, an anger I've never felt before washed over me. He's been trying to pretend he isn't as upset as I am, but I know my grandparents like the palms of my hands. Grandpa is just trying to make me feel less guilty.

And that is killing me.

My determination had already been renewed while I was still in the hospital and had promised myself I'd be the one fixing this mess, but when I got to see the real damages that were done by the fire, my mind went numb.

I saw red as I crossed the street with only one thought in my head.

To make the stupid owner of the bar pay for everything that was done to me and my family. I have no idea how I can prove he is directly responsible, but I can only hope he has some kindness in his heart to realize none of this is my fault, and therefore, I can't be expected to deal with it by myself.

As soon as I storm inside, the first person I see is the bartender behind the counter, wiping a glass, unbothered.

"I want to talk to your boss right now," I demanded, pointing my finger at his chest.

"I'm sorry, lass. May I ask who is looking for him?" he replies.

I might be imagining things, but he seems to be enjoying this more than he should. And that only makes me angrier than before.

"Just tell him he owes me a fucking new store. I don't care what he says, I'm not leaving this place until I see him," I bite back, crossing my arms determinedly.

He chuckles slightly and then his eyes dart to the corner of the bar where I see a man getting up from his chair and walking toward us.

Until now, I had no idea someone else was in the room with us. My eyes widen slightly as I realize I should've thought this through. The man coming in my direction doesn't seem to be a sweet and loving human being. If anything, he looks intimidating, gloomy, and scary in a way that has my angry, shattered heart skipping several beats.

He's wearing black pants, combat boots, and a leather jacket, his hands nonchalantly in his pockets as he stops in front of me and looks down at me.

"Anything I can help you with, *sweetheart?*" he asks with a thick accent.

Is he Irish? I've never realized it by seeing him from a distance before, but now it all makes sense. I've heard some of whom I assume are his men chatting on the sidewalk in the past, and most of them had the same accent.

However, I don't dwell too long on this because something else catches my attention.

He called me sweetheart. That is the only thing I remember hearing at the bookstore on Christmas Eve before I passed out.

Was he the angel who rescued me?

It can't be…

He looks so…so *fine.*

First of all, he is so tall that I need to look up to face him in a way that almost makes my neck hurt. He has curly, shoulder-length, dark red hair that's tied back into a loose, almost effortless, half-bun. Some strands hang free around his face, brushing his sharp jawline that is covered with a short, scruffy beard.

His nose is regal and straight with freckles scattered across it; his eyes are light brown, but they're so intense and honed on me that it makes me swallow hard.

Everything about him screams trouble. He looks dangerous and confident, and I swear there's this dark aura around him that I can't quite put my finger on, but instead of making me scared, it only makes me more curious about who this man is.

I've seen him before, sometimes even staring at the store, but never so close. I never got to realize how handsome and masculine he really is.

"Are you the owner?" I ask, ignoring the way my insides are turning with his proximity.

"I can be." He shrugs nonchalantly, his eyes hard on me. "If you calm yourself and explain to me what you need, I might be the person you're looking for."

"I'm not in the mood for riddles. Are you the owner of this place or not?" I press, gritting my teeth.

His eyes sparkle, not moving away from my face as he answers, "Yes, I am. Cal Duncan. Now, what can you tell me your name and what I can do for you, lass?"

"I'm Heidi Sullivan, from Sullivan Books," I inform him, pointing at my store across the street. "But I'm sure you already know that."

Cal raises his brows at me as if what I'm saying it's amusing to him.

"Does this sound funny to you?" I snarl, losing the grip on my patience. Why does he have to look so sarcastic?

"No, I'm just waiting for you to calm down and explain what you need. Also, you were a bit rude to my employee, so don't you think you owe him an apology?" he suggests, gesturing at the man behind the counter.

Shame washes over me, so abrupt and intense that I can feel my cheeks reddening.

I *was* rude to him. I barged in this place and yelled at him, even though he has nothing to do with my problems. If anyone does, it's his boss. Not him.

"I am truly sorry." I turn to him.

The man dismisses me with a hand gesture, but smiles softly at me. "Don't worry, lass. I'm used to way worse than that."

"Still, there's no excuse for my behavior. It's a pleasure to meet you, sir," I add, still embarrassed by my behavior.

"Likewise. I'm Ian, by the way. Can I get you anything, lass?" he offers.

I fell Cal's eyes on me, but I choose to keep my focus on Ian for now. I'm still feeling a bit uneasy with how my body is reacting to Cal's commanding presence.

"No, I'm fine, thank you. I don't intend to stay long," I reply, finally looking at Cal with what I hope it's a determined expression. "I just came to settle the issue with my shop being blown up. I hope your boss can fix it without causing too much problem."

Ian doesn't say anything else, and with my side vision, I see him fading into the background, quietly getting back to his tasks, leaving me and his boss to talk privately.

"I am truly sorry for what happened to your store, Mrs. Sullivan," Cal finally says.

"Miss," I correct.

His eyes darken, and I look away, my gaze falling on the book-store. It is a distraction, but I can't say it's a good one. I wish I didn't have to come here in the first place. I have no idea of what happened, I don't even know if I'm being fair to Cal, but I need to find the person responsible for this.

I need to hold onto anything that gives me hope because, right now, I have nothing.

In my mind, having someone to put the blame on will lessen my pain and my guilt. Even if it's not fair.

"Miss Sullivan," Cal continues. "Do you want to take a seat so we can have a polite conversation? I am all ears, and if there's anything I can do to help, I'll gladly do it."

He gestures for a table at the back of the bar, away from the windows and more reserved than all of the others.

I ponder not accepting his offer to talk. I am not even sure what I came here for. Do I want him to cover all the expenses? Do I simply want him to admit he is to blame?

What is it that I actually expect from him?

"It's just that…I…I lost everything," I blurt, unable to hold my emotions back. "I-I don't know what to do."

Tears prickle at my eyes, and I shake them away, wiping them aggressively with the back of my hand.

But one more look at Cal's intense eyes and all of my defenses collapse.

7

—————

UNEXPECTED FEELINGS

CAL

I HAVE NEVER BEEN GOOD WITH PEOPLE CRYING.

Let alone women.

To have Heidi sobbing in front of me was not something I was expecting to deal with after seeing how fiery and determined she looked a minute ago.

I don't know how to react. I don't know what to do to make her feel better.

The way the tears are pooling in her beautiful eyes is enough to make me want to go after whoever did that to her store and just make them disappear from the earth once and for all.

It's absurd how simply watching her cry is making me visit emotions I've never felt before.

She is trying to be strong, wiping the tears from her eyes aggressively, but one more look at me, and all her walls break down.

I glance at Ian, who's now pretending he isn't even here, and I consider what to do. I don't want to invade her privacy or do some-

37

thing she might find disrespectful, but I feel like she needs comfort right now.

And if I can do that for her, it might be worth a try.

"Come on, let's have a seat," I suggest in a low voice, putting my arm around her shoulders and guiding her toward the back table.

I pull the chair out for her and help her sit down, silently waiting as she recovers. She sniffles and wipes her nose in the cutest way possible, somehow managing to look hot while doing it.

I clench my jaw, cursing myself inwardly for thinking about the things I want to do to her at such a sensitive time.

Get a fucking grip, Cal.

Allowing her a moment to herself, I walk behind the counter and fill a glass of water for her. Placing it before her on the table, I sit in the chair across from her and lean back, folding my arms across my chest and waiting for her to feel ready to talk.

I don't want to press her, but I do want her to tell me everything she needs from me willingly.

Whatever I can do to help her, and lessen my guilt, I'll do it in a heartbeat.

Blue, beautiful, and intense eyes finally look up at me, and I gulp, slightly uneasy under her gaze.

"I'm sorry for acting like this. I'm not usually this... unstable," Heidi begins, her cheeks slightly pink from embarrassment.

I shake my head, dismissing her apology. "No need to apologize for anything. I completely understand where you're coming from."

Heidi clears her throat and shifts in her chair uncomfortably. Selfishly, I want to believe she's doing it because she's uneasy with my presence, in a good way, but I don't want to get my hopes up.

I can feel something in the way she looks at me, but it could also be a figment of my imagination. She's clearly not in her right state of mind, so I shouldn't be imagining such things.

"Now that you're calmer, do you mind telling me what it is you need from me?" I press softly.

"Well, I don't believe my shop was blown up by accident, not entirely at least," Heidi explains, the intensity in her eyes returning. "I mean, I saw a commotion happening outside your bar before everything exploded, so am I right to assume it is related to you, or one of your customers maybe?"

I narrow my eyes, trying my best not to scare her. I'm interested in her, more than I've ever been in a woman before, but I can't make a wrong move. I can't pretend I know everything about her. I can't tell her everything because, for all I know, she has no idea what type of life I lead.

I don't want her sticking her beautiful nose in the wrong place. Also, as much as it pains me to say it, I have no idea what her true intentions are. She seems like a great person, but the underworld has proven me wrong so many times before that I can't completely trust my instincts about her.

"You are right to assume that, yes," I reply simply.

Heidi stares at me as if she was expecting me to say anything other than that. "Uh, okay… well, then, can I ask what really happened?" she pries curiously. Nothing in her tone or body language tells me otherwise. I don't think she's asking for other reasons other than trying to understand what happened.

"We had an issue with a gang from the city. They attacked us. Cowardly, I might add," I answer cautiously. "Attacking an establishment filled with people inside is already a shitty move, pardon my language, but in the middle of the street like that, not caring if innocent people are in the way, is inexcusable."

"I can't disagree with you on that," she allows. "Was anyone else hurt?"

The concern in her voice is so genuine that I instantly know I've been right all along. She is a good person. The best kind. There's not a single bone in this woman that is evil. I can't be wrong about it.

And that makes my heart shrink with guilt, knowing she got involved in all of this because of me.

"No, luckily not. I mean… only you. And for that, I am truly sorry," I tell her.

"I'm all right. I just had to be under observation because of all the smoke I inhaled. Nothing worse happened. Not physically anyway."

Her gaze diverts to the store across the street, and she looks down at her lap. "We did lose everything, though. We couldn't save anything from the fire."

I swallow hard. I already know that, of course, but hearing it from her makes it a thousand times worse. I give her time and space to continue, remaining quiet while I look at her. She seems about to cry again, and even though I really hope she doesn't, I also find myself selfishly wanting to comfort her. She inhales deeply a couple of times, and I decide to do something bold for a change.

I reach for her hand across the table, grabbing it gently and giving it a reassuring squeeze. Heidi looks up at me, slightly surprised by my action, but she doesn't flinch or move back, allowing me to just hold onto her hand. "Does the store have insurance?" I ask.

She nods. "Yes. But they are taking their time in processing our claim. I can't continue to wait. I have no job, no home. I lost all of my clothes!" She whimpers, getting worked up again. "The few things that I owned are all gone."

I grit my teeth, realizing how fucked up her situation actually is.

"I'm so sorry. I know I might sound crazy, first coming here and demanding you do something about it, and now crying and sobbing about how lame my life is," Heidi murmurs, evidently ashamed.

I hate that she feels this way. If I could, I'd just take her by the hand and take her to a mall to buy everything she wants. I'd give her a new house and a new store, no questions or conditions asked.

But considering how good of a person she is, I doubt she'd accept it. In fact, she might even be offended by my offer. That's why I need to tread carefully. I can't act on impulse. I need her to trust me and allow me to help her. "Your life is not lame," I counter. "None of this is your fault, and you sure the hell don't deserve anything like this."

Heidi looks at me, or better yet, stares into my soul. Her eyes pierce through me as if she wants to see what I'm thinking and feeling inside my head and heart. It makes me slightly uncomfortable. Not because I don't like being the center of her attention. The opposite actually.

I don't think anyone has ever made me feel this mix of emotions at once in my life.

The way she looks at me makes me want to pin her against the wall, but at the same time, to unravel all of my secrets and share all of my worries and feelings with her.

I don't know how to feel about it, and that's why it leaves me on edge.

How does she do this to me?

"I didn't mean to put the blame on you," she carries on. "Or maybe I did. But just because I was desperate. I might have misjudged you, too. You looked like trouble when I first saw you, but you are actually quite pleasant to talk to."

Even though I can't see it, I know my eyes just darkened at hearing her words. The amount of retorts I am thinking but can't say out loud is annoying. A grin forms on my lips, and I can't hold it back. "I can be both, sweetheart," I say instead, noticing her soft cheeks flush violently. "It depends on who I'm with and what they want from me."

8

HITTING A DEAD END

Heidi

I WOULD NEVER IMAGINE CAL TO BE THE TYPE OF MAN WHO IS attentive and kind while looking so intimidating and cold on the outside. If anything, I imagined him as a grumpy, arrogant, stupid man who thinks he runs the world and that everything needs to be done according to his rules and demands.

But barging into his bar and crying in front of him—even though it almost made me die of embarrassment—has proven to be somewhat worth it.

I've never been the type of woman who was the object of desire for any man. I did have some boyfriends here and there while I was in college, but none of them ended up forming a serious relationship.

And all of them eventually cheated on me. Good thing was that I was never in love with any of them, so I can't say I suffered immensely. But it did some damage to my self-esteem. No man has piqued my interest after I graduated, and it's been like that for years. But something in Cal makes me feel different. The way his eyes drink me in makes me feel like I'm the last glass of water in the middle of the desert, and he desperately needs me to satiate himself. The way his gaze darkens and studies me makes me feel a need I've never known pooling in my core.

And he is so flirty, too. How does he do it? How can he be so sweet in the middle of a serious conversation and all of a sudden flirt with me as if we're on a date?

What did he mean when he said he can be both? Both trouble and pleasant? What does that even mean?

And why do I want to test it? What exactly is it that I want him to show me?

Do I want a man in my life who can be trouble?

No.

Do I want to know how exactly Cal can be trouble?

Yes.

I'm surprised and shocked at myself when I realize how much I want him to do things to me that I shouldn't even be thinking about at this moment.

I clear my throat, squirming in my seat, slightly uncomfortable under his gaze. The grin on his lips is devilish, and yet, it does something with my insides that I can't interpret. Or maybe I'm just not ready to.

"Uh, so, how long have you owned this bar?" I ask, biting down on my lip as soon as the words are out of my mouth.

What kind of stupid question is that, Heidi?

As if I couldn't look more awkward and weird…. Why did I have to bring up his bar? I don't even like it.

Cal leans back in his chair, looking at me with amusement in his eyes. The grin on his lips is still there, and I have to look away so I don't lose myself in it.

"Are you suddenly interested in my bar?" Cal retorts, joy evident in his tone. "You work across the street for years and never once came here for a drink. So, I'm sorry to say this, but your interest doesn't seem very genuine to me," he teases.

He's not wrong about that. If I were to be honest with him right now, he might not like what I have to say about the things I always thought of his clientele and his establishment. Not to mention him and his workers.

"Well, it's not exactly the type of place I choose to hang out in," I reply, trying not to be rude. "I'm more likely to go to the coffee shop, or a stay-at-home kind of girl." I shoot him a half-hearted smile.

He doesn't look offended, though. If anything, I'd say he's enjoying himself way too much with this awkward conversation. "Shocker," he muses.

"What's that supposed to mean?" I arch an eyebrow.

Cal simply shrugs. "Well, everything in you screams bookworm. You work at a bookstore. It wasn't that hard to figure that out, you know?"

"Yeah, well… whatever. Can we get back to the main topic and the whole purpose of this conversation?" I snap, getting a bit worked up. I hate that I can't be more composed in front of him. I'm not usually this arrogant, but this guy brings out feelings I didn't even know I had in the first place.

"Okay," he agrees with a nod, going back to what I assume is his professional tone. "I can help you, and *will* help you, but first I think we should get to know each other a little bit better."

I frown. "Why?"

Cal tilts his head slightly. "I'm not someone who trusts others easily. I'm used to a lot of people wanting to take advantage of me. I'm not saying you're going to do that, but–"

I gasp, interrupting him, too astonished with where he's going with this conversation.

"What? You think I'm here to get your money or what? I just came after justice. My family lost everything! I have no idea what type of people you're used to hanging out with, but I'm certainly not like that," I say, exasperated.

What a waste of my time….

But then again, this is my fault. I don't know what I was expecting when I came here. Truth be told, I don't think I'd take this guy's money even if he offered.

"Of course you're not. It's just that I've learned the hard way not to trust anything someone else says. However, I've also learned to trust my instincts a bit more as time's gone by. I can tell you're a good person. I was just teasing you. Breaking the ice a little. I want to get to know you a little better."

"Why?" I repeat. I don't know why I'm so on the defensive, but this guy makes me feel so vulnerable. I'm not sure I like that.

Cal shrugs nonchalantly. "Just because…"

I stare at him for a few seconds in silence. He seems genuinely interested in me. What could he possibly want from someone like me? "What do you want to know?" I test the water.

"Are you married?" he asks.

My jaw drops. "Why is that important?" I retort.

"I have my reasons."

"I don't see why this concerns you, but no, I'm not married," I finally answer.

Cal hums, leaning back in his chair a bit more.

"Is that all?" I press with my brows raised at him.

"Do you have a boyfriend?" he continues.

"No, I don't," I say bluntly.

I don't know where he's going with this, but I can't deny the fact that I'm secretly proud that a guy like him is showing any interest in me at all. I'm not sure if he's flirting with me, but to say that I don't like the attention he is lavishing on me would be a lie.

A big one.

"Where are you from?" I abruptly change the subject, not giving him the opportunity to continue with his interrogation.

"Ireland," Cal answers swiftly.

"Why did you come to New York?"

"I have businesses here."

Duh, I had figured that out by myself, I want to say. Why is he so enigmatic about himself while he's been asking about my personal life?

"This conversation is going nowhere," I point out, frustrated. I stand, adjusting the strap of my purse on my shoulder and folding my arms across my chest. "I really have to go, so are you going to do anything to help me fix this situation or not? This has taken longer than necessary already." I don't want a handout, but I do want him to take responsibility for his part in all of this and compensate me somehow.

But it seems I've hit a dead end coming here, and I should know when to stop pushing for something that will lead me nowhere.

Cal gets to his feet as well, fixing the collar of his leather jacket, his eyes set on me. "I want to help you, Heidi. You might not believe me, but I'm not a cold-hearted man. And I would never let you, or anyone else, for that matter, have to deal with this mess alone. I'm glad you showed up at my door today. I've been waiting for you."

I swallow hard, ignoring the way those last words make my core tight with need. I've been single and lonely for longer than I can remember, and being in the presence of a man like Cal is melting my brain to the point of making me think of absurd things.

"Will you follow me?" Cal offers, gesturing to a back door that leads to somewhere deeper inside his bar.

Everything in me is telling me that this is a bad idea.

But for whatever reason, I accept his offer.

9

MAKING ARRANGEMENTS

CAL

HEIDI FOLLOWS ME AS I TAKE HER TO MY OFFICE. WE STROLL ACROSS the hallway, heading for the last door on our right. Our footsteps are the only thing I can hear as I guide her, her tiny frame following me closely.

I'm trying hard to ignore how good she smells. Her sweet perfume inebriates my senses and makes it hard for me to think clearly.

And I have to figure out what I can do for her now that she finally seems willing to accept my help.

Seeing how defensive Heidi can get has turned me on more than I'd like to admit, but I can't say I don't like it. Ever since she crossed the doorway of my bar, she's done nothing but surprise me.

She yelled, cried, stood defensively and suspiciously before me, showing multiple sides of her in less than an hour. Teasing and flirting with her felt good, but considering how different Heidi is from the women I'm used to dating, I need to be cautious. And more respectful than ever. The last thing I want is to scare her away.

Her retorts only added fuel to the fire I'm feeling within me, but I don't want to take her pain for granted. I know she's going through a hard period in her life–and that's at least partially my fault. I don't want to be insensitive. So, I need to learn to control myself better when I'm around her.

"Where are we going?" Her voice echoes from behind me, and I notice a hint of suspicion and fear in her tone.

"Relax, I'm not kidnapping you or anything. I'm just taking you to my office so we can talk privately and solve your situation in the best way possible," I tell her, hoping to reassure her.

When we finally get to my office, I open the door and step to the side, making space for her to enter. "Come on in, please," I offer, gesturing for her to go before me.

Heidi passes by me, that floral fragrance leaving a trail like an intoxicating drug I can't seem to get enough of. I take a deep breath, cursing myself inwardly, then I close the door, heading for my leather chair behind my large oak desk.

"You can sit on the couch or here," I point to the chair across from me, "wherever you prefer."

Heidi seems a bit distracted with my office's decor, which I'm more than proud of. From the mini-bar, to the vinyl station where I keep my album collection; this is the place I feel most at home at, other than my apartment.

"Heidi?" I call, noticing she hasn't heard me.

"What?" Her head snaps toward me, her beautiful eyes still wide with admiration.

"I said you can take a seat if you'd like," I repeat. "Do you like what you see?"

"Yes, this place is amazing. You have an incredible collection here," she says, gesturing at my albums.

"Thank you. I'm very proud of it."

She finally seems to realize she's been standing in the middle of the room this whole time, so she hesitantly heads for the couch, her cheeks flushing slightly with embarrassment. She sits on the other edge, her purse in her lap.

"Can I get you something to drink?" I offer. Then I realize that might have sounded ambiguous, so I add, "Water or maybe a soda?" I don't want her to think I'm trying to get her drunk or anything. It's better that we're all sober for this conversation.

"Water is fine," she answers softly.

I go to the mini-bar in the right corner of the room and pour her a glass of water. She drinks it slowly, her eyes darting from one side to another of the office, clearly still mesmerized.

"I need to make a phone call real quickly. You can stay here and wait for me," I inform her. "Take your time looking around if you want."

"Oh, okay…"

Her eyes find mine, and my stomach twists aggressively. How the fuck does she do that? Good Lord…. I shake my head, shoving aside all the dirty thoughts that pop into my mind uninvited, and head out of the office, closing the door behind me.

I lean against the wall in the hallway, taking my phone out of my pocket, dialing Jackson's number, my realtor in New York. He picks up after the second ring.

"Hey, my man. What gives me the honor of getting a call from you before New Year's Eve?" he greets me

"I need your help with something," I reply straightforwardly.

Jackson has helped me acquire and sell many buildings and establishments throughout the years, and if anyone can get a nice place for Heidi on such short notice, that someone would be him. "Of course. What can I do for you?"

"I need an apartment by tomorrow. Good security, best neighborhood, my territory, of course," I explain, although he's already aware of that last part. "It doesn't need to be too large, just something cozy. I know I'm not giving you much time, but I'm sure you can pull some strings for me."

"I'm sure I can find something," Jackson replies. "Is it for you?"

"No," I answer. I consider keeping it a secret, but I guess there's no point in hiding it from him. It's not like I'm trying to hide Heidi anyway, and Jackson is trustworthy. "Someone lost their store and apartment in the explosion on Christmas Eve. I'm trying to help them get back on their feet, since you know, I was partially responsible for them losing everything."

"Oh, I see… I'll make sure to have a place for you by tomorrow morning. I'll text you some pictures and the address, then you can tell me what you think."

"Sounds good," I say.

"Is there anything else I can do for you? What about the shop? Should I look for a new place as well?" Jackson offers.

I hum, considering his question. "They're still waiting for the insurance to settle with them. I don't think they would be willing to move to another place, though. It seems they might want to rebuild or something. I'll let you know as soon as I have more information about that," I explain.

"Okay, man. I'll work on finding the apartment first then."

Jackson hangs up, and I turn to get back to my office to tell Heidi the news. But my phone buzzes almost immediately, revealing the name of the last person I was expecting to call me today.

"Tony?" I answer.

"Hey. Can you talk?" His voice is contained as usual, but the head of the Saints of Staten Island calling me is not a good sign. That much I know.

"Sure, what's up?"

"I heard your bar was blown up," he starts. "Or something like that. I was out of town, and I just got word of it. What happened?"

"Ah," I murmur. "They fucked up and didn't hit my bar but took out the shop across the street."

"Do you know who did it?" Tony presses, his tone dark.

"I know what you're thinking, and I won't tell you that the thought didn't cross my mind, but we have nothing yet," I tell him. "My men didn't find any clues about who was behind it, and the street cameras didn't manage to pick up the plates."

"It's not far-fetched to think it could be the cartel. Some of Mateo's men tried to seek revenge after his death, remember?"

I do remember. I crashed Tony's wedding to let him know about it a few months ago, right after the head of the Cartel De La Cruz was killed by Tony. I helped him with that mission, and some of Mateo's men were not happy about it, making me a target also.

But that was an easy problem to solve.

Tony and I barely had to lift a finger.

The truth is, after Mateo's death, word on the street is that his men have been fighting to take his place. But as far as we're concerned, none of them have had the guts or the power to take full control.

Until now.

The idea that some of them are responsible for the attack on my bar has rippled through my mind ever since it happened. But since none of my men managed to get any evidence, we're still stuck at square one.

"Until they try something again, we can't do anything, lad," I point out. "You know that."

"Yeah. Well, it doesn't hurt to be prepared. Let me know if you hear anything or if you need my help," Tony insists. "I owe you one. For everything you did for me and Chloe."

"I'll keep that in mind. Now, go enjoy your family," I say gratefully.

Tony has become a great friend, one I'm proud to have by my side–personally and professionally.

"Okay, fine. Keep me posted. Happy New Year's, man," he replies.

"Happy New Year's, lad!"

10

DO WE HAVE A DEAL?

CAL TAKES ME TO HIS OFFICE, AND I FIND MYSELF SLIGHTLY SUSPICIOUS while at the same time, an anticipation builds within me that has everything to do with the fact that he's taking me somewhere private to have a conversation.

While we were talking at the bar, his barkeep pretended he wasn't listening to us, but I'm sure he was.

Now, we'll be alone in his office, and that seems... weird. I'm not supposed to be feeling like this.

Cal is everything I should keep myself away from in a man. He's handsome, intimidating, sexy, flirtatious, not to mention he's mysterious in a way that keeps me wanting to know more about him. If the novels I read have taught me anything, I should know better than to want to have any kind of relationship with Call. I know I came after him for help, but in my defense, I had no idea who he was. After I was already here and made a scene out of myself, demanding to talk to him, well... I couldn't back down.

I'm waiting in his office, admiring his decor and the shelves filled with albums and a vintage aesthetic that I can't seem to get enough of. He has such good taste.

I also have to admit that, even though I've hated his bar for so long, after walking inside for the first time, I was surprised to see the place actually has a great atmosphere. Sure, his clientele is off-putting most of the time, not to mention I'm almost positive that Cal turns a blind eye to illegal business taking place here, but... I don't think bar owners have that much control over who attends their establishments all the time.

What's bugging me the most is how he makes me feel when he looks at me. The way his eyes stare into my soul, the way his lips turn up in a devilish grin, the way he seems to know the effect he has on me whenever he talks to me.

It's overwhelming.

I'm constantly on my toes when he is near me, scolding myself to get a grip and put my head in the right place. I don't know how to feel about it. A part of me likes the attention, but the other part knows this is a dangerous path to follow.

A few minutes later, Cal comes back, his hands shoved in his pants pockets nonchalantly. "Sorry to keep you waiting," he says, closing the door behind him. "I might have good news for you, though."

His scent hits my nostrils right away, spice and leather, and I clench my hands over my purse, urging my brain to focus on the matter at hand. "Sure, it's not a problem. What is the good news?" I press, forcing a polite smile. Hopefully, he's not aware of how much hotter the room became just because he entered it.

"Well, other than this bar, I have businesses around town. And I have a realtor that helps me whenever I need to acquire or sell real estate," Cal explains, walking toward his chair.

I almost let out a sigh of relief when he walks away from me, sitting on the opposite side of the room. "Okay..." I trail off, nodding at him to signal I'm paying attention.

"He might have an apartment available for you tomorrow, if you're interested," he continues, his eyes never leaving my face. The room is dimly lit, casting a shadow across his eyes that keeps me on edge. Or maybe I'm just overthinking. I've been here for longer than I intended. Way longer. "Ah…" I let out, taking in what he just said.

What does that even mean? Am I supposed to pay for it? I don't have enough money saved up to pay for anything, let alone an apartment. And the insurance company hasn't given us anything to pay for the damage done to our establishment. How does he expect me to afford an apartment?

Or perhaps… is he offering to give it to me? Is this his way to pay me back for the damage caused to my family's store?

If it is, am I ready to accept it? What would that even entail? Will I be tying myself to him forever by accepting his favor? Or should I simply consider it a payback and leave it at that?

"Look, Heidi." Cal saying my name in such a serious and firm tone makes my head snap toward him so fast that I get whiplash. Not to mention that yearning sensation deep within me, which I try as hard as possible to ignore. How am I supposed to make such a serious decision with him staring at me this way? I can't focus. I can't think clearly. This is a nightmare.

"I don't want to overstep any boundaries, and I definitely don't want to hurt your ego and pride," Cal continues, his face stoic. "But I do want to help fix the mess I caused. Indirectly that is," he states. He leans back in his chair, casually leaning on the armrests. "If you let me, I'd like to give the apartment to you," he informs me, making my jaw drop, even though I was already expecting that to come out of his mouth. Hearing it is another story though. "If not permanently, at least until you get settled with your store and everything. I know how hard it is to get money from insurance companies, and I don't want to keep living the guilt of knowing you have nowhere to stay."

He sounds genuine about wanting to help me. He probably doesn't feel guilty about many things in life, but my instincts tell me he really wants to help this time. I do need a place to stay. Living with my aunt is anything but ideal. I like her, but she has this habit of insisting that everything is done a certain way, and it's hard for me to adapt, so I'm on my toes all the time while I'm at her house.

After living with my grandparents my whole life, I was kind of looking forward to getting the place all to myself. I wasn't expecting it to be so soon, but now that they have decided to move to the retirement home, I don't think I can live with anyone else.

I came here demanding some help from Cal. I didn't intend for him to deal with all the damage by himself, but from what I'm seeing, he seems to have a great deal of money. Perhaps I wouldn't call him a millionaire, but considering the expensive boots he's wearing, his vintage album collection, the brand name watch on his wrist, and the bar he owns, I don't think money is an issue for him. I don't want to make assumptions based on appearances, but he wouldn't offer it if he couldn't afford it, right?

"So, what do you say?" Cal presses, watching me intently. "Will you let me help you?"

"I just want to make clear this isn't what I was after when I barged into your bar. Sure, I wanted you to be responsible somehow, but just because I was angry and desperate," I clarify. First impressions are important, and I definitely didn't create a good one, but for some reason, I don't want Cal to think badly of me. "I'm not that kind of person–"

He chuckles, the sound surprising me and catching me off guard "You don't have to worry about that, Heidi. I won't think you're a gold-digger or anything."

I gulp, not sure if I should take that as a compliment or not.

"I want to help you, and you need help, so let's just leave it at that," Cal concludes, standing and walking toward me. I watch as he strides through the room, crossing it in three steps. He is so tall, his legs are so long, and...

Focus, Heidi!

"Okay, I..." I stammer, rushing to my feet, suddenly feeling the need to disappear from this place before I do something I'll regret. "I think I can accept your offer then."

"Good," Cal murmurs with a grin.

God, I'm getting annoyed with his flirting. He probably doesn't even notice he's doing it. He must be so used to flirting with women, it just comes naturally to him. I hate how that thought only makes me jealous, for whatever stupid reason. I shouldn't be feeling anything but anger and hatred for him.

But, surprisingly, it's the complete opposite. I don't think I've been this attracted to a man before in my entire life.

I clear my throat, shifting on my feet uncomfortably.

"I think we have a deal then, right?" Cal asks. "I'll keep you updated on the apartment. Do you want to give me your number?"

YES! is the answer that pops into my mind, but I shouldn't want him to have my phone number.

But how else will he let me know about the apartment? I definitely do not want to come here again tomorrow. I don't think I can take this situation twice in less than a week. Cal is too much for me to handle.

"Ah, sure," I finally reply, taking his phone and saving my number in it. "There you go."

Cal takes the phone from my hand, and our fingers brush, making my entire body shiver.

Oh, God!

What did I just get myself into?

11

WORK IT OUT

Cal

Having Heidi in the same room as me this entire time has proven to be nothing but a bad idea. Even though she's left, her scent lingers in the air, which makes it almost impossible for me to focus on anything other than her right now.

I'm glad she accepted my help. Giving her a new apartment isn't the only thing I wanted to do for her, but it does lessen my guilt to know she'll be safe and able to get back on her feet with a roof over her head.

I wish things hadn't gone bad for her in the first place, but since I have no control over the past, I might as well accept this is all I can do for her—for now.

Sure, I can give her way more than just an apartment, but considering how hard it was for her to accept that, I doubt she will even listen to any other offers. I think I can get her to open up to me eventually, although I have to be patient and careful.

She doesn't seem to trust people easily, and I can't pretend I didn't notice how skeptical and suspicious she was around me the whole time she was here.

I also noticed a certain uneasiness, and a selfish part of me wants to believe it has something to do with the connection I felt between us. Heidi seemed somewhat uncomfortable to be feeling the same thing, almost as if she was trying to fight herself, if the way her cheeks reddened and her body stiffened are any indication.

I drop myself onto the couch she has just vacated, regretting it immediately. The scent of her sweet, intoxicating perfume is stronger here than anywhere else in this room.

I need to leave my office before I go insane.

I have so much work to do–especially finding out who the fuck attacked my bar, but my brain isn't able to focus lately. I should be able to get shit done now that I know Heidi is safe and out of harm's way, but seeing her has triggered feelings I've been trying to keep buried.

Whenever I close my eyes, I imagine how it would feel to have my fingers tangled in her smooth, long hair, what it would feel like to have my lips on her soft porcelain skin, and how great it'd be to hear her moan my name, begging me to fuck her into oblivion–

Get your shit together, Cal!

"Fuck!" I murmur to myself, propping my elbows on my knees and rubbing my face with my hands, frustrated.

I need to vent all of this pent up energy.

I'll definitely go nuts if I remain here.

Pushing myself off of the couch, I walk out of my office and head for the second door on my left. I've never been more grateful that I built a gym inside the bar than right now.

The room is smaller than the one I have at home, but it serves its purpose. It's helped me on the most difficult days when I need to keep my head clear to make the right decisions.

I have added some dumbbells, pull-up bars, a bench press, and a punching bag. An hour or two in here should do the trick.

Slamming the door behind me, I don't even bother turning on the lights. I strip out of my leather jacket and shirt, toss them over the bench press, and head for the punching bag. Before I start, wrap my hands to prevent myself from splitting my knuckles.

The first few punches aren't so sharp. My mind is still foggy with images of Heidi I need to force away. But when I get the hang of it, my body starts getting familiar with the movements, and I lose count of how many punches I've thrown.

A knock on the door takes my mind off the training. I snap my head back to see Sam peeking his head into the room.

"Is everything all right, Boss?" he asks, his tone firm despite the little smirk on his lips. "Why are you training in the fucking dark?"

I grit my teeth, already knowing what's coming my way.

Fucking Ian might have told him what happened.

I groan in response, unwrapping my hands and heading for the pull up bar. I hear Sam walk inside and close the door behind him, and through my peripheral vision I see him sliding my jacket off the bench press and sitting down, facing me.

"Little bird told me you had a visit earlier," he begins, his tone teasing.

If I had a dollar for every time my assumptions about him were right, I'd be fucking retired right now.

"That little bird seems to want to have his tongue cut off," I retort through clenched teeth, my frustration making a comeback.

Sam chuckles but isn't done teasing me. "Am I right to assume things went badly, judging by your foul mood?" he asks, testing the water.

"Not exactly."

"Ian told me she was quite determined to hold you responsible for the damages to her store," Sam continues, a hint of curiosity in his voice.

I turn my head in his direction, my brows raising with amusement. "So your little bird has a name then, huh?" I joke, getting flipped off in return.

I laugh and throw my head back, grateful for the distraction. Sam always knows how to make me feel better whenever I'm in a sour mood. He's not just my second, he's my best friend, and for good reason.

"So, are you going to tell me what has you throwing punches in the middle of the afternoon, or should I make the assumption based on what I heard?" He gets to his feet and walks toward me, leaning against the wall and facing me with his arms crossed over his chest.

I grab the bar above my head with a firm grip and pull myself up, my muscles straining with the effort. My movements are fluid, although I'm still slightly distracted. "Heidi has made a–" I grunt after my thirtieth pull-up, "a great impression."

"So, Bookgirl finally has a name." Sam laughs.

I pull myself up again, my chin barely reaching above the bar this time. I'm getting tired, but my brain seems to think I'm high or some shit like that. It's like I need to drain myself of all the energy bottled up inside. I don't answer him.

"Okay, so what else? Did she put up a fight and win you over?"

"Exactly."

I drop down on the floor, wiping my hands on my pants. Leaning against the bar to catch my breath, I watch as Sam walks to the mini fridge next to him and grabs a bottle of water. He throws it at me, and I catch it midair, thanking him with a nod. I ignore his teasing look as I gulp down half the liquid in the bottle.

I'm contemplating the idea of keeping my conversation with Heidi from him, but if anyone would be able to help me navigate these stupid emotions I'm feeling, that someone would be him.

There's no one in this world who knows me better than Sam. And although I hate his teasing and fucking smirks, I know it comes from a good place in his heart.

"She demanded that I take responsibility for the explosion, but I don't think she was expecting me to accept it so quickly," I explain, taking deep breaths to compose myself. "When she realized I wouldn't put up a fight or ignore her completely, she started crying, explaining to me how she lost everything…"

"Everything?" Sam frowns. "I mean, I know the place is beyond repair, but–"

"She lived in the apartment upstairs," I tell him. "The insurance company is not giving her any useful information on when or how much they'll pay for the damages yet, and apparently, she has nowhere to live."

"Fuck," Sam murmurs, more to himself than to me.

"Yeah." I nod. "I have Jackson looking for a place for her right now. It took her a while to accept my offer, but ultimately, she accepted my help."

"That's nice of you," Sam replies.

I wipe my face with the back of my hand. "It's the least I could do. She lost everything because of a fucking enemy of ours. And although we have no clue who did it yet, I couldn't let her get back on her feet by herself. It wasn't her fault." I walk toward the locker on the left wall and grab a towel to better wipe the sweat dripping down my face and neck. I need a fucking shower, and perhaps a cold one will do the trick, finally wiping Heidi's image from my mind.

"Well, if she accepted the apartment, why are you working out like your life depends on it?"

I clench my jaw, knowing this question would come at some point during this conversation. I consider telling him that I can't stop picturing Heidi in my bed, but I don't want to provide that much information.

So instead, I say, "I'm just uneasy with this situation. We need to find out who did this. We still haven't gotten any leads?"

Sam's expression darkens instantly as he realizes it's no longer the time to be teasing or fucking around.

"Not really. We're trying to track down some of the Belgian guys from our last run-in, but to be honest, I don't think they're behind it," Sam informs me. "It's not really their style to cause that much of a mess. The Russians? Maybe, but they had it out for the Italians, not us."

I nod, agreeing with him. The negotiation with the Belgians was our last business deal that went somewhat bad, but we didn't finish it with a disagreement. I don't think they would have caused this much trouble over it, anyway. They're like us–the little guys. The groups that get the scraps leftover from the Italians and Russians who run New York City. And Sam's right, it's not their leader's style to blow a place up like that.

Hitting dead ends over and over during our investigation has put me and my men on edge this entire week. It's like we're constantly waiting for the next bomb to drop, not even knowing what direction it will come from.

My phone buzzes in my pocket. I fish it out. There's a text from an unknown number, and I almost consider ignoring it. If it wasn't for the imminent threat we're facing, I'd probably delete it.

But something tells me this is important, so I open it.

My blood freezes in my veins as my eyes take in the picture on my screen. Heidi is walking out of my bar, wearing her long coat, black boots, and green scarf. It was taken an hour ago when she left my office.

There's nothing else attached to the message. No threat, no text, no nothing.

Only her picture.

And that's enough to send me raging again.

12

NEW DIRECTION

"WHAT IS IT, BOSS?" SAM ASKS, BUT HIS VOICE SOUNDS DISTANT AND muffled.

When he moves to stand in front of me, his eyes studying me cautiously, I realize I was so angry, I wasn't paying any attention to him at all.

"Who is it? What happened?" he insists, his gaze darting to my phone and back to my face.

I turn the screen for him to see the picture, but by the way his brows crease, I can tell he doesn't understand what it means.

"This is Heidi leaving the bar," I explain expressionlessly, my mind numb with a type of fury I've never felt before..

I'm doing everything in my power to suppress the outrage threatening to overcome me.

I shouldn't have reason to be afraid for Heidi. If someone's watching her, which is evident by this photo, I could, in theory, shrug it off as someone trying to bait me by thinking the hottest girl to ever set foot in my bar is someone attached to me. A girlfriend, perhaps. A mistress.

It wouldn't be the first time another group has pulled a stunt like this. Mafia wives and girlfriends are the easiest targets, the targets that hurt the most when something happens to them.

But I had a brief conversation with Heidi. My mistake was that most of the conversation took place within view of the street.

However, there's no reason for anyone to think she's significant to me. As far as everyone knows, we just met. I had never talked to her, or even crossed paths with her, before today. Before the day when I saved her from the fire, anyway.

But that was different.

I would have done that for anyone.

Was someone watching me while I saved her and misunderstood my intentions? Is that what this is about?

"Why do you think they sent you that?" Sam asks out loud the same question in my mind.

I shake my head, my brain still struggling to find the right answer for that.

"I have no idea," I finally confess. "I mean, we just met. Do you think someone saw me saving her that day?" It's a stupid question because, of course, we were seen. My guys and the fucking feds were crawling all over the street that day. I handed Heidi over to a paramedic in view of every high rise and apartment building within the block.

Sam seems to consider my question for a second, then shrugs. I don't need his answer.

My mind reels as he says, "Maybe. But why would they assume you have anything to do with her just because of that?"

"They could be trying to scare me, blindly aiming at people around me." It comes out more as a question than a proper suggestion, but I honestly can't understand why they would pick Heidi over anyone else.

Even my men.

Then it hits me—like a ton of bricks.

I do care about her. I've been watching out the window nonstop ever since she was taken to the hospital, hoping, wishing to see her alive and well. Every time the bar door opened, I secretly hoped it was her walking through it. I have been drawn to her like a magnet ever since I first laid eyes on her, but it's not as if I ever acted on any of my feelings for her.

The eagerness to have her for myself, even for an hour, isn't like anything else I've ever felt for a woman before. Maybe it's the challenge of trying to get a different type of woman, someone who isn't interested in dating or my money, that has me like this—excited to see her.

But no one knows that.

It only came to me at this very moment.

Why would those motherfuckers who attacked me think otherwise when I hadn't even realized it myself?

"I can ask the guys if they've noticed anything different lately, people following them or shit like that, but it'd be expected that they would report it to us as soon as it happened," Sam notes, and I can almost hear the rusty gears in his brain turning as he tries to come up with an answer that makes sense.

"Do that," I order with a nod.

Sam's head rocks back and forth, but he doesn't move from his spot.

We remain in silence for a couple of minutes. My eyes are still glued to Heidi's picture on my phone, but I don't dare make a move without thinking it through.

I can't make any mistakes.

Especially since Heidi is now somehow involved.

I can't put her through any more shit. She's suffered a lot already. The last thing she needs is people following her and threatening her because of me.

But what if that's already happening?

"Do you think she's being followed?" I turn to Sam, the fear in my voice evident.

I don't even try to hide it this time. I'm too fucking on edge that something might happen to her while she's out of my sight that I can't think clearly. Let alone pretend I'm unbothered.

"I think that it could be a possibility. Maybe they're watching everyone involved with you, directly or indirectly," Sam tells me. "They might be keeping an eye on the bar and some of your other establishments, watching who's coming and going? Until they know for sure who you care about and who you don't, we need to be careful. Especially since we have no clue who is after you and why."

I hate the way my stomach twists with his words. He's right. It fucking sucks to be in the dark like this. Having a lot of enemies always leaves you on edge and prepared for shit to happen, but normally I know who is after me.

As I try to form a plan in my head for my next moves, Tony's words from a couple of days ago pop into my mind uninvited.

"It's not far-fetched to think it could be the cartel. Some of Mateo's men tried to act after his death, remember?"

The explosion and the attack was something that Mateo would do.

But he's buried six feet deep. And to think his men could be behind it isn't indeed far-fetched, but why would I be the one being targeted? Tony doesn't seem to be dealing with anything lately, or he would have told me.

So, why would I be in the aim of Mateo's men?

"Forget about the Belgians," I order to Sam, my gaze still stuck on my phone screen.

"Do you have a better idea?" He sounds curious, and when I look at him, his face is turned down in an ugly frown.

"Keep an eye on the Cartel De La Cruz," I reply.

His frown deepens. "Do you think they're behind it? None of their guys have been seen in the city in a while."

"Maybe. I don't know." I shrug. "But they acted right after Tony's wedding, and they could be coming for us now since we had his back. Until we know for certain, we need to make sure we're not taken by surprise again."

"It makes sense. What do you want us to do?" Sam's voice becomes more serious and firm as he waits for my orders.

"Have Pirate and Mouse trace this number and track down the person who sent it." I hand him my phone. "Let's see if we can get any information that way since we got nothing from the cars on the day of the explosion. Maybe this will lead us somewhere."

I hope I'm right. I need something—anything—to guide me.

Because right now, it feels like I'm in the middle of a fucking black hole–blind, deaf, adrift, waiting for the next bullet to hit me.

I hate to feel like I don't have control of things. It leaves me fucking anxious.

And now that Heidi is being used to get to me, it's only making me angrier and more eager to find who is behind this.

"Consider it done, Boss." Sam straightens up, his grip on my phone tightening as he stares at me. "What are you going to do about Bookgirl? If they're really following her, she might be in danger."

I swallow the bitter taste in my mouth at the thought of Heidi being under their watch, vulnerable to them, and my fists clench beside me.

"I'll keep an eye on her myself," I inform him, the idea coming to me on the spot.

I don't trust anyone to watch over her. And I won't be at ease knowing she's out there being targeted by my enemies.

"Do you think she'll accept it? If the way she dealt with everything that's happened is any indication of her character, it might be an issue for you to be on her tail," Sam wisely observes. "Or do you intend on doing it behind her back?"

I take a deep breath, determined to protect her no matter what. "I'll do it anyway, whether she wants it or not," I reply.

1 3

INVITATION

I lug my only suitcase inside the new apartment. It's stuffed with new clothes that I bought over the week.

Since nothing was salvaged from the fire, I had to make a list of priorities of what to buy. My computer is gone, and I've yet to replace it. I spent an entire day at City Hall getting a new social security card, then the DMV for my driver's license despite the fact I never use it to drive. Getting a transit card for the subway was easy, at least, but I had no clothes to wear that didn't smell like smoke, and I also had to do grocery shopping so I'll have something to eat at *home*.

Since I left the hospital, I've been eating only fast food—quick slices of pizza and hot-ham-and-cheese from the corner bodega. Sometimes my aunt would offer to cook something for us, but I knew she was only doing it because I was there. She's not very fond of the kitchen, and if I weren't at her house, I'm sure she would be eating out, too, and I didn't want to be any trouble.

I grunt as I pull the luggage inside the cozy, tiny apartment Cal arranged for me.

I don't want to tell my grandparents the details of how I got this place so quickly because I don't want them to worry about me. I'm sure they will freak out to know I accepted help from a man I don't even know, let alone the owner of the bar who got us into this mess in the first place.

I wonder what type of clients and lifestyle Cal has in order to afford renting an apartment for me. Surely, that dingy corner bar can't be that profitable. I hardly ever see it packed, and if it is, it's not the kind of clientele that looks like they drink high-price cocktails over whatever cheap beers on tap.

I decide to call my grandmother anyway, to see how she's doing, and tell her I've got a place to live. "How were you able to find a new apartment so quickly?" Grandma asks on the phone

"I... I found a broker, Granny, and with the little money I saved from my paychecks, I managed to pay for the first month and the deposit," I explain. It's a lie, but I believe I'm doing this for her own good. "At least until I figure out what to do, it is a great place to stay. It's close to where we lived, so it's convenient."

"Oh, that is good, sweetheart," Grandma informs me kindly. "Please don't hesitate in asking for money, Heidi. I would be very offended if you needed something and didn't ask. New York City can be so expensive."

I smile to myself, walking to the living room window and opening it to let the air of the city inside.

The place Cal found for me is perfect. It's a small, corner one-bedroom on the next block, close to where the bookstore and my old apartment were, so everything around the building is basically the same neighborhood I was used to back in my old home.

The living room is cozy, with a plush white sofa and a small coffee table. There's a simple, sleek bookshelf filled with a few books, which was something that made my heart beat so fast I thought I was having a heart attack.

I was so moved to know Cal was thoughtful enough to have bought me some books. He didn't say he did it, but I know they didn't come with the apartment. He had to have known how much I was missing my books and didn't want me to feel all alone in such a new space.

The kitchen is tucked into one corner with a compact stove, a mini fridge, and a small counter. The bedroom barely has enough room for a full-sized bed, but it's perfect. The white linens are crisp, the duvet soft, and the bed is framed by light gray walls, with a couple of plants in the windowsill.

I love how the morning light floods through the windows, spilling across the wooden floors. It's simple but feels like home already.

I was astonished when I saw it for the first time yesterday when he brought me here. Of course, I didn't come *with* him; I met him here instead. I still need to keep my guard up whenever Cal is around, and taking a ride from him would've set off alarms in my head.

"I will let you know if I ever need it, Granny. I promise," I tell her.

"Also, the insurance company called your grandfather this morning," she adds.

I stop in my tracks. "Oh, really? And what did they say?" Anxiety washing over me.

"Well, they will pay us in a few weeks, but it's not enough to cover everything we lost, of course," Grandma explains. "It will help us rent out a new store, though, if you want it, that is."

"If *I* want it? Doesn't Grandpa want it, too?" I frown, even though she can't see me.

"He wants what you want, sweetheart. Now that you have no obligation to the store whatsoever, it's time to decide what you want for your future. You don't have to do it just because you think this was your grandfather's dream. We only want what's best for you."

I feel my heart tightening with gratitude for them but also with sorrow. I hate that this outcome was forced on us.

"But I did love that store. I can't see myself doing anything else," I confess. "None of this was an obligation to me, Grandma. I was proud to be the one to keep the store going."

"I know. That's why this will be a decision for you to make. Think it through. See what you want to do. If you want to get a new place or rebuild this one, it's up to you. We're here to give you our opinion if you need it."

A smile returns to my face as I drop myself on the couch, closing my eyes and feeling the sunlight touching my skin. "Thanks, Grandma. I'll visit you both this week after I get settled into the new place," I tell her. "I still need to get some new stuff, so I might be busy for the next couple of days."

"Okay, sweetheart. We'll be right here waiting for you. Your Grandpa is asking you to bring those Magnolia Bakery's cupcakes he likes so much," she requests, but then her voice sounds muffled when she starts speaking with Grandpa instead. "You should take this as a sign to stop eating sugar, Glen. You're almost diabetic," she scolds, and when I hear him complaining in the background, I chuckle. I'm so happy they didn't let this whole mess ruin their lives. They sound happy, and that's all I care about. "I'll talk to you soon, honey. Have a great day," Grandma says before hanging up.

I open my eyes and stare at the ceiling as I consider what to do next. I have to go to the shopping mall to get some more necessities, but I feel so tired.

I've been barely sleeping lately since the fire. When I do fall asleep, my dreams are full of smoke and heat. Moving to a new apartment has just made my life more complicated. Cal's help was more than useful, with him using his connections to make everything quick and smooth, but it's still a lot to adjust to. I didn't have a lot to bring, but the fact that he got this amazing apartment so quickly is astounding.

It strikes me that tomorrow is New Year's Eve, and for the first time in my life, I have no plans.

Not that I used to have big plans before. Ever since my parents died, I would spend it with my grandparents until they went to bed right after midnight, sometimes earlier. And then I'd go out to see the fireworks by myself, enjoying the alone time I had to make a list of goals for the new year.

But this year, I haven't had time to make plans. I might spend it at home, organizing my stuff and maybe drinking a bottle of wine to drown my sorrows.

At least I have some books now to keep me company, thanks to Cal.

My phone buzzes in my hand, and when I look down, I see his

name flashing on the screen as if he heard me thinking about him. My entire body stiffens. What could he possibly want? Maybe he just wants to make sure I got moved in all right. He might just be checking on me to make sure I don't need anything else.

Stop overthinking, Heidi!

"Hello?"

"I don't want you to think I'm stalking you or anything, but am I right to assume you moved into the new place already?" he asks straightaway, his sexy accent disorienting me for a second.

I hate how that alone is enough to tempt me with desire for him.

"Uh, yeah, I just got here," I chuckle, scolding myself inwardly for being so easy to win over.

I should be treating him with coldness. Everything that happened was because of him, and even though I have no proof that he was involved, the fact that he's paying for this apartment is enough to make me believe he's to blame.

He didn't deny it either, so….

For whatever reason, I can't be mean to him. Or indifferent.

Whenever he's near me, all I can think about is how badly I want him to pin me to the wall and ravish me with those inviting lips of his and—

"Heidi?"

Oh, shit.

"Yes? Sorry! I was distracted for a moment, what did you say?" I ask, glad he can't see my face blushing with embarrassment.

"I asked if you have plans for New Year's," he repeats calmly.

"Uh, not really, no."

"Would I be overstepping if I invited you out to dinner? A friendly dinner, that is. I'm not trying to buy you off or anything, I just wanted a chance to get to know you a bit better, and well, I might also have another offer for you."

That piques my interest.

I don't want him to be able to buy me off or whatever he said either, but I can't pretend I don't like the fact that he seems to want to spend time with me.

On New Year's Eve.

Doesn't he have someone better to spend his time with? Why would he want to spend such an important holiday with someone he just met?

I should say no.

I should reject his invitation.

But everything in me wants me to go.

And thinking about staying in this apartment by myself tomorrow sounds awful.

My life is quiet enough already as it is. I don't need to add another night of solitude. If I can at least finish this year with a little fun, I should take the opportunity.

"No, you wouldn't be overstepping," I finally reply, determined.

"Good. I'll pick you up tomorrow at seven. I'll send you something to wear."

And with that, he doesn't even wait for my answer, hanging up on me and leaving me alone with my inappropriate thoughts about what tomorrow night could lead to.

14

MAN TO MAN

That was a shot in the dark.

I didn't expect Heidi to agree so quickly to my invitation to spend New Year's Eve with me.

If anything, I assumed she wanted nothing to do with me and that she only accepted my help because she was desperate. But maybe, just maybe, my selfish hope that she, too, felt something between us isn't an illusion after all.

Maybe my flirting skills aren't as rusty as I thought they were.

However, Heidi is different. It will take a lot of effort to finally get her to tear down the walls she's built to protect herself. She's clearly afraid of me because of the dealings she's witnessed from a distance at my club over the years.

She doesn't know exactly what I do for a living, but she's right. Getting involved with me is not a good idea. I should be the one keeping my distance from her, knowing what that could mean for her life and her safety. I can't imagine her being harmed again because of me.

But deep down, I'm a selfish man.

Despite my best efforts, now that I finally got to meet Heidi, the more I want to be with her and get to know her more. I shouldn't do this, and I was expecting her to be the one to draw the line. But to my surprise, she agreed to go out with me.

I have no clue if she thinks this is simply a dinner to close a deal, since I told her I might have a new offer for her, or if she also thinks this is a date–like I hope it is.

Now that I have a *yes* from her, I want to do everything I can to impress her.

I don't know a lot about impressing a woman like Heidi. The ones I normally go out with don't take a lot of effort on my end, considering they seem to be already impressed by my status and money.

But Heidi is not like that. And she kind of reminds me of Tony's wife.

Chloe was born into this life, though, so it's not like she was unaware of the dangers surrounding her.

I can't say the same about Heidi. But I can't be honest with her, either. Not entirely, at least.

I can't tell her what I do for a living. But keeping myself close to her right now is the only way I can protect her.

Grabbing my phone and searching for Tony's number in my contact list, I head for the kitchen. The lights are out in my apartment making it seem like it's uninhabited. When I got home tonight, I went straight to my office to get updated on my latest business deals and ended up trapped in a plan to meet up with Heidi.

After the call, I spent fifteen minutes trying to come up with a good idea of a restaurant to take her tomorrow, but nothing came to mind.

Maybe Tony will be able to help me.

"Hello?" he answers, his voice a bit distant.

"Hey, lad. Are you busy?" I ask, grabbing a bottle of whiskey from the bar and pouring a glass for myself.

"No, I'm just putting Ellie to bed while Chloe finishes dinner, but I can talk. I'm on the speaker though," he informs me, and it makes sense now that I can't hear him properly.

"I can call some other time. It's not that important," I offer, although I hope he doesn't take me up on it. I really need some help, and I already feel sheepish to be calling him for this.

"Just shoot, man. I could use a distraction. Chloe is driving me insane with all the preparations for tomorrow, and Ellie seems to have taken the week to decide not to sleep," Tony pleads.

I chuckle, walking back to the living room and standing in front of the large window, watching the car lights on the streets below and the skyscrapers of New York's skyline in front of me.

"I need help finding a nice restaurant for tomorrow night," I begin, but my voice turns firm and serious when I add, "somewhere private and safe."

That seems to pique Tony's interest because the next time he speaks, his voice is closer to the phone and clearer than before, which makes me assume he took the call off speaker.

"Is there a problem?" he probes, his voice low.

The picture of Heidi on my phone sent by an unknown number comes to mind, but I shake my head, thinking it best not to tell Tony about it. I know he'll freak out and demand I let him help figure out what's going on.

But even though the idea of keeping it from him sounds satisfying, I know better. If this really is the De La Cruz cartel, this will become his problem as well.

"Do you have time? It's kind of a long story," I tell him.

"Yeah, hold on a second."

The soft shuffle of footsteps on the other end tells me that Tony is moving around, then murmurs of a faint conversation are heard, although I can't quite make them out.

Everything goes quiet for a moment before he speaks again, this time, his voice clear and focused. "All right, we're good now," Tony assures me. "Now, tell me what is going on."

I clear my throat, deciding where to start. I'm usually a man of few words, but I need to update Tony on the latest events, so I start from the day of the explosion, telling him exactly what happened. Then I briefly explain how Heidi became a part of my life and how I've been keeping an eye on her ever since.

"Ah, I knew there had to be a woman involved," Tony murmurs when I finish telling him about getting Heidi a new apartment.

"Yeah, well, keep the teasing to yourself. I haven't finished yet," I interrupt, already knowing I'm feeding him enough information to harass me for the rest of my life. "An unknown number sent me a picture of her leaving my bar the other day. I have no fucking clue who did it, but I know they're watching her. I don't know why they thought she was important to me, but I don't think that's relevant now."

Tony remains silent for a minute, and I almost think he hung up on me, until I hear a loud intake of breath on the other end. "That's fucked up," he finally says. "You know how hard it is for us to get involved with other people, right? You saw how difficult it was for me and Chloe to be together, and she was already a part of this life. Being born into it, she's always known what it takes."

I grunt to myself, not needing him to repeat what I already know.

"I can't ignore her, pretend I never met her. I can't simply walk away knowing they're on her tail. What if they aim at her thinking they can get to me?"

"They clearly can, right? You're into her, aren't you? You wouldn't do all of this if she wasn't somewhat important to you," Tony points out.

I hate that he can read me so well. "I can't tell you I'm not," I confess, my tone low and somewhat hesitant.

"What are you planning on doing? If this really is the cartel, we don't know what they are capable of, now that Mateo is dead," Tony notes darkly. "If the explosion is any indication of how they deal with their shit, we can't expect them to play fair and clean."

"You know better than anyone how hard it is to walk away." I don't say this as a way of poking an old wound, but if anyone can understand my feelings, that'd be Tony.

"I know, man. I'm not telling you to. I'm just warning you to be careful. Although, I agree with you in a way. Staying close to her right now might be the only way to keep her safe. At least until you know what you're up against. Or who."

"Thanks. I have my men looking into who might be running the cartel now. Hopefully, we'll have information on it soon."

"Send it to me as soon as you hear something new," Tony requests.

I nod, even though he can't see me. "Will do. Now, can you give me a recommendation on the restaurant or what?"

Tony chuckles, the atmosphere in our call changing drastically. "Sure. I own a restaurant in Staten Island with a view of the city. It does wonders to impress a woman," he suggests, and since I know Tony has exquisite taste in food and decor, I immediately agree.

"Can you get me a reservation?"

"Consider it done."

15

IS THIS A DATE?

HEIDI

NEEDLESS TO SAY, I BARELY CLOSED MY EYES LAST NIGHT.

I don't know why I feel so anxious to have dinner with Cal. He never once mentioned this was a date. Not officially, at least. Would I be wrong to assume it is if he didn't expressly say the word *'date'*?

In my experience, if a man wants to spend New Year's Eve with a woman, he probably has romantic intentions.

No matter how polite and respectful Cal is, I don't believe for a second that this is strictly a business meeting. Or, maybe I'm just thinking about it too deeply.

I'm probably not the type of woman he's used to dating. I imagine him with someone who has tattoos, piercings, and isn't afraid to hop on a bar and dance... But the way he looked at me the past few times we came into contact makes me wonder if he might be interested in me, the way he's constantly orbiting around me, wanting to know more about me.... There's no way I'm imagining it.

I shake my head and look around. I've finished unpacking my things and organized everything in the closet in my bedroom. I also

85

organized the groceries I bought this morning and cleaned the entire apartment, so it feels like I'm finally ready to start the new year in my new, *temporary* home.

Except now I have to hurry to get ready. It's already past 5:00, and I have so much to do. I totally lost track of time while I was cleaning. Rushing to the bathroom, I get into the shower and wash my hair in record time. Wrapped in a towel, I return to the bedroom, blow drying my hair and pulling it up into a bun so it has smooth curls when I untie it.

Then, I begin my makeup, which is definitely not my strong suit. Times like this make me wish I had a girly friend to teach me how to make myself look pretty. Or, better yet, someone who could do it for me. My friends growing up were into books and horses, not perfecting the perfect cat-eye. I've tried learning through YouTube tutorials over and over, but this is definitely not my forte. However, I do make myself look presentable with red lipstick, mascara, and a peachy blush. It's not exactly what I would call a look to die for, but it will have to do.

At least I have the dress that Cal sent me. Holding it up against my body and looking in the mirror, I have to say, it *is* to die for. When I pulled it out this morning, I couldn't believe it. The green silk runs through my fingers like flowing water. For a moment, I imagine Cal's fingers flowing over my body. I need to push those thoughts aside. This man is *trouble* with a capital T.

With a dress like this, I don't need a bra, so I'm wearing a lacy new thong I just bought–ignoring why I would do such a thing–and pull the dress over my head, feeling the smooth material slip effortlessly over my skin. It settles against my body, enveloping me like a secret. Looking at myself in the mirror, I finally let out a faint, "Wow."

I don't think I've ever looked this beautiful before in my entire life. The dress hugs my waist perfectly, draping over my hips and falling almost to the floor. The neckline brushes against my collarbone, feminine and delicate. The way it clings to my body makes me feel like a completely different woman. I have to remind myself I'm still the same old bookworm on the inside.

Untying my bun, I let my long hair fall over my shoulders and down my back, deciding to let it loose for the night. If there's one thing about me that I like, it's my hair.

I stare at my reflection, completely astonished.

It's obvious that I've completely lost my mind.

My brain exited my skull the night of the fire, didn't it?

My phone rings on my bed, startling me back to reality.

"Hello?" I answer, taking a last look in the mirror before sitting on my bed to put on the silver strappy heels that Cal sent along with the dress. Considering I usually wear sneakers, I imagine I will fall and look like an idiot at some point, but I can hardly wear sneakers with a dress.

The heels will have to cooperate with me.

"Are you ready?" Cal's voice greets me, and I almost curse at how sexy he sounds.

What is going on with me tonight? It's gotta be his accent. His Goddamn sexy, Irish accent.

"Yeah, just grabbing my purse," I tell him.

That's when the buzzer rings. Seeing as I don't have a doorman, Cal is likely standing outside my apartment right now. My heart seizes, and suddenly my dress feels a touch too tight.

"That'd be me, by the way," he says with a chuckle.

I hang up on him, take a deep breath, grab my purse, and walk to the door, feeling both nervous and excited at the same time.

As soon as I open it, my eyes meet Cal, and I suddenly forget how to breathe. There he is; this tall, broad-shouldered, effortlessly handsome, masculine man staring back at me, staring at me like I'm the most valuable piece of art in the *Louvre*.

He's dressed in a sleek, tailored suit with a simple white shirt beneath it, the collar open just enough to reveal his toned chest and what looks like the tip of a tattoo. His dark red hair is slicked back, the slight shadow on his sharp jawline making him look more mysterious and sexy than ever.

Cal leans against the doorframe, his light brown eyes scanning me from head to toe. For a moment, the world tilts on its axis.

His gaze is slow, deliberate, savoring the view. The corner of his mouth twitches into a smile, and his eyes hold a darkness that makes my pulse quicken. Heat pools in the pit of my stomach, and I try to suppress the rush of arousal washing over me by clenching my thighs together. But it's almost impossible to act unbothered when he's looking at me like that.

It's like he can touch my skin with only his gaze.

It's magnetic.

"I knew that dress was made for you the second I saw it." His voice is low and smooth. We're standing so close, the heat of his body and the intensity of his stare makes something within me come to life, like an animal that has been hibernating for years has finally woken up.

Good Lord. Help me.

How can I spend the entire night with this guy without surrendering to his charms? The man is a professional when it comes to charming women. He's barely spoken a dozen words to me, and I feel like I've already climaxed at least once.

I'm putty in his hands, just like every love-sick heroine in the books I love so much.

There's no way this night can end with me coming home early to cozy up with a good book, that's for damn sure.

"I really like it. Thank you," I reply instead of letting on that he's getting to me. I notice how hoarse my voice sounds and hope he doesn't catch onto the nerves threatening to shatter me into pieces.

The last thing I need is to give Cal this much power over me, but he might already have it. If he were to tell me to back up, to guide me to my bedroom, and take off my dress… I'd do it.

He smiles at me, revealing his perfect, white teeth. I didn't think he could look more handsome, but here he is, proving me wrong. "Are you ready to go?" he asks, his gaze stopping for a split second on my lips.

I bite down to prevent myself from saying anything or making sounds I shouldn't. I don't doubt for a minute that Cal could drag a moan out of my throat with only his eyes undressing me like that.

"Yeah," I agree with a nod.

He offers me his arm in the most polite and elegant way possible. I would never have guessed the guy in a leather jacket who owns a sleazy bar in Manhattan could be this much of a gentleman, but Cal seems to be willing to prove me wrong over and over.

I take his arm, letting him guide me down the hall, to the elevator, out of the building, toward the front of the building where a sleek sports car is parked. I gulp, looking up at him with wide eyes.

"Is that your car?" I ask, my mouth agape.

I don't know why I'm so surprised, considering I already knew he was rich, but damn, I was definitely not expecting him to own a car like this.

"Yeah," Cal replies humbly.

"Is that a Maserati?" I blurt, my gaze stuck on the beautiful black finish reflecting the streetlights above.

Cal's brows rise as he looks at me. "Didn't take you for a car girl," he notes with amusement in his tone.

I shrug slightly. "I'm not. My dad used to talk to me about them all the time, though. I got to learn a few things unwillingly. I was the son he never had," I laugh, the memory of endless conversations with Dad about vehicles invading my mind.

"Well, you have a good eye," Cal remarks, opening the passenger door for me.

This simple gesture makes me forget about childhood memories immediately, replacing them with rated R scenes instead.

With a slow, deliberate movement, his hand grazes the small of my back as he guides me inside. The touch is light; yet, it sends an electric current through me. "Madam," he murmurs, his voice low and steady, laced with that confidence that makes my breath catch.

As I slide into the seat, his hand leaves my waist, and I immediately miss his touch. He closes the door with a soft click, but the weight of his gaze lingers on me as he walks around the car.

Cal slides into the driver's seat a few seconds later, and his scent wraps around me like a cloak, making everything feel blurry. My pulse quickens as I inhale his musky cologne, leaving me acutely aware of how close we are in the confined space. He glances at me, his eyes dark and knowing, and the corner of his mouth tugs upward into an evil smirk.

Shit, I'm doomed. I swallow, trying to find my composure, but his presence is overwhelming. *What is wrong with you, Heidi?*

At times like this, I wish I had someone telling me this was a bad idea from the start. A good friend would warn me that keeping myself away from Cal is the wisest choice.

I've watched enough movies and read enough books to know how dangerous guys like him are.

But what I fear most right now is not what he can do to me. What could possibly be worse?

Going back home without getting a taste of him.

16

GETTING TO KNOW HER

HEIDI LOOKS STUNNING IN THE DRESS I PICKED FOR HER, EVEN BETTER than I imagined. As soon as my eyes fell on that dress wrapped around her beautiful curves, I knew it had been made for her.

I hadn't prepared myself to actually see her in it, though. It took everything in me not to jump on her as soon as she opened that door.

Until that moment, I had only seen her in jeans, sneakers, and big sweaters, nothing too revealing or sexy, and that had been enough to leave me drooling and waking up in a cold sweat. But this dress…

Even now, as I drive us to the restaurant that Tony reserved for us, I'm struggling to keep my eyes on the road instead of on her. Her presence is consuming all of my senses, her intoxicating perfume invading my nostrils and making it hard for me to breathe.

The way the silk fabric clings to her tiny frame makes me wonder what it would feel like to run my fingers along her curves, hold her in my arms, and…

"Where are we going?" Heidi asks after minutes of pure silence.

I was starting to think she's not comfortable being here, considering she hadn't spoken a word until now, but maybe she's just timid? She's an enigma to me, and the more time I spend with her, the more I want to know her. *Really* know her.

"It's a surprise" I reply, shooting her a sly grin.

It doesn't seem to work on her. She folds her arms beneath her chest and stares at me, her brows creased. "I'm not very fond of surprises," she informs me. Her tone is not angry or disapproving, though. There's a small smile forming on her lips, and I wonder if she is playing with me.

"Do you really want me to tell you then?" I pry.

Heidi pretends to consider my question, her finger moving to her chin in a contemplating pose.

"All right, maybe not. I'm sure you're trying to impress me, so I won't ruin your fun," she finally says.

I glance at her briefly, and Heidi looks at me, her intense eyes hypnotizing. This girl *is* playing with me.

I was slightly frustrated after I picked her up from her apartment and she remained quiet for longer than I'd like. I am not used to indifference from women. Heidi is making me work harder than I expected, but surprisingly, it's not a bad thing. If anything, it only makes me more determined to make her like me.

I've never given a fuck if anyone liked me before.

"You got that right. You're not easily wooed though, right?" I retort, smiling at her before returning my attention to the road ahead.

Traffic is insufferable tonight. New York City is one of the hardest cities to drive in, but tonight, because of the holiday, it seems like every single citizen decided to go out at the same time, filling taxis and ignoring crosswalk signs all together. Even the highway to Staten Island seems to be busier than usual. It might have been better to take the ferry, in retrospect.

I'm really grateful that Tony reserved a spot in his restaurant for us. Otherwise, I can't even imagine where I'd take Heidi for a more private dinner. While the Irish Kings have sway in the city, it's still run by the Italians. I'd have to grovel on my knees and kiss serious ass to secure any kind of invitation to the swanky, upscale restaurants if it weren't for Tony.

I'm used to dive bars. I'm used to dollar slices and cold beers in brown paper bags.

I'm used to not feeling a thing doing whatever with some girl I'm trying to pick up, to take home… but not Heidi. I want to impress her, and I think it has a lot to do with the fact I was the reason her world crumbled.

As far as I'm aware, only VIP clients can get reservations at this restaurant, so I'm expecting it to be quiet and somewhat reserved. Hopefully, I don't hate it, and she enjoys herself. Either way, I owe one to Tony for this. Knowing him, he'll have me in the field spying on the Triads while he and his guys drink scotch and eat cold cuts in that dingy basement he still uses as an office.

"Am I easily wooed? It depends," Heidi replies calmly, her voice soothing beside me. "If you're asking me if I'm wooed by money and luxury, I'm not. That's not the kind of thing that does it for me, you know?"

The monster inside of me snarls with lust at the unspoken challenge she just tossed at me. It's almost like she is prodding me to find out what *does* do it for her, what gives her butterflies, what brings her to her knees.

I hum, considering what to say next. I don't want to offend her or sound invasive, let alone want her to think I'm only trying to get her into my bed because, surprisingly, that's not the only thing I want from her.

Of course, I'd be lying if I said I'm not attracted to her, and the idea of having sex with her is something that doesn't leave my mind for more than mere seconds. But something about Heidi also makes me want to learn more about her tastes, her hobbies, her dreams, and even her fears. I've never felt this way about any woman before. I think she might make a good girlfriend. I figured I'd have one eventually. I didn't think much of it until recently, when she barreled into my bar demanding answers. I'd like her to be the only woman in my passenger seat from now on, but….

She has no idea how I can afford this car. She has no idea how I can afford a five-thousand dollar dress and shoes worth as much as the monthly rent on her apartment. She has no idea who I am, and I'm sure if she found out, she'd run.

I wouldn't blame her.

"Yeah, I figured money didn't matter to you. You do look like someone who is waiting for Prince Charming to come on a white horse and sweep her off her feet," I tease, receiving a narrowed glance in return.

"Or maybe I'm looking for a mafia boss to show up at my door and fuck me until I forget my own name," she bites back, making me slam on the brakes, causing the tires to squeal against the concrete.

Thankfully, I do it before I crash into the car in front of us that has just stopped because of a red light.

Heidi looks ahead, slightly alarmed and making sure we're not in trouble. Then she turns to me again, her brows slightly raised.

My mouth is suddenly dry, and my pants feel a bit too tight in the crotch. That was too fucking close. Not almost crashing my car… but the truth. Has she figured me out?

To my utter surprise, Heidi chuckles, tilting her head back against the headrest.

I take the opportunity to pull myself together. She has no idea how close to reality she got by saying that–or does she? If I could, if she'd allowed me to, I'd do exactly what she said in a heartbeat. I'd pull the car over right now and fuck her.

"You should see your face," she says between laughs. "I was just kidding," she explains, a bit too late.

I clear my throat, focusing on driving now that the light has turned green, and the car in front of us is starting to move.

"I was just caught off guard," I rasp, throwing her a sharp look. "You don't look like the kind of woman who could handle something like that, anyway." Trying to get back on my game is the only thing I can do so I don't look as stupid as I feel.

Heidi snorts, and I'm certain that it's the cutest sound I've ever heard.

"What do you mean by that?"

I grind my teeth, wondering how far I can take this line of conversation. "You'd probably start whimpering and saying you couldn't handle it, *a mhuirnín.*"

"I–what does that mean?"

"It means don't tempt me with a good time, because I'd show you–"

"Not that," she says just above the whisper then proceeds to absolutely butcher the Gaelic pet-name that inadvertently left my lips.

"Sweetheart," I reply, glancing at her, watching the way her eyes glow beneath the lights of the bridge. It's not exact–but it's close enough.

"How do you say *fucking dickhead* in Irish?"

"Gaelic," I correct, snorting a laugh. "It sounds better in English, I'm afraid."

"Well, that's what you are." She giggles, and I think she's teasing me–to a degree.

"I've been called worse."

"You don't know anything about me, just so you're aware."

"Not yet." I shrug. "I'm sure I can change that soon."

I feel her eyes on me, but I can't look at her right now. Not while I'm still trying to forget about what she said. I knew asking her out would be a big challenge to myself, but I wasn't aware of how much. Staying with her in this confined space is more than I can handle.

I'm this close to making a mistake and doing something I'll definitely regret.

"Is that really what you want?" she asks, her voice now low and curious. "To get to know me, I mean."

"Of course. Why else would I invite you to spend New Year's Eve with me?"

"I don't know. You said you had an offer for me," Heidi reminds me.

"That could've waited until tomorrow. Or even the day after that," I point out. "I wanted to spend this night with you. And I thought you might like the distraction as well. I'm glad you had no other plans with someone else."

"I don't have many friends, and my grandparents are at their fancy retirement home. There's going to have this huge party for the residents which makes me realize their lives are way more exciting than mine." She sighs.

I look sideways at her, making sure she's giving me permission to ask personal questions before I dive deeper into it. I don't want her to think I'm invading her space or prying too much into her life.

"You don't have many friends?" I ask, doing my best to sound casual and not judging. Which I'm not. I don't really have many friends either, just a few that I can count on the fingers of one hand. In the underworld, it's hard to trust anyone other than yourself.

"Not really," she replies. The sad tone in her voice doesn't go unnoticed, but I remain silent as I allow her to elaborate more.

Heidi takes a deep breath before continuing. "I was really shy when I was in high school, and while I was in college, I focused too much on helping my grandparents during my free time, so I didn't have much time left to go out with the other students. No one ever showed much interest in me anyway, so… I have no friends."

"I am sorry to hear that. It must be lonely sometimes." I'm not good at any of this, but I hope I'm conveying my genuine and honest feelings to her.

She shrugs, sinking back in her seat.

"Sometimes. Is it sadder to say I got used to it?"

"No, I get it." And I really do. "It is good that you have your grandparents though, right?"

"Absolutely. I don't know what I'd have done if I didn't have them. Life was really hard when I lost my parents."

I open and close my mouth, pondering if I should ask more. I can sense her body stiffening and tensing up beside me, and I don't want to bring up sad memories on New Year's Eve. I don't want to ruin our night by making her tell me about losing her parents, so I make a mental note to start that conversation at another time.

For now, I'll focus on making this an unforgettable night for

Heidi. And if I'm lucky enough, I'll finally be able to put a smile–an honest one–on her face.

Luckily, I don't have to think about what to say because we arrive at the restaurant, just in time for our reservation. There's a significant queue forming on the outside, but Tony instructed me to go in through the side door, telling the host that I have a reservation under his name.

I open the car door for Heidi and offer her my arm. Her hand wraps around my forearm, and the fact that she's touching me has my entire body on high alert.

We go inside the building, and a woman in a black suit guides us to the elevator.

"The restaurant is on the rooftop, sir. You can press this button, and someone will greet you up there and take you to your table," she informs me, stepping aside so the door closes.

When it opens again, it reveals the most beautiful view of Manhattan in the distance, the night sky clear and beautiful. I send a mental 'thank you' to Tony when I realize how mesmerized Heidi seems to be as she looks around and takes in one of the most beautiful views I have ever seen.

"Wow," is the only thing that comes out of her mouth as I gently place my hand on her lower back and guide her toward our table.

17

THE TASTE OF HIM

Heidi

This has to be the most beautiful place I've ever been to in my life. Not that I get out that much, but I don't think I would have had the opportunity to dine in such a luxurious restaurant with a spectacular view of Manhattan if it wasn't for Cal.

I'm glad I didn't push him to tell me where he was taking me because I actually *do* like surprises. When they're good surprises, anyway. I wasn't necessarily lying when I said I don't normally like them, but then, I wasn't expecting a surprise from him to be this magnificent.

He really managed to surprise me.

The fact that we've gone all the way to Staten Island is one thing, and then the view through these enormous glass windows is breathtaking. From this distance, with the water separating us from the mainland, Manhattan seems peaceful somehow, not the chaotic city I'm used to.

"Do you like it?" Cal's voice reaches my ear, and only then do I realize how close to my neck his lips really are. It causes an electric current to course down my spine, and I swallow hard before turning to answer him.

"It's amazing," I say honestly. "The city looks incredible from afar. I don't think I've ever seen it quite like this."

Cal nods, pushing my chair in for me when we finally reach our table. The restaurant is practically empty tonight, which strikes me as odd, given that it's New Year's Eve.

After settling in and ordering us a bottle of wine, we pick up our menus. It takes a while for me to choose because everything looks so delicious, but once I've made up my mind, he calls the server over, and she promises our food will be out quickly.

I sip my wine, admiring the outside view while Cal takes off his jacket and leans back in his chair. I try as hard as I can not to stare, but I can't ignore the way his muscles flex under his shirt. He looks exceedingly relaxed–and unbelievably hot.

The man is so effortlessly attractive, it's astounding.

How did I end up on a date with someone like him?

Well, that is, if this is really a date. He told me on the way here that he was interested in spending time with me and getting to know me, so that means this could be a date.

If the way he took me in when I opened the apartment door earlier is any indication of his intentions, I'd say he's just as attracted to me as I am to him. The energy and the sexual tension running between us is palpable, I admit. I'm definitely not wrong about that.

I wonder if he's having the same sort of inappropriate thoughts about me as I'm suddenly having about him.

Cal grabs his glass of wine from the table and lifts it to his mouth, slowly savoring the red liquid. I'm momentarily lost in the way his lips touch the rim, his Adam's apple bobbing up and down as he swallows, his tongue darting out to lick his lips…

Good God, what is wrong with me tonight? You have barely even started to drink, Heidi!

If I don't control myself, I can't even imagine what will happen once the wine starts kicking in.

"So, I have some news," I blurt out, trying to distract myself from his presence.

His brows shoot up, and he sets the glass down to pay attention to me. His gaze is so intense that I almost forget what I intended to mention to him.

"My grandma said the insurance company will be paying them soon," I tell him. I didn't want to talk about this tonight, but I don't know what else to talk about with him, and I don't want to overstep and end up asking about topics he's not willing to share with me.

"That's good news," he agrees with a sharp nod. "What do you intend to do with it? Are you going to reopen the store?"

"Yes, of course. I just don't know where to begin." I blink, feeling a little less on edge and take a sip of my wine. "I'll need to find a new storefront, of course. Then I'll need new inventory, new shelving, new… everything. But yes, I'll be reopening the store."

"Start small," Cal suggests, his eyes darkening as he stares at me.

"It's New York City," I remind him. Even when he's saying something obvious, which I could be offended by, my body responds to him. The intensity in his look is so strong that it's making my need for him almost impossible to hold back, and we're literally talking about books right now, not something… sexy. I swallow hard, adding, "Everyone has to start small. Plus, I'm just–I've only ever been a bookseller. It's all I know how to do, all I am. I'm not–I'm not good at these kinds of things."

"What kinds of things?"

"Being a business-woman."

"I will agree to disagree with that," he murmurs, his voice raspy and sexy.

"I mean it," I retort, chuckling to hide my embarrassment. He's so good at flirting, it's disconcerting. "I'm just a bookseller. *Was*," I correct.

"You're wrong about that. You're remarkable. What you do for a living has nothing to do with it."

How can he be so good with his words? Maybe he spends more time reading than he lets on to be so articulate.

"It must be nice to know you got game, huh?" I tease, sipping from my wine, hoping it gives me some liquid courage to navigate this conversation in the best way possible without embarrassing myself in front of him.

"You're making me work harder than ever," Cal replies with a smirk. "But it's worth it if it means I get to spend the evening with you."

"The whole evening?" I smile around the rim of the glass, noticing his eyes dart to my lips for a split second.

Cal shrugs. "Sounds like a good plan to me."

"Let's see how dinner goes," I say boldly.

I have no idea where this courage is coming from, but I think the wine is starting to do its job of helping me navigate through this. I don't know how to interact with a man like Cal, but whatever it is I'm doing, it seems to be working on him.

Our food arrives quickly, but that doesn't stop us from flirting and teasing each other. I'm shocked at my ability to keep up the banter with him when I have so little experience.

I don't have enough experience dating to say whether or not it's like me to want to sleep with a man on the first date, but Cal is doing something to me I've never experienced before. It's almost like my mind has no choice. My body is attracted to him, and my ability to reason is out the window.

I just wonder if he feels the same way.

Once dinner is over, he takes me outside to the rooftop to watch the fireworks. The place is empty, and if it wasn't so far-fetched to even consider it, I'd think he somehow reserved it for just the two of us.

It's a privilege to be able to watch the fireworks from here, only the two of us, but I'd be lying if I said I care about the fireworks when I have Cal by my side, his hand on my lower back causing shivers to run through my entire body.

I look up to tell him this has been such a memorable night and that I really liked it, but when I realize how close he is, our lips almost touching, the words get lost in my throat.

"I hope you'll forgive me for what I'm about to do," he whispers, his breath fanning against my lips, "but I can't hold myself back anymore."

And with that, he closes the distance between us, sealing our lips in a passionate, almost desperate kiss.

I respond instantly, my breath hitching as he pulls me closer to him.

Every cell in my body is on fire, begging for more. More of him. More of this.

He tastes like wine and mint, with a subtle undertone of something smoky.

A moan escapes my throat when his free hand grabs the nape of my neck, holding me steady against him. As if sensing my needs, Cal deepens the kiss, his lips moving against mine with hunger.

I lift my hands, one curling lightly into the fabric of his shirt while the other rests on his shoulder. I press myself closer to him, and he responds, his arm wrapping completely around my waist, holding me tight against him.

His touch is hot against the cool fabric of my dress, enticing me, my nipples hardening under the silk as he brushes his chest against mine.

"I don't want to overstep," Cal mumbles against my lips, pulling back just enough to look into my eyes, "but what do you say we get out of here?"

I don't think I've ever agreed so quickly to something in my life, but I nod aggressively as I pull him back for another kiss, already missing his lips on mine.

18

THE BEGINNING OF SOMETHING

The drive back to Manhattan is excruciating. I can still feel Cal's hands on me, his lips hungry on mine. Every cell in my body is alert, anticipating the continuation of our kiss on that rooftop.

I can tell he feels the same. His grip on the wheel is so tight that his knuckles are turning white. Neither of us says anything, the sexual tension inside this car making it hard to breathe.

I don't ask where he's taking me. I just look outside the window, hoping we get there as soon as possible or I'll combust right here against his leather seat.

When Cal pulls the car inside the underground parking garage of a luxury apartment building in Midtown, I realize he's taking me to his place... not back to mine. A part of me scolds myself for agreeing to go to a man's apartment on a first date–a guy I barely know–but I shove that unwelcome thought aside.

I don't want to think tonight.

I just want to feel.

I just want to let Cal treat me like the woman that I am,

someone who deserves attention, someone who deserves to be treated like a queen. I know for a fact that is exactly what he has planned.

We get out of the car and head to the elevator, but he doesn't wait for us to get to his apartment. He pins me against the cold metal wall of the small compartment, his hands darting to my waist and holding me flush against his toned body.

I wrap my arms around his neck, pulling him closer, hoping he never lets me go.

The door opens again a few seconds later, and he guides me inside his penthouse. But I barely have the chance to look around.

The place is stunning, I can tell that much. It has high ceilings and ceiling height windows, with a beautiful view of the skyscrapers of New York, but his mouth on my neck distracts me from taking in the rest of the details.

"This is… a very nice… apartment," I mumble, closing my eyes when he nibbles my earlobe. A moan escapes my lips, and Cal turns me in his arms, making me face the window instead of him, his arms keeping me close to him, my back against his hard chest.

He caresses my stomach, down to my hips and up again until he reaches my breasts. Through the fabric, his thumbs find my hardened nipples, and I lean my head back, resting it against his shoulder and closing my eyes in pure bliss.

My legs are weak. I'd fall to my knees if he wasn't holding me upright.

His mouth finds my earlobe again, and he sucks it before trailing down my neck, pressing hot kisses to my skin.

I'm putty in his hands, and he knows it. He knows exactly what he's doing to me.

Every touch is honed to my pleasure like he already knows me—knows what makes me tick, what makes me wet, what he needs to do to have me totally, completely at his mercy.

I can't even remember my own name.

Cal massages my breasts, squeezing them harder when I moan and pulling me closer to him when I cry out his name.

"If you keep doing that, I won't last long, sweetheart," he warns me, his dark tone causing a new wave of shivers to course through me.

My panties are already soaked, but I can't make myself move out of this position. I'm afraid to take one step forward, out of his grasp, and end this magnetic, almost magical feeling.

"If you keep doing that, I won't last long either," I tell him, my voice almost unrecognizable.

Cal chuckles darkly behind me. "I've barely started with you."

Shit.

I don't think I'm ready for all he's promising.

He releases his grip on my breasts, but my protests are choked when he lowers his hands to my waist, slowly pulling my dress up, teasing me.

"You know, I really love this dress on you, and I'm struggling to decide if I should rip it off," he tells me, placing kisses up and down on my neck, making my vision blur.

"I don't think I can help you with that decision," I say, boldness creeping up in me once more. "But I can encourage you by saying I'm wearing a new thong I bought to match the dress."

Cal hisses against my ear before swirling me around to face him. A grin spreads on my lips as I notice his eyes scanning me up and down before he decides what to do.

"That's good," he agrees. "Off it is then."

He grabs the hem of my dress and pulls it over my head, tossing it aside. Thankfully, it doesn't rip. Shyness overtakes me for a split second when I realize I'm only in my panties in front of him, my chest completely bare and exposed.

But one more look at his hungry eyes is enough to make me feel powerful and confident.

"Fuck," Cal hisses. "That was the best choice, indeed."

"I'm glad you like what you see," I reply in a low, smooth voice.

It's incredible how he can make me feel so beautiful, so wanted, just from the look in his eyes.

But when he touches me again, his hands directly on my skin this time, it's like a new Heidi is born. No man has ever made me feel this desired before. No one ever lavished me with this much attention and devotion.

His hands dart to my breasts again, and while he teases me with his fingers on my nipples, I decide to do something to make him feel just as good as I'm feeling. I'm not as experienced as he is, that I'm sure of, but there is a thing or two I know about men.

I reach for his pants, finding his bulge and squeezing him, drawing a moan out of his throat for a change. Cal squirms under my touch, his grip on my breasts tightening involuntarily as I massage him.

"Shit, Heidi," he murmurs. "That's…" he trails off, and I chuckle to myself, satisfied to have done something right.

"Good?" I pry in a teasing tone.

"Better than good," Cal corrects, and with a swift movement, he tosses me backward onto his leather couch.

It's a huge piece of furniture, and I sink into it. Cal climbs on top of me, his muscular frame covering me entirely. But he doesn't lower himself on me, rather holding his weight up as he watches me.

"What?" I ask, my voice cracking with need.

"Just admiring the view for a second," he replies with a smirk.

"Care to speed that up? I really want to continue." I hate how needy I sound, but at this point, I couldn't care less.

"In a rush, huh?" he teases, pecking my lips.

I wrap my legs around his waist and pull him down on me as I get tired of waiting.

"I'm not really a patient girl, you know?"

Cal adjusts himself on top of me so that he's between my legs, and even though his pants and my underwear are still on the way, the small friction itself is enough to entice me even more.

"I can tell that," he notes, claiming my lips again with the same desperation and hunger as before.

I tangle my fingers in his hair, mussing it slightly and making him look hotter than ever. He seems to like the feel of my hands on him, too.

His kiss moves to my jaw, down my neck, and then to my collarbone. When the stubble on his face grazes the soft skin of my breast, I swallow down a moan of anticipation.

Then he takes one breast in his mouth, sucking and nipping at it, making me see an entire universe of stars.

I buck my hips, desperate for more, anything that will make this pent up energy lessen, but Cal seems to be taking his time like he said he would. One hand is on my breast while the other moves up my calf and thigh, reaching close to where I need him the most.

His finger grazes the lace of my panties, and I close my eyes, preparing myself for what's to come. He pushes the fabric aside with one finger, just enough so he can access my soaked folds, and when his thumb brushes my clit, I moan his name. Loud.

"You like that, sweetheart?" he asks in a provocative tone.

I can't provide an answer. I can only hope my moans and squirming under his touch are enough to let him know I want more.

I need more.

He starts working his fingers faster and harder on my most sensitive area, his thumbs circling and adding pressure, making me moan louder.

My limbs start to go weak, my entire body preparing for the wave of pleasure about to hit me.

I don't dare open my eyes, allowing myself this selfish moment of satisfaction. I can lavish him with attention afterward.

But as soon as I feel the beginning of that electric wave approaching, Cal pulls back, getting on his knee and staring back at me.

"Shit, what are you doing?" I ask, shocked and incredulous.

He's not leaving me like this, is he?

Cal shakes his head, reassuring me that he isn't done yet. Then he finds the hem of my panties, sliding them down my legs, leaving me completely naked before him.

"I told you I'm only getting started," he tells me, before leaning down on me, this time his mouth replacing his fingers.

19

TAKE ME TO PARADISE

Heidi

"Oh, my..." I trail off, unable to finish my sentence while Cal's tongue flicks out and ravishes my clit with enthusiasm.

My whole body shivers, my muscles tightening and breaking into spasm as my orgasm finally reaches its peak. Every cell inside of me is so sensitive to his touch, I wouldn't be able to form a proper sentence at the moment, even if my life depended on it.

My fingers are tangled in his hair, keeping his head trapped between my legs, even though he doesn't seem to be ready to get out of there yet.

I drop my head back, closing my eyes to savor how good it feels to reach climax with only his mouth on my body. If he's this good with his tongue, I can only imagine what he can do with his dick inside of me.

The wave of pleasure starts dissipating when Cal pulls back, and I allow myself to take a deep breath. If I want this to keep going–which I absolutely do–I need to pull myself together first.

I feel my cheeks burning when I realize Cal is staring at me, completely vulnerable and naked under him. I'm sure I look anything but sexy now, spread on his leather couch as if he just sucked the life out of me, which honestly, that's exactly what it feels like.

It must feel good for a guy to know he was able to make a woman moan his name over and over, delirious with lust, only using his fingers and his tongue.

"That was… something else," I finally manage to say, looking up at him. Normally, I wouldn't like to inflate someone's ego like this, but to be fair, Cal deserves the credit.

His eyes still hold that hunger and darkness that makes my insides churn with desperation.

Of course, he's not done yet.

He made me feel good while all I did was stroke him a little. I'm positive that it didn't do as much for him as it did for me.

Cal chuckles, shifting uncomfortably on the couch. My gaze lowers to the bulge in his pants. I'm glad it's still there, which means he's ready and waiting for me.

I don't want to disappoint him or leave him hanging. The guy just gave me the best orgasm of my life, and he's promising to give me way more tonight.

Cal doesn't reply to what I said, giving me the time I need to compose myself. I ponder waiting until my heartbeat settles back to normal, but I don't want this moment to end. If I take too long, it might break the spell surrounding us, and I'm not ready for the night to be over yet.

I can think of the consequences and regret it all tomorrow. But not tonight. Not *now*.

So, without saying another word, I get to my feet, gathering all the courage and determination I can to move toward him.

I crash my lips into his before either of us can say anything else. It's like we never separated. I'm still sensitive to his touch, my skin burning as his hands roam over me and pull me toward his hard chest.

I reach for his belt, unbuckling it. Cal's breath catches in his throat as he pulls back from our kiss and looks down at what I'm doing. I'm grateful that my hands aren't shaking as I open his button and work his pants down, leaving him only in his black boxers.

My eyes widen slightly as I get a better look of what's underneath the thin fabric, anticipating having it all inside of me.

"Need some time, baby?" he teases with his eyebrows raised.

I look up at him, a grin forming on my lips.

"Nah, I think I'm good," I reply, kissing him again.

I reach for his length, and while moaning against my mouth, Cal pulls me and walks us backward, holding me tight and guiding us to another room. I hope it's his bedroom. I could use a comfortable bed to get lost in him. The couch was great, but I'm sure his bed must look and feel a thousand times better.

As soon as my back hits the soft mattress, I find out I'm not wrong. It's like I'm lying on a cloud.

The room is completely dark except for a dim lamp in the corner, which is the only thing allowing me to see Cal. His eyes are darkened by shadows and lust, and I spread my legs apart, giving him enough room to fit his tall frame between my legs.

"You're so fucking hot, Heidi," he tells me, starting to slide his boxers down his legs.

I watch him, swallowing hard as I wait for him to finally get rid of all the layers of clothing and get back to me.

The whole scene is so sexy and effortlessly arousing that I can't recognize myself and my dirty thoughts. It feels like a scene straight out of one of those steamy romance books I like reading so much. Having read so many of them is coming in handy right now. Otherwise, I'd have no idea what to do to make Cal feel as good as he's making me feel. I don't want to be selfish and focus only on my own pleasure

"You're very hot, too," I say, licking my lower lip in what I hope is a sexy way.

"Am I?" he asks, amused, his thick accent working me up even more.

I nod. "Yeah. You got me on my back on the first date. That's a first for me."

A glimpse of desire crosses his eyes and face, and Cal finally moves forward, adjusting himself between my legs, his body completely naked against mine.

There's nothing between us anymore, only our skin brushing each other, causing sparks to erupt between us.

His mouth finds my neck, causing my eyes to roll backward.

I feel his hardness against my folds, his tip playing at my wet entrance and causing me to moan in protest. I bulk my hips toward him, looking for any kind of stimulation, feeling more than ready for him again.

Cal chuckles against my skin, clearly enjoying himself by provoking me and making me desperate.

"You like making me beg, don't you?" I complain, locking my ankles together behind him and pulling him down on me further.

"Can't say I don't," he replies, kissing me hungrily.

Our tongues play together while Cal slides his dick up and down my slit, deliciously circling my sensitive clit in a slow dance.

My brain is foggy, my heart beating so fast against my chest that I can hear the blood thrumming through my ears. I'm aching with need, and if he takes too long, I won't be able to wait for him.

"You're so wet for me," he murmurs against my lips, his voice rough.

"I am," I reply, slightly frustrated it's taking him so long. "What you're going to do about it?"

Cal pulls back just enough to look into my eyes, and for a moment, I wonder if he's going to give up.

I hold my breath, waiting for him to make the next move, even though my insides are burning up, and my mind is numb.

"Are you sure about this?" he asks me, his voice firm and his expression suddenly serious.

Is he kidding me? I love a man who asks for consent, but I wouldn't be able to hold back now even if I wasn't.

Instead of answering him with words, I grind myself against him, my wetness sliding against his length easily. "Is that enough of an answer for you?" I retort breathlessly.

Cal swallows hard. He reaches for his drawer, retrieving a condom from it. I silently thank him for thinking about it, because at this moment, if it were up to me, I'd make the mistake of having sex without protection.

That'd be stupid of me, of course. But Cal has that effect on me. I can't think properly. I don't even feel like myself when I'm around him.

He returns his attention to me and as if a switch has been flipped, his actions become more aggressive, more purposeful. He trails hot kisses from my neck to my breasts, making me arch off the mattress, providing him full access to me.

I gasp, gripping his shoulders as he expertly, but carefully, enters me, slowly filling me. At first, his thrusts are slow, and he's watching me to make sure I'm not in any pain.

But as soon as I let out a loud moan, my hips in sync with his, Cal seems to have the reassurance he needs to speed up.

My legs tremble with anticipation as his fingers find the flesh of my hips, gripping me so tightly that I'm left on the edge of oblivion.

"You're so fucking tight," he whispers against my ear, our chests pressed together. My nipples are hard, rubbing against his muscles and sending shivers down to my core.

The familiar feeling of an orgasm building is unmistakable, and I close my eyes, allowing myself to enjoy the ride. I don't think I've ever experienced pleasure in such an intense way.

I feel like I'm floating away to heaven. And if that was the case, I'd gladly accept my demise, wrapped in Cal's strong arms. He's holding me so tightly, it seems he never wants this to end.

If only he knew I also hope to stay here as long as I can.

As I teeter on the brink, my inner walls throbbing around him, I feel Cal's length pump inside of me as he also reaches climax.

"Holy shit," he murmurs against my neck.

I can only nod in agreement with him, unable to do anything other than enjoy the wave of pleasure that engulfs me like a tsunami.

With a final, deep thrust, Cal presses a single kiss on my lips before collapsing on top of me, completely worn out.

ALARMING PHONE CALL

Cal

I can't wrap my mind around the fact that I finally got to have Heidi to myself. Taking her on a date had been a surprise already, but when she agreed to coming here with me, I was stunned.

I thought she was going to freak out once she realized I'd brought her to my apartment, but one look at her and her expression told me she was *more* than pleased.

I didn't think it was possible for her to look sexier than she had when I first picked her up, but she managed to prove me wrong.

A completely different woman showed up in front of me once I began to entice her. The look of lust, desire, longing, and yearning that crossed her face had me on my knees. Literally.

I've had plenty of sexual partners in my life, lots of different experiences, but even so, Heidi brought out things in me that I've never felt before.

I couldn't get enough of her.

And never once have I brought a woman to my apartment, let alone my bed.

This is my safe harbor. My home. The only place I feel like myself.

For reasons I can't explain, I brought her here without a second thought.

Even now, while I caress her smooth hair, watching her chest move up and down slowly as she sleeps peacefully in my arms, I can't say I made a mistake. I'd do it all over again in a heartbeat if I had the chance.

This is the best way I could possibly imagine beginning the new year—with Heidi in my arms, waking up to the sunlight beaming through my window, her sweet scent invading my senses and making me feel at peace.

Something I haven't felt in a long time.

She hums softly beside me, shifting lazily and leaning her head against my chest. I wrap her tightly against me, taking the opportunity to hold her in my arms while I can.

As much as I try to convince myself this should mean nothing, and that after today, I should leave her the hell alone, I don't want her to wake up because she'll likely return to her senses. She might regret staying here. Hell, she might regret having sex with me.

I hate to admit that it would kill me to know she feels that way.

The truth is, I don't want to stop whatever this is. I'm not ready to break away from her. To not see her again.

"Good morning." Her sweet voice reaches my ears, and I look down, finding her beautiful blue eyes looking at me expectantly. She blinks slowly, her eyelashes moving as if she's trying to hypnotize me.

"Good morning," I reply softly. "Did you sleep well?"

A smile spreads across her face, her cheeks turning pink and giving her a rosy glow. Effortlessly, she is so fucking sexy. "Like I haven't slept in a long time," she confesses.

I tighten my grip around her, pulling her close to me. I inhale sharply, taking in the smell of coconut and lavender from her hair.

God, this woman will be the death of me.

"Glad I could provide you a good night's sleep," I say playfully.

Heidi slaps me softly on the shoulder, rolling her eyes at me. "I knew you had a big ego hidden somewhere," she muses, locking her gaze with mine. "You just tried to hide it last night, didn't you?"

I laugh, placing a kiss on her forehead. "I was trying to give you a good first impression," I tell her, hopping on her banter. "Did it work?"

She hums again, closing her eyes once more, feeling the sun touching her skin. I drink her in, watching the way her body fits perfectly within my embrace. It's like she's molded specially for me. "Yes, it did," she murmurs in response.

Her leg slips over mine, and with my fingers, I start drawing lazy circles on her bare back. Touching a woman like this would provoke an instant arousal for me in other circumstances, and even though Heidi's scent is working against me right now, a huge part of me just wants to enjoy this moment like this, with no sexual tension or anything like that. It's just us, carefree and relaxed, not worried about our next move or what to say.

It just feels…natural.

"What are you thinking about?" she pries, looking at me.

"Nothing, really." I shrug. "I'm just enjoying this moment."

And it's true.

But like anything in my life, nothing comes easy. Every time I feel a glimpse of happiness, the universe feels the urge to warn me I'm not *supposed* to be happy. Nothing is supposed to be this easy, this carefree.

I'm a fucking mafia boss.

My phone buzzes on my bedside table, and I close my eyes, taking a deep breath and cursing myself inwardly for not turning it off last night. Who would call me on the first day of the year at… what? What time is it? It must not even be seven in the morning, judging from the amount of sunlight shining through the windows. A moan of complaint escapes my lips as I try to ignore the call.

But Heidi shifts beside me, clearly bothered. "Aren't you going to answer it?" The hint of curiosity in her voice amuses me, but I can't focus on it too long because the phone doesn't fucking stop.

"Shit! What's a guy gotta do to enjoy a single morning without being bothered?" I grunt, turning to grab my phone.

Tony's name flashes on my screen, and my stomach twists at the sight of it. Why is he calling me on a holiday? Shouldn't he be enjoying the day with his family? Even a guy like him isn't working today, right?

"Yes?" I answer, not hiding how irritated his call makes me.

"Sorry to bother you so early. I think you'll want to know what I have to tell you," he informs me cryptically.

"Get to it then," I grumble.

"Can't risk it over the phone," Tony explains.

Fuck.

Of course he wouldn't give me confidential information over the phone. The guy is a fucking vault.

"Does it have to be now?"

"Not if you're not in a hurry to catch the bastards after you and your girl," he replies sarcastically.

I look down at Heidi, who's still staring at me expectantly, although she tries to hide it by looking away from me as our eyes meet. It's fucking endearing, and I hate the fact that doing what Tony wants means leaving her behind. But his words hit me hard. The photo I received of Heidi leaving my bar forms inside my mind, and I know I can't ignore it.

Not if it means it will get me closer to whoever is threatening me— and her. Tony wouldn't disturb me if it wasn't important. I know that much. And as much as I hate myself for agreeing to it, I have to go.

"Fine, I'll meet you at the bar in thirty minutes," I inform him before hanging up. "I'm really sorry, but something came up," I tell Heidi, watching the way her expression hardens.

She's still as beautiful as always, but I'd take the glowy Heidi anytime of the day if that meant I didn't have to see the look of disappointment in her face staring back at me now "Oh, sure. Of course. I didn't mean to overstay my welcome anyway," she says, struggling to get out of my grasp. But I hold her harder, keeping her against me and forcing her to look me in the eyes.

"You're not," I emphasize. "It kills me to have to leave this bed–and you–but I can't ignore it. I promise I'll make it up to you, if you'll allow me, that is," I add, unsure if this is indeed what she wants.

For all I know, she could simply want to forget this night ever happened and just go back to her life without speaking to me ever again.

Heidi stares at me, searching for something in my face that I can't quite interpret. I just hope she finds what she's looking for so I can see her again. She nods slightly, and I take that as a yes, not wanting to give her more time to change her mind.

"I'll give you a ride to your apartment," I tell her, finally releasing her from my grip and sliding out of bed to look for my boxers and grab some pants.

Heidi does the same, dressing at the speed of light. Her face is turned from me, but I can tell by the way her muscles are tense and from her body language that she's disappointed in me.

But how can I blame her?

I'm being a major dick for ditching her like this after having the best night of my life with her.

The words are stuck in my throat, though, as I finish getting dressed, watching as she pulls her dress over her head and buckles her shoes, not daring to look at me again.

Not even once.

And because of that, I know I fucked up. Hard. I wonder if I can ever make it up to her and convince her to forgive me.

Tony's information better be good for have fucking cost me this time with Heidi–especially if she doesn't forgive me.

21

TASTE OF DISAPPOINTMENT

HEIDI

BEING PRACTICALLY DRAGGED OUT OF CAL'S BED AND HIS APARTMENT IS not the way I imagined ending our date. I hadn't originally planned to sleep at his place either, but after the best sex of my life, I didn't have the strength to leave his arms, get dressed, and call for a cab.

I didn't think Cal would have let me do that even if I'd wanted to, but now that he's basically told me to leave, I'm starting to doubt my instincts.

He reassured me that he didn't want to go either, and I could tell by his expression that he was being honest with me. But as he drives me back to my apartment, I wonder what got him out of bed so early.

I don't think our relationship is close enough for me to ask him—even though we've seen one another completely naked and vulnerable—so I stay quiet the entire time, watching the empty, snow-covered streets out the window. Even with my coat on, and the heat from the car, I'm shivering.

I also think it has something to do with Cal's eyes on me. I feel his gaze every once in a while, like he's checking on me to make sure I'm not angry.

I can't say I'm not. I get that he has work to do, and I'm not a priority in his life. For all I know, I am just a one-night stand, which is something he probably has all the time.

But what can I do? I can't force my feelings to bend to my will. I can't pretend I'm not upset that we couldn't wake up in each other's arms and maybe have a nice breakfast together. Maybe even go for a second round before he had to drop me home.

Yes, perhaps I fantasize too much. Grandma always says I'm a hopeless romantic, and I'm starting to believe she's right.

I can't fall for a guy like Cal. We have absolutely nothing in common. My life is boring, uneventful, and I'm sure I was far from the best sex he ever had.

On the other hand, Cal must be a man with an adventurous life, an exciting job every night at the bar with women falling at his feet. What could we possibly have in common?

You're ridiculous, Heidi.

"Hey..." His voice pulls me out of my thoughts, which is a good thing. I tend to overthink everything, and to be fair, this is not the type of situation I should be overthinking. Cal and I spent the night together, and that's all. Nothing else is to be expected.

So, why can't I force myself to believe that and just move on? Why does it feel like he's holding my heart in his hands and intends to grip it until it stops beating?

"Heidi?" Cal calls, his tone more emphatic this time.

"Yes?" I turn to look at him, my eyes slightly widened with surprise. I hadn't noticed how distracted I was.

"Is everything okay?" he asks, his brows creasing.

That look on his face is concern, isn't it? Why is he concerned about whether or not I'm okay? Does he care if I'm upset or disappointed?

"Yes, everything is fine. I'm just a bit tired," I lie.

Cal doesn't seem to believe me, but he doesn't say anything else, focusing on the road ahead and taking his eyes off me.

I almost let out a sigh of relief, but I don't think I'll be able to do it until I leave his car and can take a deep breath without feeling inebriated by his scent.

"Listen, I–" Cal begins, but whatever it is he has to say is interrupted by his phone buzzing.

Who the hell is calling him so early? What is it that he does that requires his presence so urgently on the first morning of the year? His bar isn't even open yet.

Unless he has other businesses, which I guess he probably does. But can't it wait?

Cal curses to himself, reaching for his phone in his pocket. I look away, staring out the window so he doesn't think I'm paying attention and eavesdropping.

"What?" he answers sharply. He doesn't even hide the annoyance in his voice. "I'm coming. Just entertain him and tell him to wait," he adds before hanging up on whoever called him. "I'm really sorry about that."

I look at him, pretending I'm not feeling rejected. I have no right to feel that way. Last night, Cal made me feel like the most desired and worshiped woman on this planet. But that doesn't mean he still feels that way about me this morning. I don't know why I'm so emotional today.

"It's okay. You have nothing to apologize for," I tell him, glad my voice doesn't betray my conflicted feelings.

"Yes, I do. I meant it when I said I would never leave that bed if this wasn't urgent," he explains firmly. "Do you think I can see you again tonight?"

My insides churn when I remember everything we did together last night, anticipation pooling at my core. Do I want to see him again? *Yes*. Do I want him to do all of that to me again? *Fuck yes*.

An alarm goes off somewhere deep inside me as a reminder that I'm not able to control my feelings when it comes to Cal, but I choose to ignore it. Now doesn't seem like the time to be worried about getting hurt. If he wants to see me again, it means I did something right last night. And that he likes me, at least a little, if he wants to spend his precious time with me again.

If anyone could hear my inner monologue, they'd think I'm desperate for love and attention, but that's not it. I don't know what it is, but something about Cal has me feeling like a teenager again, wanting to take the opportunity life is throwing at me to be with a guy as sexy and kind as him. I haven't known him for long, but ever since the incident with the bookstore, he has done nothing more than help me. I didn't give him much of a choice at first, but he didn't have to do all he did. He's been such a gentleman–attentive, thoughtful, and caring with me. None of the men I got involved with in the past were half as respectful as Cal is proving to be. I do want to spend more time with him if I can.

"You don't have to do that just to make it up to me," I reply instead. "I promise. Everything is fine. You owe me nothing."

But Cal shakes his head. "That's not what this is. I had a really nice time with you last night, Heidi, and I want to see you again."

That sounds more believable. I don't need much more than that, but I can't help but want to make him try a bit harder. Hiding a grin from him, I shrug nonchalantly. "It wasn't anything special, was it?"

A shadow crosses his eyes, and a relentless smirk forms on his lips as we finally reach my building, and he parks out front. "Nothing special, huh?" he echoes, reaching for the nape of my neck and pulling me closer to him. "I don't think I can agree with that." His hot breath fans my lips and makes a shiver run down my spine.

Oh, God, if he wasn't in a hurry, I wouldn't mind if tossed me into the backseat and took me right here and now–in the middle of the street.

"Maybe a thing or two," I admit.

A smile threatens to appear on my lips, but Cal claims them with his mouth before it happens. His tongue crashes against mine in a desperate, passionate kiss, as if he wants to commit how I taste and feel in his arms to memory.

He traps me against him with one hand on my neck and the other on my thigh, and a moan escapes me when I feel the heat radiating from his body.

He pulls away from our kiss, leaning his forehead against mine. "I'll make sure to remember that later and change your mind," he promises me before giving a peck on my lips and leaning back in his seat.

A bit numb, I swallow hard, adjusting my hair and dress before I climb out of his car. My cheeks are burning, and the butterflies in my stomach are throwing a party.

But Cal is in a hurry, and I need to get out of his way.

"I'll call you later. Be ready after sunset," he adds before I open the door, and we part ways.

2 2

HEATING UP A CHILLY NIGHT

Taking Heidi to her apartment this morning and being forced to leave her after the incredible night we spent together was one of the hardest things I've ever had to do, and that's saying a lot.

I cursed Tony the entire way to my bar, but I have to admit it ended up being the right choice after all. I don't know how he did it, considering none of my men succeeded when they investigated it, but Tony managed to confirm that Mateo's cartel was involved in the attack on Christmas' Eve.

He didn't confirm who took that picture of Heidi leaving my bar, but that wasn't necessary. I have all the confirmation I need already.

When I asked him why he couldn't tell me this news over the phone, he showed me a picture of two cars, one of them which I immediately recognized as being the one who attacked me that same night.

Tony gave me some confidential information on how to track down Mateo's men and told me he's trying to find out who is leading them now and why they are targeting me and not the Saints.

My mind is a fucking mess every fiber of my being wanting to return to Heidi and forget about this part of my life. The fact that she managed to give me some semblance of peace last night, and made me feel like myself, is something I can't put aside.

Not after having tasted her.

During my meeting with Tony, we discussed our next steps, and after I gave orders to all of my men, I left the bar and headed to my apartment to take a shower and get dressed to meet Heidi again.

Her scent is still all over the place when I get back, and it is painfully excruciating to return to my bedroom and not find her there, waiting for me.

After making sure I look presentable, I rush to her apartment, the engine in my car roaring to life as I pull out of the garage and onto the street. Heidi is already waiting for me at the same place I left her this morning, only this time she's not as dressed up, although she still looks sexy as hell.

She's wearing a plain, white T-shirt with a leather jacket over it, which kind of reminds me of the way I was dressed when I first met her. It's fucking sexy, and I bet she knows the effect it's having on me. Her outfit is completed with black pants and combat boots. Her hair is tied up in a ponytail, and although I love her hair falling down her shoulders, and how it feels sliding through my fingers, this look causes the monster inside of me to snarl when I spot the skin of her neck exposed.

I watch as she gets inside the car, grinning at her as she fastens her belt and turns toward me. Her beautiful blue eyes stare back at me with amusement, and I know she can tell I'm fucking aroused. I shift uncomfortably in my seat, my pants feeling a bit too tight all of a sudden.

"Hey, you," she greets me with a huge smile on her seductive, plump lips....

I consider pulling her to me and kissing the life out of her, but I know once I touch her, there won't be a stop to it. I won't be able to control myself, and for now, I want to be able to spend some time with her and make up for practically kicking her out of my bed this morning.

"Hey," I reply, driving away from her building. "How was your day?" I ask, trying to keep things light while I take us somewhere nice.

I haven't thought this date through. I've been too eager to see her. If nothing comes to mind, I can just drive back to my apartment and order something for us to eat while we drink some wine and spend some quality time together watching the city sky from the balcony. I know she loves beautiful views, and my penthouse has a fucking good one.

But I've never done this before. My "dates" have always been with women picked up from my bar, women who know who, and what, I am. I've never gone on a second date.

Until now, I've never wanted to.

"My day was fine. I just took a nap and watched a movie," Heidi answers with a shrug. "I hadn't realized how tired I was until I sat on the couch. That was a big mistake." She chuckles, making me smile at her.

She makes life sound so simple and easy. For a moment, it makes me want to have that too. *With her.*

"I guess I am partially to blame for not letting you get a good night's sleep," I admit.

"It was worth it," Heidi fires back with a sexy grin.

Fuck, she's hot. If we weren't in the middle of the street, I would pull over and just claim her right in her seat.

"I thought you said there wasn't anything remarkable about it," I tease.

She hums, shrugging and focusing her attention on the buildings flying by outside her window. "I was wrong."

I take us to Central Park, parking several blocks away and buy us both an ice cream. We walk around the park, enjoying the cold night air while she tells me about some ideas she had for the bookstore.

I give her all of my attention—or as much as I can, struggling to keep my hands to myself while seeing her dressed like this—but it seems to be enough for Heidi, who looks more excited than I think I've ever seen her.

"I'm sure whatever you do will be a success," I tell her, finally unable to resist her anymore and pulling her toward me. Thankfully, this part of the park is nearly empty now, so I pull her into a shadowed nook of trees just off the trail. A quick look around tells me that there's no risk of anyone seeing us, so with that in mind, I kiss her.

Hard.

As if she is the air that I need to keep living.

My hands dart to her ass, and I press her against me, showing her how needy she makes me. That simple friction is enough to make my toes curl with arousal.

"God, I need you," I murmur against her mouth.

She doesn't say anything, but her actions are enough for me. The way her fingers find my hair and entangle in it, and the way her mouth responds to mine is all the answer that I need.

"Can we go back to your car?" she asks, breathlessly, pulling away from a kiss.

I take a step back to look at her, not letting go of her completely. "Do you want to go already?" I don't hide the concern from my expression. I don't want her to think I asked her out only for this, but I also can't hold back anymore.

She drives me insane.

Heidi shakes her head, tugging at my shirt. "No," she murmurs against my lips. "But I don't want to give anyone here a show."

Ah…

"Sure, you're right. I'm sorry. I didn't mean to–"

"Shut up and stop apologizing." She grabs my hand and runs back to where I parked the car, dragging me along with her. This section of the lot is dark and there's no one milling around, which only leads me to dirty thoughts. I unlock the car, but before I suggest anything, Heidi opens the back door and climbs inside.

I look from one side to the other, making sure there isn't anyone around, and hop in after her. Normally, I wouldn't be this careless and bold, but Heidi makes me feel like I'm a fucking teenager again, horny and desperate to get my dick inside of her.

I close the door, and before I know it, she's on my lap, her legs straddling me. My dick throbs inside my pants, and for the first time in my life, I regret buying such a small car. We can barely move in here.

Heidi kisses me, her moans enticing me even more than before.

I reach for her jacket, getting it out of the way and tossing it into the front seat.

I'm happy to see she is just as eager to get me inside of her as I am to be there. Her hips rock back and forth, begging me to make her see stars again. I'm dying to hear her moaning my name. That's all I've been thinking about the entire day.

With such limited space, I try my best to please her. Her clothes reminded me of just how hot she is, but right now, they are a fucking nuisance. There are too many layers between us and not enough space to get rid of them.

I tug at the hem of her shirt, struggling a little to pull it over her head. Her breasts welcome me from behind her white, lacy bra. It's a beautiful, delicate piece, but right now, I don't have enough patience to admire it.

I pull it down, too hungry to unfasten it properly. I find her hardened nipple, sucking at it voraciously while I cup and squeeze her other breast.

"Shit," Heidi hisses on top of me, arching her back and offering herself to me. "I should have chosen a skirt instead. These pants are so tight and hard to take off," she complains, her nails sinking into my shoulders.

"I fucking hate this car," I grunt against her breast. I wrap my arms around her waist, and I pull her closer to me, trying to erase the little distance between our bodies.

She's right. Her pants are in the way, and I can't do anything about it here.

"Maybe we should go to a suitable place. I don't want to fuck you in the middle of a parking lot." I pull away.

I'm stunned with my self-control. I have no idea how I managed to put some distance between us, as hard as I am. I can't even think clearly. My mind is consumed with lust and passion.

But Heidi deserves more. I don't want to have sex with her as if she means nothing to me. And even though I don't want to give my brain enough time and space to consider what this means, I know for a fact that this is not how I want this night to end.

"It's okay, I don't mind," Heidi says, her voice low and breathless. But her eyes hold a different glow now. If I didn't know better, I'd say she's touched by what I said.

I don't know her well enough to know who she truly is on the inside, but I know one thing—she's the type of woman who deserves everything. All the attention I can lavish her with, all the care I can offer her; she deserves to be worshipped. And that's exactly what I plan on doing.

But not here.

"Come on. I'm sure we can find somewhere safer," I tell her. It takes everything within me to get her off my lap and climb back into the driver's seat, but ultimately, I manage to do that, and she gets back into the passenger seat, putting her shirt back on but not her jacket.

Every nerve ending in my body is worked up, all the pent up energy threatening to burst from inside. But I hold on tight to the steering wheel as I navigate us out of the lot, stealing glances of Heidi every now and then to make sure she's still on the same page as me.

We're getting close to my apartment building when I spot something that makes my blood freeze in my veins—a black SUV in the lane to my right. It looks suspicious. I don't know why I think that, but there's no way I am wrong about this.

One look at the plate, and that's enough to confirm my suspicions. This is the same vehicle that was involved in the attack on the bar. The same vehicle that Tony showed me a picture of this morning. The same vehicle that was driven by the person responsible for blowing up Heidi's bookstore.

My fingers tighten on the wheel, my knuckles turning white as I consider what to do.

I don't want to scare Heidi, and I sure as hell won't take her to my apartment now—or hers, for that matter—so I need to think of a plan B.

There's only one place I can take her where I'll be certain she's safe, and I'll have my men to take care of these bastards if they try anything.

I turn at the next corner and head toward the bar.

2 3

———

DISTRACTION

"I DIDN'T THINK YOU MEANT YOUR BAR WHEN YOU SAID 'SOMEWHERE safer,'" Heidi points out with a note of amusement in her voice as I guide us inside through the back door.

I managed to shake whoever was following us, but I don't think I lost them completely. They might be somewhere near, watching my next moves. They know I own this place, but I can't show Heidi any sign of worry or fear right now.

I can only hope they don't have ulterior motives tonight other than keeping an eye on us. An attack would be a fucking mess with Heidi here with me.

"It wasn't my first thought, but considering you really liked my office the last time you were here, I figured, why not?"

Heidi seems surprised by my answer, but her expression softens as soon as I open the door to my office, and she finds everything exactly as she remembers it.

"Make yourself comfortable," I tell her, pecking her on the lips,

137

one hand gripping her waist. "I'll just send my men away and get us both something to drink," I lie.

I will get us something to drink, but I don't plan to send my men away. Or… maybe I do. I need to have them on the cartel's tail. It's the only clue we've had in a long time, I can't risk losing it.

"I'll be right back."

I close the door behind me, leaving Heidi alone in my office as I head upstairs to find Hunter or Sam, or anyone who can go after the SUV I just saw.

"Ian!" I call, finding the barkeep in his usual spot behind the counter.

The bar isn't crowded, and the staff is already getting ready for the night shift, which will be much busier.

Ian looks at me with concern in his eyes as he notices my serious tone and expression.

"Where are Sam and Hunter?" I ask bluntly, not bothering to lower my voice.

Everyone nearby is part of the Irish Kings, so thankfully I don't need to be careful with what I say. At least, not if Heidi does as I said and keeps her beautiful ass inside my office until I get back.

"Hunter is out grabbing the stock of beer for tonight, and Sam went to the storage room," he tells me with a frown. "Is everything okay, Boss?"

I nod, already turning on my heel and heading for the storage room. As he informed me, I find my best man squatting down, grabbing a box of whiskey from the bottom shelf.

"I need you to go on a mission," I say, not even bothering to greet him properly.

Sam turns to look at me, getting to his feet in an instant. "What happened?" he asks, the box of whiskey already forgotten.

"There was an SUV from the cartel tailing me and Heidi," I explain, lowering my voice in case someone wanders by who doesn't need to hear all of this.

"Are they here?" Sam frowns.

"I managed to outwit them, but I'm sure they know I came here since they know the location of the bar. I brought Heidi here with me, so I need you to get the guys and track them down," I order. "I'll stay here and entertain her until it's safe to take her back home. I don't want anyone finding out where she lives." That thought alone makes my insides churn. The fact they already know about her existence, and that they dared to threaten me with a picture of her, is more than enough. The last thing I need is to give them more ammunition.

"I'll get to it, Boss. Don't worry," he reassures me with a sharp nod. "What do you want us to do? Should we get them or just watch their moves?"

I consider his question. Do I want them to make a mess and bring the guys here for a one-on-one interrogation while Heidi is inside? Definitely not. But this might be our only chance to do it.

"I'll leave you to make that decision. Depending on what they are doing, you can just follow them and find out where their headquarters are in the city. We can form a plan afterward," I say. "If things get ugly, get them to our warehouse in the port. Keep me updated."

Sam nods once more before leaving the storage room.

I take a deep breath and head back upstairs, asking Ian to prepare Heidi a cocktail. The bar is busier now, and some patrons crowd the bar, ordering their beers. Others are playing pool or sitting at the tables.

A few minutes later, I get back to my office with Heidi's drink in hand, finding her seated in my chair, her feet lazily resting on my desk as if she owns this place.

My dick twitches in my pants as I kick the door behind me closed.

"I took the liberty of snooping around since you took so long and left me here by myself," she informs me, shooting a smile in my direction.

I put her cocktail down on the table in front of the couch and stride toward her, my steps slow and cautious, like a lion stalking its prey.

Her eyes are stuck on me as she watches me close the distance between us. One look at her, and all my worries are forgotten, the black SUV vanishing from my mind completely.

But before I'm able to put my hands on her again, she gets on her feet, brushing past me and heading for the couch. She takes the cocktail from the table and sips the colorful liquid, her tongue darting out to lick her bottom lip.

The whole scene is fucking sexy as hell, but it's like she doesn't even realize the effect she has on me. Heidi looks so innocent, so fragile and pure at first glance, but knowing what she is capable of doing with her mouth, and that perfect body of hers, I can't look at her and imagine myself doing anything else other than fucking her to oblivion.

"I was thinking... I'd like to have a bookstore where I could add my own design, everything I like. Kind of what you did with your office here," she notes, gesturing around the room. "I love what you've done here, and I think it'd be nice to do something similar in my new shop. What do you think?"

Her asking my opinion catches me off guard, but surprisingly, I feel happy that she did. It's like she cares about what I think, and somehow that tells me a lot about how she sees me and the position I have in her life.

"I think that's the best idea you've had so far," I tell her honestly.

"I don't know what I'll do yet, but being here makes me feel at peace. Like I belong," she continues, sipping her drink again. "And you could help me. Maybe tell me where you bought all of these nice pieces."

"You can take it all if you want."

Her eyes narrow at me, but she doesn't look pissed. "I don't want you to give away what's yours. I can buy the things I like, I just need you to tell me where to find them," she retorts.

"I know. But I'm willing to give them to you anyway."

She studies me, silence enveloping us for a moment. I hold my breath, wondering if I said something to ruin our night. Her eyes hold an intense gaze, and if I could guess, I'd say she's just as eager for me to get into her pants as I am, but I don't want to make a wrong assumption.

When she swallows down another gulp of her drink and walks toward me, I know I'm right.

Her mouth collides with mine, and she wraps her arms around my neck, pulling me toward her. I devour her, feeling alive now that I can taste her again.

I'm glad I told Ian not to show up here or allow anyone to come after me because this time, I don't intend to stop. I need to keep Heidi distracted–as well as myself–until I can take her home, and thankfully, this is the best way I can possibly think of.

Her jacket is on the floor in less than a minute. She doesn't wait for me to help her with her boots, kicking them off while I pull her shirt over her head. Wearing only her bra and her pants, I take her in, my eyes roaming over her from head to toe.

"You're overdressed," she complains, tugging at the bottom of my shirt and undressing me.

She slides her fingers across my abs and caresses my muscles, causing shivers to course through my body. I watch as she slides her hands down, until she gets to the waistband of my pants. She looks up at me, her eyes mischievous as she opens the button, and her hand delves beneath the fabric of my boxers.

I hiss when she wraps her soft, delicate fingers around my shaft, massaging me, pumping me up and down excruciatingly slowly.

Wanting something to do with my hands and needing to touch her, I cup her breasts while her ministrations leave me on the edge of insanity. Tired of her pants, I unzip them and slide them down, finally getting to see her beautiful, toned legs.

The lingerie set she's wearing leaves little to the imagination, but I intend to get rid of that as quickly as possible, too. I allow Heidi to remove my pants, and when I'm only in my boxers and tired of this make out session, I look at her, determined to start playing for real.

24

BLISS

HEIDI

THE STEAMY SESSION AT CAL'S CAR ONLY GOT ME WORKED UP ENOUGH to be desperate for him to take me. So much that I didn't even bother that he took me to his office out of all places. When he said he wanted to take me somewhere safer, I thought he was talking about his apartment, but to my surprise, I was even more aroused when he took me to his bar.

I never had sex in an office before, but I've read enough books to keep my imagination vivid and wanting to give it a try.

Standing in his office in nothing but my underwear turns me on more than I expected. The simple fact that someone could barge in at any minute and catch us excites me more than I'd like to admit.

God, I was never like this before. I wonder how Cal manages to turn me into this hungry woman who can only think about having sex.

Sure, I do want more from him, but right now, having sex with him leaves me fully satisfied, and if that's all I can get, well, I might as well take it while he is offering me.

The intense look of passion in his eyes is enough to make my core pool with need. Everything in me is already tense and sensitive, as if my body knows what he is about to do to me. The expectation and anticipation seems to be too much for me to handle, but I urge myself to get a grip so I can enjoy it further. I don't want it to end too quickly.

Cal is good at foreplay, and if last night was any indication of what he can do to me, I can expect he will take me over the edge again more than once tonight.

He finds the nape of my neck with his mouth, licking and sucking at the skin and making me moan his name.

He moves us backward until I'm against the wall behind his desk. Being pressed between his toned body and the wall leaves me breathless, but I can't find it in me to push him away so I can take a breath.

He seems to be the only oxygen I need right now.

His large hands roam the back of my thighs, and he easily pulls me up, as if I weigh nothing. I wrap my legs around his waist, twining our bodies together. His hard length brushes against my core, adding just enough pressure to make me choke on a moan.

Cal grunts against my skin, his teeth grazing at the soft flesh of my collarbone as he pushes himself harder against me.

"You should have taken those off, too," I complain, gesturing to my panties which are in the way of me getting what I so desperately need.

He looks at me, his eyes darkened by the shadows of desire, and that devilish smirk I like so much makes an appearance.

"Don't worry. I'll take care of that," he informs me, and to illustrate what he means, his fingers slip under the thin lace, immediately teasing me, circling my clit with expertise.

I bite down on my lower lip hard, preventing a loud moan from escaping my throat. My fingers sink into his shoulders, as I try to hold onto the last glimpse of reality I am struggling to keep.

My toes curl as his fingers speed up, slightly increasing the pressure on my sensitive nub.

"I-I won't last long if you keep doing that," I warn him.

A dark chuckle escapes him, but he doesn't stop.

I can feel the electric wave approaching me, so intense and brutal that I close my eyes to prepare for it to hit me. And when I think I am already on the edge, Cal slides two fingers inside of me.

A surge of heat courses through me, and for a few seconds, I'm frozen in place, feeling my walls throbbing around his fingers as I come.

I drop my head on his shoulder, taking deep breaths to compose myself. Cal patiently waits for me, holding me in his arms, his fingers still inside of me.

When I pull back to look at him, he releases me. The emptiness I immediately feel inside when he moves feels like a loss, but I know he won't leave me hanging for too long. To prove to me he isn't done, he sticks his fingers to his mouth and sucks on them, his eyes on me.

"You taste so good," he purrs. "Now," he continues, setting my feet down on the floor and turning me so that my back is now against his muscled chest.

Before I know it, my face is on the hard wood of his desk as he bends me over it. His hands slowly and deliciously caress my hips and ass. I brace myself, anxiously anticipating his next move.

Cal finally slides my underwear down my legs, taking his time to do it, and torturing me in the process.

"You're really patient," I mumble breathlessly.

I don't care if he knows I'm eager for more of him. At this point, I could even beg him to fuck me, and I wouldn't care if he thinks I'm too desperate.

He wraps his hand around my ponytail and tugs on it, finding my earlobe with his mouth and biting down.

"Why would I want to rush this?" His voice is hoarse and heavy.

While one hand holds me by the hair, the other snakes around my waist, finding my clit again. I'm still wet and slightly sensitive, his touch causing shivers to run through me, but the sensation is so overwhelming I feel ready for him to make me come again.

He keeps moving his thumb while he bends me over the desk again. With his free hand, he grips my hips, guiding me into position. I hear the sound of plastic being ripped, which I'm assuming it's from the condom wrapper, and I know I'm closer than ever to getting what I spent the entire day dreaming about.

A gasp escapes my lips as Cal thrusts into me from behind, my wetness allowing him to sink himself to the hilt. Still rubbing my swollen clit, Cal increases the speed of his thrusts with unrestrained enthusiasm, making me whimper loudly.

I must look like a savage, like an animal reaching primary pleasure, but I couldn't care less. I can only hope this room is soundproof because I can't control my moans anymore.

"There you go, sweetheart," he whispers against my ear, his dick pumping in and out of me, making me hold onto the desk hard.

His grip on my hips tightens as his movements get more erratic. Then, with one final thrust, his length pumps inside of me, my inner walls wrapping around him tightly. A grunt escapes him as he holds me against his hard chest, his skin hot against mine.

"That was…" I trail off, too exhausted to say anything.

"You're fucking perfect," Cal muses against my ear.

My heart is racing while I try to catch my breath. It's hard to do so with Cal holding me against him like this, but I'm glad he is because I'd surely fall on the floor if he let go of me. My legs feel like jelly, and I can barely feel them. My insides are deliciously sore, and if we were in his bed right now, I would probably fall asleep right away.

"Are you okay?" he asks me attentively.

I nod, leaning my head on his shoulder. "More than okay. I feel like I died and went to heaven."

A chuckle reverberates through his chest, and Cal places a soft kiss on my neck.

He carefully removes a strand of hair from my sweaty forehead. The touch feels so intimate and gentle after what we just did that it leaves me astonished for a split second. It's shocking how Cal can go from a wild, sexy man to a romantic and gentle one within the blink of an eye. And it doesn't come as a surprise to me that I like both versions of this man.

He turns me to face him, his arms still wrapped around me and keeping me close to him. And even though I don't think there will ever be a moment where this sexual tension between us doesn't exist, I love that we can also have a peaceful moment like this where no words are needed, just us staring at each other in silence, showing our affection through our eyes.

"So, what do you want to do now? Should we go for another round here, or should I take you to my place?" He wiggles his brows at me, his offer sounding more like a suggestion than anything else.

I laugh, kissing his lips. "I think I should go home tonight. We can meet tomorrow if you want, though. That way I can keep you wanting me even longer."

"As if that's necessary. I don't think I'll ever get tired of you," he says.

And with those words, I'm sure I'll have a lot to dream about tonight.

2 5

─────

CLUELESS

CAL

HEIDI AND I GET DRESSED AS I CONSIDER WHAT TO DO. I CHECK MY phone, expecting to see a message from Sam telling me that the path is clear for me to take Heidi home, but he hasn't texted me yet.

I need to keep Heidi here for a little longer, until I know for sure we can head out without the risk of being attacked.

"I'll get something for us to eat before I take you home," I offer, fixing my hair and adjusting the collar of my shirt.

Heidi arches an eyebrow at me, considering my suggestion. I'm sure she must want to go home, and I can't deny I also want to be alone so I can find out who the fuck was following us earlier, but unfortunately, she'll have to wait.

Reluctantly, she scoots back on the couch. "Fine, I'm starving."

"Want me to order some pizza?" I ask, grabbing my phone and opening the delivery app.

"Yeah, I could eat some pizza," she agrees.

Her cheeks are still flushed from our previous activities. Seeing her skin glowing like that makes me want to do it all over again.

Fucking her bent over my desk wasn't something I had even imagined until I was doing it. I've never mixed business with pleasure before, and I never once brought a woman into my office.

Until Heidi.

It frightens me a little to realize how much of an effect she has on me. I didn't even hesitate before bringing her here.

The pizza takes approximately an hour to arrive, for which I'm grateful. It's more than enough time for me to receive an update from Sam. When I'm grabbing my third slice of pizza, watching as Heidi licks her lips and savors the melted cheese, my phone beeps in my pocket with a text message from him.

"All clear, Boss. You can take her home now if you want. We'll follow just in case you need us, but there's no sign of them around anymore."

It's not exactly the message I wanted to receive, but it'll do for now.

I'm sure whatever information he got from all of this, he will tell me personally later.

I text a quick reply, telling him I'll be on my way out in fifteen minutes, and then focus my attention back on Heidi as she finishes a slice.

For a split second, I find myself wanting to take her back home with me instead of to her apartment. It's an unfamiliar feeling to me, but I choose to blame it on my sexual appetite. It's like I can't get enough of her, and that's the easiest path to follow at the moment.

I can't–and won't–get attached to her.

Or anyone for that matter.

I saw how fucked up it was for Tony and Chloe, how much they suffered to be together, and that's not something I aim to do to myself. Or Heidi, for that matter. She deserves so much better. After everything she went through, I hope she can get all the happiness she deserves and everything she ever dreamed of.

But selfishly, I also want her for myself.

All of her.

Even though I know I can't have it.

"Is everything okay? You look distracted," she points out, her sweet voice pulling me out of my thoughts.

I look up to see her blue eyes staring at me intently, although there's a small smile on her face. "Yeah, I'm just a bit tired," I tell her.

Heidi nods, wiping her mouth with a napkin. I imagine myself doing it with my tongue instead, but I shake my head, pushing away that thought for another moment.

"We could both use some sleep tonight," she agrees. "That's why I want to go home. Because I know staying with you will be anything but relaxing," she laughs, leaning her head back slightly.

"I can do relaxing," I joke, although inwardly I must agree with her. There's no way I can have her by my side, in the same bed all night, without getting in a few more rounds with her.

"Right, of course we can," she muses, her smile widening even more.

As I told Sam, fifteen minutes later we're heading out of the bar through the back door. My car is still in the same place I left it when we arrived.

"Why are we taking the back door?" Heidi asks, confused.

"It's the best way to leave without walking through the bar filled with clients," I lie.

She seems to buy it without pressing me for more answers.

The entire drive to her apartment, I'm on full alert, my eyes shifting back and forth between the rearview mirror and the side mirror to make sure we're not being followed. I spot Sam's vehicle a few cars behind us, which leaves me a little less anxious, but knowing someone might be following us and finding out where Heidi lives still leaves me on edge.

I park in front of her building a couple of minutes later, and she turns to look at me, her eyes sparkling.

"I had a really nice night," she says softly.

It astonishes me how she can be both endearing and fucking hot at the same time. The way she's looking at me almost makes me change my mind and drive us to my penthouse instead. But I respect her wishes and allow her to go, at least for tonight.

Tomorrow may be another story.

"I had the best time," I reply firmly. "Can we see each other again?" Anticipation creeps up on me. Why am I so eager to see her everyday now? The sex is fucking good, I know that, but is this the only reason why I want to spend all my free time with her?

"Uh… sure, I guess," Heidi replies, a bit hesitant. Her face screams surprise, and I know she must be wondering why I'm asking her out every day.

I don't even recognize myself.

"Unless you don't want to," I add, unsure.

"Oh, no!" She dismisses me immediately with a dramatic wave. "That's not what I meant. I just didn't think you'd want to see me again after today," she confesses.

I frown at her. "Why not?"

"I don't know." She shrugs, a chuckle escaping her beautiful lips. "I thought you'd get tired of me after one night, but technically, we spent two nights together, so… maybe I was wrong."

"You were," I admit, my voice firm and my expression resolute. "I want to see you as much as you allow me." Her cheeks redden with embarrassment, and it's one of the cutest things I've ever seen.

"Okay then. I'll text you tomorrow." She leans forward, kissing my lips, her hand already on the door handle.

I deepen our kiss, finding her neck with my hand and keeping her trapped against me. It's only when I hear a honk behind us that I let her go.

"I'll be waiting for your text."

With that, Heidi leaves the car, and after I make sure she's safely inside, I head back to the bar.

Sam meets me in my office with Hunter on his tail. "What did you get?" I ask, not waiting for them to start the conversation.

I sit in my chair, pictures of Heidi naked on the desk in front of me occupying my mind for a split second before I force myself to focus on the two men inside the room.

"They are indeed the cartel. It's the same car that attacked us on

Christmas' Eve," Sam begins, making himself somewhat comfortable on the couch.

Hunter remains standing, leaning against the wall beside the door, his arms crossed over his chest.

"Okay, we already knew that," I note.

"They were driving around the neighborhood, clearly looking for you, but once they realized something was off, they left," he explains.

"Did they see you?" I ask with my brows creased.

Hunter shakes his head. "No, but I think they knew we were watching them. We waited to see if they would head back to their headquarters, but they stopped at a motel, probably to try to outsmart us."

"Do we have any news from Mouse and Pirate on that unknown number?" I recall.

Both shake their heads, their mouths turned down in disappointment at telling me something I don't want to hear.

I nod, trying to decide on our next move. We have nothing on them yet, and Tony hasn't reached out to let me know if he found out anything new, which is a sign he must be on the same page as us.

"Let's keep an eye on the bar and the surroundings," I order. "Make sure every establishment and business we own has the security reinforced, without catching more attention than necessary. Let's keep it quiet but also keep our eyes wide open. I don't want any more surprises."

Both men nod sharply in agreement.

It frustrates me to know so little, but for now, there's nothing more I can do. I get some work done and then go back to my apartment.

I sleep well for most of the night, except for some nightmares of faceless men getting to Heidi and taking her away from me. But other than that, the other dreams I have with her are enough to make me forget about the cartel for a while when I head to work the next morning.

Heidi hasn't texted me yet, so I have no idea if she plans on meeting today, but since I don't want to suffocate her, I decide to focus my energy on my businesses, which are somewhat lacking my attention lately.

Most of the day goes by with me driving from bar to bar, casino to casino, port to port, checking on things and making sure nothing happened that I'm not aware of. A couple of meetings are the last thing on my list before I head back to my office, eager for a shot of whiskey.

As soon as I step inside, I greet Ian, who's preparing to open the bar, and my phone buzzes in my pocket. A text message from an unknown number pops up on my screen, making me clench my teeth hard as I read it.

"You will do well to protect what's yours."

"What the fuck?" I mumble to myself, my jaw tense.

"All good, Boss?"

I rush to my office, not caring to answer Ian, my mind racing a thousand miles per minute.

Should I warn Heidi? Should I tell her someone might be watching her, following her steps? Should I check on her?

I don't want to scare her, but right now, I know nothing. I have no control over the situation. I can't protect her.

It's too late to step away from her and whatever we have going on between us. The cartel must already know she means something to me, and they won't let go of it now that they know they are in control.

I don't know how long I've been in my office, brooding, when there's a knock on the door.

"Yes?" I grumble.

Clara pops her head into the room. "Sorry to disturb you, Boss, but your girl is at the bar upstairs, probably waiting for you."

2 6

———

FLIRTING

Cᴀʟ

I ꜰʀᴏᴡɴ ᴀᴛ Cʟᴀʀᴀ, ᴍʏ ʙʀᴀɪɴ sᴛɪʟʟ ᴀ ʙɪᴛ ꜰᴏɢɢʏ. I ᴅᴏɴ'ᴛ ɴᴇᴇᴅ ᴛᴏ ᴀsᴋ who she is referring to. At this point, everyone who works for me knows I'm seeing Heidi.

"I'll be right there," I tell her, getting to my feet and checking my appearance in the mirror.

I don't feel tired, but the dark circles under my eyes say otherwise. I'm sure Heidi will notice it as soon as she sees me, but I don't want her to worry. I'll probably have to lie to her if she asks. It wouldn't be the first time I've kept something from her.

The idea of keeping the truth about my life from her is starting to bother me to the point I'm considering risking everything, telling her what I do for a living. But I know the moment I confess and she realizes how dangerous it is, she'll be out of my life in a blink of an eye.

And I'm not ready for that.

I wonder if that's how Tony felt when he got married to Chloe to protect her from the cartel. He told me one time that he was afraid to

155

involve her in all of this mess, and even though I could see his point back then, I can understand him completely now.

I finally head to the bar, finding Heidi seated at the same table I took her to the first time we met—when she barged into my bar and demanded I do something about her blown up bookstore.

Contrasting drastically to the outfit she was wearing yesterday, tonight she is wearing a flowery dress, her collarbone exposed, her beautiful skin glowing under the dim light. The hem of the dress brushes her thighs, causing me to thank her internally for making it easier for me to have access to her. A grin forms on my lips when I remember how she mentioned how unfortunate it was that she chose to wear pants yesterday when we were in the car. I'm glad she chose something simpler tonight–but equally sexy.

Heidi sips a cocktail through a straw, her eyes roaming around the bar as she watches the clients. She seems to be entertained, not even noticing when I approach her.

"Now, that's a surprise," I mumble, leaning down and placing a kiss on her cheek.

She flinches, being caught off guard, then a chuckle escapes her. "You scared me," she says, smiling at me.

God, she's so beautiful.

"Sorry. I didn't mean to," I admit, gesturing to Ian to get me my usual drink–whiskey on the rocks. He nods at me, turning to pour my drink.. I turn my attention back to Heidi who is looking up at me with a different glint in her eyes.

"Why didn't you tell me you were coming?" I ask curiously.

She shrugs, taking another sip from her drink. "I wanted to surprise you. That seems to have been a success."

"Indeed. I was not expecting to see you here tonight," I tell her, sitting in the chair across from her. "I'm glad you came, though."

"Are you really?" Her voice sounds somewhat hesitant, even though she maintains a confident expression. "I was worried I'd disturb you while you're working."

I lean forward, capturing her lips and kissing her slowly but passionately. She lets out a soft moan, and I pull back, staring into her eyes. "You could never disturb me." Then I straighten up and sit back. The small distance I just created between us is met with protest from my body, but I ignore it, not wanting to put on a show for my clients and employees. What I want to do to Heidi can only be done behind closed doors, with no one else but the two of us around.

She's flushed from the sudden display of affection, her cheeks reddening ferociously as she takes another drink from her glass, this time without using the straw. She clears her throat next, pretending she isn't deeply affected and shifts in her seat uncomfortably. "How was your day?" she asks, trying to make small talk and clearly distract herself.

I smirk at her before shrugging. "Busy. Boring. Lots of meetings and rounds around the city to check on my other establishments," I explain, making sure I don't give her too much information about exactly what I did. "Nothing worth mentioning, to be honest. How was your day?"

"Well, I walked around the neighborhood, looking for places that are for sale. I loved this shop in Greenwich Village, but it's very expensive. I don't think I'll get enough money from the insurance company to buy it." She looks and sounds disappointed, which is something that doesn't sit well with me.

"I can help you, if you want," I offer, even though I know she won't accept it.

She's already shaking her head before I finish the sentence. "No way. You've already done so much for me. I can't even begin to imagine how I'll pay you back."

My eyebrows shoot up, and I grin at her. "I can think of a couple of ways you can do that, don't worry. But seriously," I continue, noticing Heidi play with her hair to hide her shyness. "I wouldn't mind. I really don't mean to brag, but you know I can do it in a blink of an eye. You just need to give me the word, and I'll get it done."

"I know. But I feel like it isn't fair to you, you know? You've helped me a lot already."

"Well, take your time to think about it. We can figure something out. You can consider me your sponsor, if that'd make you feel better," I suggest.

Clara approaches our table with my drink in hand. It doesn't escape my notice how she looks at Heidi and shoots me a grin afterward. I'm sure all my men and employees are dying to tease me, but I glance back at her with the scariest look I can muster, and she vanishes from my sight, heading to another table.

"Okay, fine. I promise I'll think about it," Heidi finally concedes. "Just because I really loved the place."

"Whatever suits you, sweetheart. I just want you to be happy." My words catch me off guard, and I take a sip from my whiskey to wet my suddenly dry throat.

What's wrong with me? What is it about Heidi that brings out this awkward, romantic side of me that I didn't even know existed?

"Thank you, Cal. I don't know what I'd have done without you. Ever since the fire and my grandparents moving away, I've been feeling so lonely. It's nice to have someone to spend time with," Heidi confesses, her eyes roaming over my face.

My heart shrinks at the thought of her spending her days alone, her grandparents being the only ones in her life. I feel like Heidi wants to open up to me, share her thoughts and feelings, but I honestly don't think this is the right place for her to do it. I want her to feel like she can trust me with her whole heart. I want to give her the space she needs to tell me her fears and dreams, and if there's anything I can do to help her and provide for her, I want to do it.

"I'm here whenever you need me." I catch her gaze with mine, making sure she understands this is coming from my heart.

Heidi only nods, swallowing hard. That's when I notice her eyes are filled with tears. I'd hate more than anything to see her cry. I wouldn't be able to stand it.

In an attempt to prevent her tears from falling, I ignore everyone around me, and all the possibilities of being harassed by my staff later, and move my chair closer to hers, wrapping my arm around her shoulder and pulling her close to me. With my free hand, I smooth a lock of her hair behind her ear, watching as her blue eyes study my face.

"You know, I think tonight's outfit is a much better choice than the one you picked yesterday," I murmur, my eyes lowering to her exposed thighs. "Not that I didn't love seeing you in a leather jacket and combat boots. Because I did. It gave me enough content to dream the entire night about you."

Heidi chuckles, nudging me slightly with her shoulder. "You did not dream about me. I bet you crashed as soon as your head hit the pillow."

"You couldn't be more wrong," I reply, although she is correct that I fell asleep pretty quickly. "You've been occupying my mind even when I'm sleeping. It's a bit invasive, if you ask me."

She laughs harder this time, her head falling backward, revealing her elegant neck to me. I take the opportunity when no one is looking in our direction, thanking the heavens that this is the most private table in my bar, and kiss on the neck, nipping at her soft skin and feeling her body shiver under my touch.

"Cal," she scolds, pushing me away, although with little intention of actually being successful. "We're in a public place, remember?"

"So? It's *my* place, remember?" I tease back.

"Regardless..." Heidi looks around, her cheeks pink with embarrassment.

"Okay, so..." I lean down, my lips brushing her ear and causing another wave of shivers to course through her. "What do you say we get out of here and go somewhere more private?" I suggest with a deep chuckle. "I really want to get you back in my bed."

27

SHARING MY FEELINGS

MY FACE HEATS UP WITH HIS OFFER, AND I CAN'T FIND IT IN ME TO reject it. I was trying to be bold and surprise him by coming here, and I would be lying if I said I didn't have any plans on returning to my own apartment tonight.

But I was also telling the truth when I said I liked to spend time with him, no sex involved. Cal makes my days much better, especially now that I'm living by myself and barely see my grandparents. New York is a big city, but it can feel so small when you're alone.

Whenever I'm with Cal, it's like time freezes, and I can simply enjoy being around him. He makes me feel wanted, heard, cared for. Nothing about what we have feels fake or forced.

I don't know what we are–and I would never dare to say we're together–but I can't lie to myself anymore. I believe I'm falling for him. Or better yet, I think I have already fallen. Deep. Beyond redemption.

"So, what do you say?" His hoarse, sexy voice whispers in my ear, and I remember I didn't give him an answer.

"You want to go to your apartment?" I narrow my eyes at him. "To get me into your bed?"

Cal feigns being offended, his hand darting to his chest in a dramatic way. "I'm not that type of guy, sweetheart. I'll get you something to eat first."

I laugh, pushing him away again. "Okay, fine. You got me with the promise of food. Are you sure you don't need to get back to work though? I feel like I took you away from something important."

He dismissed me with a shake of his head, clearly unbothered. "I'm glad you came here to distract me. I was drowning in paperwork, and I can honestly use the break. I've worked nonstop today," he replies, getting to his feet. "I think I deserve to be pampered."

"Yeah, right…" I stand, following him outside and toward his car. He waves at some of his employees and talks to someone on our way out, although I can't hear what he's saying.

Cal opens the door of the car for me, and I slip into the leather seat. His musky cologne hits my nostrils immediately.

The drive to his penthouse is calm, the two of us deciding what we want to have for dinner. I end up offering to prepare us some pasta that Grandma taught me how to make a while ago. I feel like doing something in return for everything he's done for me, but since I don't have money, I can only shower him with affection and food.

Once we're inside his kitchen, Cal shows me where everything is, and I start preparing the ingredients for the sauce. He opens a bottle of wine and pours a glass for each of us. He hands me my glass, but before I can take a sip, he presses me against the counter, his mouth claiming mine, his tongue invading me with a heated kiss.

He finds the hem of my dress, and before I know it, he pulls it off me and lifts me from the floor and sets me down on the marble. I feel the coldness of the marble against my ass, but Cal's hands roam freely up and down my thighs, making it hard for me to focus on anything else other than the heat of his skin on mine.

"Cal," I say against his mouth, pressing against his hard chest and pushing him away, thoughts of making him dinner still on my mind.

But he devours me more hungrily, not giving me the chance to say anything.

He grips my ass, squeezing my flesh like he wants to take a piece of it for himself, and pulls me forward, positioning himself between my legs. He spreads them further apart so he can fit between them, and I feel need pooling at my core.

I should be preparing our food, and now it feels like I'm about to become the meal instead.

His lips move from my mouth to my jaw and down to my neck, while his hands slide up my stomach, finding my breasts and cupping them through my bra.

The fabric is thin enough for me to feel his fingers against my nipples, making me choke on a moan. I'm glad I chose this bra this afternoon.

Before Cal gets any further with this, I force myself to put an end to it so I can have our dinner ready. If we continue, we won't be eating any food tonight, and I'm sure Cal probably hasn't eaten anything during the day.

I want him to be in his best shape for whatever we have planned for later, and I also need him to be healthy.

With that in mind, I push him harder this time, his dark eyes finding mine with coated desperation.

"I need to prepare dinner," I tell him, as if he doesn't already know this.

"We can do that later," he murmurs, planting his face back on my neck, biting down on my flesh and making me momentarily forget about what I was saying.

But then, with renewed determination, I push him away again and jump back on the floor, putting a safe distance between us.

"We can eat first, and then we can do whatever you want later," I inform him, grabbing my dress and putting it back on before he can stop me. Then, I pick up the knife and start to cut the onions for the sauce.

Cal grumbles but ends up accepting it. "Do you need my help?" he offers.

I shake my head, not removing my eyes from my task. "I can do it by myself while you take a shower and get changed. You've been out the entire day. You're probably dying to get cleaned up and put on something more comfortable before we eat," I point out.

"You're right," he agrees. "Okay, I'll be right back then."

An hour later, we're both seated on the stools around the kitchen counter, facing each other and diving into the pasta I prepared–which I must admit tastes delicious.

Cal spends the first five minutes complimenting my food but eventually stops talking and finishes his meal in silence.

We continue to drink the wine he opened, and half the bottle is already gone without us even realizing it. Cal puts on some background music while I fill our glasses again, and then we move to the living room, the inviting, soft couch calling for me.

I get comfy, pulling my legs up, my glass of wine in hand as I watch Cal take his place by my side.

"So, I've been wanting to ask you, and I don't mean to overstep, but…" Cal starts, drinking from his wine before continuing, "how did you end up living with your grandparents? What happened to your parents?"

A twinge of pain hits my heart at the mention of my parents. Remembering them still has that effect on me. It's been long enough since I lost them, but I still miss them like crazy.

I swallow before sharing the worst pain of my life with him. For some reason, I feel like telling him everything. I know Cal will hear me out and share my pain with me, taking the burden off my shoulders for a moment.

"They died in a car accident," I explain. "We were driving back from Connecticut, where we went to spend Christmas with my mom's family. I was in the back seat, and I honestly don't remember much of what or how it happened. All I know is that I got this stupid scar." I point to my cheek. "While they lost their lives." My voice cracks while I say this out loud for the first time since the accident.

"So, that's where you got the scar from…" Cal murmurs, more to himself than to me, while he gently traces the scar on my cheek. His soft touch sends shivers down my spine, but more than that, it makes my heart lurch in my chest at how kind he is as he studies my face carefully. "I was always curious about it," he confesses, his voice so low I barely hear him.

"You were curious about my scar?" I frown, narrowing my eyes slightly at him. "Why? Because it's so ugly?" For a long time, I was ashamed of it. I would try to hide it as much as I could, but having it was always visible, no matter what I did, so eventually, I simply started ignoring it. When I was younger, I blamed it for not having any friends. I thought everyone would be disgusted by it, but as I grew up, I realized I was being stupid and illogical.

I didn't have any friends because I pushed myself away from people. I hid from them most of the time, preferring to stay by myself than in the presence of anyone else. It felt overwhelming most of the time to be surrounded by people.

"There's not a single part of you that's ugly, Heidi. You're the most beautiful woman I've ever seen in my life," Cal says, his voice firm and serious.

His gaze is heavy on my face, and I can't force myself to look away. There's so much honesty in his eyes that I convince myself he can't be lying or saying these things without meaning them.

"I've been interested in you ever since I laid eyes on you from across the street years ago. And I always wondered what caused you to have that scar. I wanted so badly to get to know you, even if we could only be friends."

His admission hits me so hard that I forget how to pronounce proper words for a second. I wasn't expecting Cal to be so honest and raw. I never realized he was interested in me until I met him at his bar that day I barged in. I never really paid attention to him or his place before that. If anything, I despised it, thinking whoever owned that place was a troublemaker who made it hard for me to draw more clients into the bookstore.

Obviously, I was wrong.

Cal has to be the most caring person I've ever met—except for maybe my grandparents. And for that reason, and the fact that I can't express my gratitude and my overwhelming feelings through words right now, I put my glass down on the table and climb on his lap, straddling him and trapping him on the couch.

WHO'S FOR DESSERT?

Heidi

Cal looks up at me, his eyes slightly widened in surprise as if asking me what's gotten into me.

"That was the sweetest thing anyone's ever said to me," I explain, my heart beating rapidly against my ribcage.

"It's the truth," he tells me honestly, caressing my cheek with tenderness.

I'm sure my heart is about to jump out of my chest. Why do I feel so emotional? Everything he says and does to me seems so genuine, like he truly wants to make me happy.

I don't think I've ever felt this way toward another man before. It's an unknown feeling to me, but if I could dare say it, I'd guess it's love.

Or at least something similar to it.

He might not feel the same way about me, but right now, I don't mind. I just want to be with him and enjoy whatever time I have with him all to myself. Being with Cal makes me happier than anything else I've ever experienced in my life—even getting lost in a good book.

Tired of the distance between us, I lean forward, and our mouths crash together. Cal's hands immediately find the bottom of my dress. He slides his fingers up my thighs and reaches my hips, sinking into my skin and causing a wave of heat to rush down to my core.

Slowly, he moves his hands up to my ass, gripping and pulling me toward him. I gasp when I feel his bulge brushing against me. I'm glad he chose sweatpants after the shower. This way, I can feel him better, even with all the layers of fabric between us.

I rock back and forth on top of him, enticing both of us even more.

"Fuck, don't do that," he hisses, placing kisses against my collarbone.

"Why not?" I ask, teasing him, rocking myself against his hardness.

I feel his fingers sinking deeper into my skin, making me move my hips even more. His words are still echoing in my head, making me forget about reason completely. I just want to show him how much he means to me. And I can't think of a better way to do it other than using my entire body and showering him with attention.

"You like to play with fire, don't you?" he asks, his voice hoarse with desire.

"I do," I reply, a grin spreading on my lips.

I reach for his pants and push them down to his thighs, realizing he is not wearing boxers this time. His shaft is erect and waiting for me.

Slowly, I get off his lap. Cal's eyes follow me, a dark hunger crossing them as he watches me get on my knees in front of him. I look up at him through my eyelashes before lowering myself on him, enveloping his tip with my warm mouth.

He hisses when I lick him, his hand darting to my hair as he entangles his fingers between the strands and tugs at it. "Fuck, Heidi," he mumbles, his voice cracking.

I smirk against him, delighted that I can drive him just as crazy as he drives me. I grip his thighs as I tease him before taking him fully into my mouth. He tugs harder on my hair, guiding me as I take him deeper.

"Holy shit," he moans.

I feel him growing even harder, his breathing becoming more ragged as I work him up. My panties are soaked with need at this point, and when I realize he's close to climax, I gather all the strength I can muster and pull away from him, standing.

My gaze is trapped in his as he watches me tug my panties down to my ankles and kick them away.

Cal produces a condom from his pocket and slips it on. "Come here," he orders, reaching for me and pulling me onto his lap again. "That was fucking amazing."

"I'm glad," I answer as I adjust myself against him, moving my hips forward, feeling him hard against my slick slit.

Then, I slide myself down, letting him fill me up completely to the brim.

Cal grunts under me, his hands gripping and guiding my hips, and after my inner walls embrace him completely, I start riding him.

My moves are slow at first. At this angle, he's hitting my clit so perfectly, I can't think straight.

"Oh, God, Cal" I cry, my head falling backward as I close my eyes.

"You drive me crazy, Heidi," he purrs. "I don't know how you do it, but I can't seem to get enough of you."

I know what he means because I can't seem to get enough of him either. No matter how much time we spend together, it never seems to be enough.

In a swift movement, Cal pulls my dress over my head then unhooks my bra, leaving me completely naked, my breasts exposed to him. I arch my back, keeping my eyes shut as I feel his tongue playing with my nipples, his teeth grazing them, causing me to moan his name.

I'm already breathless, panting as I speed up my pace.

"You feel so good around me," he rasps, bulking his hips up to meet mine.

When I feel his thumb circling my swollen, sensitive clit, arousing me even more, I tighten around his shaft, that familiar sensation of explosion approaching. "Yes. Shit! Yes!"

I reach for support on his shoulders, my nails sinking into his skin as I try to steady myself. I feel like I'm dying and on my way to heaven, my vision blurring as an electric current courses through me, making me momentarily numb with pleasure. I bite down on my lip, preventing a loud cry from escaping me as I reach climax.

Despite the chill of being naked, it feels like my body is on fire, every inch combusting with my orgasm. My walls are throbbing around Cal, but I still feel him hard as a rock inside me.

Then I realize he hasn't come yet.

"Are you okay?" I ask, still panting, my eyebrows shooting up with curiosity.

"I'm perfect. I just like watching you come for me, moaning my name like that," he informs me while getting to his feet and carrying me like I weigh nothing.

He kicks off his pants and walks us through the apartment, both of us still connected, his dick pumping slightly inside me.

"However," he continues, a grin forming on his lips as he kicks the door to his bedroom open. "I'm not done yet."

I chuckle. "I sort of figured. It's kind of hard to miss at the moment."

He chuckles and grunts as he moves a bit inside of me. "You ain't seen nothin' yet, baby."

Cal tosses me on the bed, separating us for a split second before he lowers himself on me again, his dick sliding inside me once more. With his hands, he spreads my legs wide open to position himself between them, his hips thrusting hard against me.

I lock my ankles behind his waist, trapping him, ready for our second round.

I grip his ass, squeezing and pulling him even deeper inside me. Cal's gaze finds mine, and he brushes a strand of hair from my sweaty forehead with a gentle touch. There's something different in his eyes this time, although I can't quite interpret it.

"You're perfect," he murmurs, kissing me once more, his tongue dancing against mine, exploring every inch of my mouth. I feel his muscles tense under my fingers as his thrusts increase in speed, and he gets closer and closer to coming. He cups my breasts again, sending another wave of pleasure coursing through my body. Soon enough, with a guttural grunt of pleasure, he finally releases himself inside me.

I follow him, unable to hold myself any longer. I feel sore all over, all my senses enhanced because of all the pleasure he has provided me with.

Cal pulls out, lying on the bed and pulling me close to his chest, embracing me, caresses my hair softly, lulling me into sleep.

My brain is foggy as usual whenever Cal and I have sex. And even though I should know better than to let something like this slip, the words escape my mouth before I can even think of holding them back. "I love you," I whisper, my voice dragging as I close my eyes.

His arms tighten around me, as if he fears I might escape if he doesn't hold on tight. I'm falling into the abyss of sleep, my body too exhausted to be able to think properly and realize I might have fucked up whatever we have going on between us.

If he responds at all, I don't hear him before sleep carries me away.

29

BEST FEELING IN THE WORLD

CAL

I've had other women say they loved me before—after we had sex and I'd taken them to paradise and back. It's not uncommon. However, I know that Heidi's words carry a different meaning than all of the rest. I'm absolutely positive she didn't say that just because she was in post-coital bliss. She meant it. Every word. I only know because I can feel that whatever we have going on between us is different from anything I have ever experienced before.

Which is why it freaks me the fuck out.

This wasn't supposed to get this deep. This was supposed to remain an infatuation, a brief curiosity. Something I could chase, experience, and set aside. Because I'm a dangerous man, and that danger lurks in every facet of my life. She'd never be safe.

But deep down, the selfish part of me is thrilled to know she loves me. I never thought I deserved someone's love, but Heidi makes me feel like I do. Like somehow I deserve to be with her and have her by my side. That's the kind of effect she has on me. One that I don't know how to face.

She falls asleep fast in my arms, and I ponder what to do. I'm not sleepy at all. If anything, I'm more anxious than ever after hearing her confession.

So, gently, I pull the blanket over her naked body, being as careful as possible not to wake her. Even though it kills me to have to step away from her now, I need to take in some fresh air and maybe get myself another glass of whiskey to numb my nerves so I'm able to think clearly. I can't allow myself to fall into the giddy feeling of love. It's counterproductive and distracting.

I edge out of the bedroom and head to the kitchen, pouring myself a glass of whiskey before walking to the balcony. The city lights are incredibly beautiful tonight, like stars against a blanket of black velvet. It reminds me of home for a moment–Galway–where the air is clean and fresh, and the sky is wide and open. I take in the cold air around me and imagine I'm back there, walking into my ma's house, shrugging out of my coat while bustling Heidi in behind me. I'm not sure why that crosses my mind but…. She's the one, isn't she?

What the hell am I supposed to do with her now?.

The type of life that I lead in the underworld is not something that I would wish for anyone. Let alone someone like her.

Heidi is so pure, innocent, genuinely kind… how could I put her through the danger that I face on a daily basis? How would I ever be at peace knowing she might be in danger because of me?

Deep down, I'm mostly afraid of what she will say and do once I decide to come clean with her and tell her the truth about my career and my role in the mafia world. So far, she hasn't asked about it. She doesn't seem to care why the owner of a dive bar has the money for a nice car and a penthouse apartment.

Would she listen to my reasoning and try to understand them? Or would she accuse me of being a liar and using her, shattering her heart with my omission?

I take another huge gulp of my whiskey, finishing the contents of my glass as I stare at the tall buildings ahead of me. Reality hits me like a ton of bricks. I should give her the opportunity to choose. But if Heidi broke up with me because she couldn't accept what I do for a living, that would crush me.

Because the truth is that I also love her–whether I'm willing to admit it to her yet or not.

Her words still echo in my mind. The moment I heard them, I was paralyzed with fear, but also thrilled to know she had such deep feelings for me.

I've never loved a woman in my life. I've never met a woman who made me think of settling down, of giving up everything I've built. But Heidi makes me think of those things. Things I never considered myself doing. Ever.

Getting married, having kids, building a family… that's not something I'm allowed to have.

Tony's family comes to mind, and it makes me wonder why can't I have the same thing? We have the same lifestyle, and yet, he manages to keep his family safe just fine.

Sure, it wasn't always easy, and I'm sure that won't always be the case. He'll be constantly looking over his shoulder, making sure he's in control and that his family is out of danger. I can also do that, can't I? I can keep Heidi safe.

A voice in the back of my mind sneers, telling me I can't. I can't even find whoever is threatening me. I can't say Heidi is safe right now, lying in my bed, either. I have no clue what their plans are, what they are after, and when they will get to me, catching me off guard. It's fucking frustrating. I sigh, running my fingers through my hair.

It sucks to be out of control, unsure of what to do. But I realize there's no way I can come to a decision tonight. I'm tired, and more than anything, I want to enjoy having Heidi in my bed. So, with that in mind, I head back inside, leaving my empty glass in the kitchen sink and returning to my bedroom.

Heidi is still asleep, entangled in my sheets, her smooth hair covering her face. I climb back in the bed, carefully adjusting myself on the mattress so as not to wake her. However, she must feel the movement beside her, Heidi opens her eyes lazily, finding me staring at her with a guilty expression.

"Sorry, I didn't mean to wake you," I whisper.

But she only hums, scooting closer and lying her head on my chest. I willingly embrace her, pulling her tight against me.

"Are you okay?" she asks in a whisper. I can barely hear her.

"Yeah, I was just getting some air," I explain, kissing her head and closing my eyes.

Having her here with me, like this–her legs intertwined with mine, her soft, warm skin against me–makes all my worries and concerns vanish from my mind completely. Her scent calms me, and I inhale sharply, taking in as much as I can. She's like a drug I'm addicted to and can't get enough of.

"I thought you left," Heidi confesses, her voice dragging.

"I'm not going anywhere," I reassure her, looking down and finding her eyes closed again. "Now, go get some sleep. I'll be right here when you wake up." I intend to keep that promise. Waking up to find Heidi beside me might be one of the best feelings in the world. And I can't wait to experience that, and so much more with her.

Eventually, sleep catches up to me, and I feel my eyes grow heavy. I fight it for a while, not wanting to let go of this feeling of holding Heidi, but if I'm right about one thing is that this won't be the last time I have her here, in my bed, all to myself. With that, I finally allow myself to fall asleep.

Surprisingly, when I open my eyes again, the sun is already up, its rays passing through the curtains in my bedroom window.

Heidi's scent hits me, and I look to my side, finding her breathing peacefully, her chest moving up and down without a care in the world. As I had imagined, it's one of the best sensations in the world to watch her like this. She's so beautiful, and I know I'm lucky to have such a wonderful woman in my bed.

When her eyelashes start to flutter slightly, I dart my eyes to the ceiling, pretending I haven't been staring at her for about an hour. In my peripheral vision, I see Heidi stretching her arms above her head, moaning quietly as she wakes up. "Good morning," she says, her voice raspy from sleep.

I look at her, a smile tugging on the corner of my mouth. "Morning, sweetheart," I reply, not daring to move. If I do, I'm afraid I might touch her naked body under the sheets and I won't be able to get out of this bed in time to get to work. "Did you sleep well?" I ask, watching as she blinks slowly, her eyes glowing under the sunlight. She looks perfect in the morning, her eyes bright blue and her skin like porcelain. She's something to behold.

"I don't think I've slept this well since the incident with the bookstore," she admits, rolling to her side and facing me. Her right leg slowly wraps around mine, and I feel my entire body stiffen with tension as she caresses my leg with her foot.

I swallow hard, closing my eyes and letting the sensation wash over me. "I'm happy I could provide you with a good night's sleep for a change," I joke, trying to lighten the mood before I can't stop myself from taking her again.

She chuckles beside me, and in the blink of an eye, she's naked on top of me, straddling me with her toned legs.

Heidi grins at me, teasing me with her hips. "So, do you have to go to work immediately or do you have time for more?"

3 0

SECRET CLOSET

Opening my eyes to find myself in Cal's bed with him by my side is even better than any dream I've ever had. His scent is all over the room and the sheets, and the heat radiating from his body is almost too much for my sleepy mind to handle.

He looks even hotter after waking up, and I need to control myself not to jump on him. Which, eventually, I end up doing anyway.

I'm on top of him before I know it. Having morning sex feels somewhat different, and I'm slightly embarrassed that he gets to see me with my puffy, sleepy eyes and disheveled hair, but he doesn't seem to mind and is eager to please me.

Our skin is damp with sweat after I ride him and give us both a morning to remember. I roll off him and stare at the ceiling, too tired to stand up and get started with my day.

"I really have to go to work," he tells me, his tone expressing how annoyed he is to have to leave this place.

I don't blame him. I wish he didn't have to go either. I wouldn't mind having the day off, to spend it entirely with him without a care in the world. It's not like I have much to do anyway, other than look for locations for the bookstore. I might have to call Granny and ask her for updates about the insurance situation. I also owe them a visit, so I should plan to do that soon.

"Okay..." I say softly.

After a couple more minutes of cuddling, Cal finally gets up from the bed and heads for the shower to get ready for his day. I remain in the same position, memories of last night invading my senses.

Suddenly, a thought pops into my mind. Did I say what I think I said to him before I fell asleep last night? I cover my mouth, hoping that it wasn't real, that it was part of a dream.

I told him I love him!

God.. that had to be a dream. I couldn't have really done something that stupid, could I? "Fuck," I hiss, glad he can't hear or see me.

Why the hell did you do that, Heidi?

I have no idea how Cal managed not to freak out and leave me here by myself. I should've woken up to nothing but an empty space beside me in bed. Any other man would have done that. So, how come I didn't scare him with my confession?

As if on cue, Cal steps out of the bathroom with a towel wrapped around his waist, his chest and toned abs on display, little droplets of water shining on his skin. He smirks at me, crossing the room and heading to his closet. Seeing him like this is enough to make me forget what I was freaking out about.

He comes back wearing jeans, a black shirt, a pair of boots, and a leather jacket. His hair is wet and loose, curling around his ears. He's so effortlessly sexy.

I'm still naked, wrapped in his sheets, feeling self-conscious all of the sudden. "I should probably head home too," I say as Cal walks toward me and presses a kiss to my lips.

"You can stay here as long as you want," he tells me. "I'll be home later tonight. We can watch a movie or something if you want."

The offer is tempting. I really don't feel like going home. I could stay here, doing some research on my phone while I wait for him. I could also call my grandparents, catch up on my favorite TV show, and make something for us to eat for dinner. "Are you sure?" I ask. "I don't want to impose."

Cal shakes his head, kissing me one more time before pulling away. "You're not. Make yourself at home."

And with that, he walks out of the room, leaving me alone with my thoughts. I hear the front door closing, and as soon as he is out of the apartment, the whole place suddenly seems too big for me.

So, I finally get out of bed, grabbing my dress from the floor and putting it back on. Then I go to the kitchen to make something for breakfast. I settle for eggs and black coffee. I'm really not that hungry, and it'll be lunchtime before long anyway.

Walking to the balcony with my mug and plate in hand, I enjoy the sun warming my skin, its unseasonable heat embracing me like a comforting hug. My mind is still reeling over the fact that I told Cal that I loved him—and he didn't mention it this morning. Was he pretending I didn't say anything? Was he doing that so I don't feel embarrassed? Why didn't he bring it up? Should I even want him to?

Maybe I should just pretend that it didn't happen at all. That would probably be best for both of us–and whatever we have going on between us. I'm not ready to stop seeing him, that's for damn sure.

I finish my breakfast and call my grandparents. We spend over an hour catching up, and before I hang up, I promise them I will come to see them sometime this week.

Then I lose track of time as I start looking for places to rent in New York. Not to mention the amount of time I spend on websites that sell vintage decor and on Pinterest, looking for inspirations for the bookstore.

Only when I hear my stomach growling do I realize how late it is. I order some food to be delivered, and after I eat it, I finally head for the bathroom to take a shower. I should have done that as soon as I woke up, but I was busy with everything else, not to mention that I could still feel Cal on my skin, and I wasn't too eager to get rid of that feeling yet.

I turn the hot water on and step inside. The warm water washing over me instantly relaxes me. I wash my hair and take my time to scrub my skin. Surprisingly, Cal has a lot of products in his shower, which intrigues me.

I wonder if he leaves them here for other women, for when he brings them in, but I don't allow myself to delve on that for too long. I shouldn't be worried about what Cal does with his personal, romantic life. Most of them aren't girly anyway.

Besides, he never promised me anything. We're not exclusive, even if it sometimes feels like we are.

Getting out of the shower, I dry off and wrap myself in a towel before walking back to his bedroom, looking around for something to wear. I could put my dress on again, but it feels dirty after taking such a great shower. My eyes fall on his closet door, and I ponder if I should grab something of his to wear. I don't think he would mind. It astonishes me how comfortable and at home I feel in his apartment, and even though he told me to make myself at home, I also don't want him to think I'm imposing.

I can't be naked the entire day either, so I finally decide to walk into the closet. Only then do I realize how big of a closet it actually is. It looks like just a small room at first, but now that I'm inside, I'm struck by how many compartments this closet has—neatly divided for shoes, shirts, suits, jackets, and accessories.

It'd be a dream to have such a closet in my apartment.

Looking around, I find a pile of shirts that seem to be a bit worn out and grab the one on the top. It's a simple white shirt with a NY Knicks logo in the front. It only comes down to my thighs, but since I'll be staying inside, that won't be a problem.

When I decide to return to his bedroom to find my underwear, something odd catches my attention. At first, I think I'm hallucinating. But as I move closer, I confirm I'm not imagining things. I hesitate before cautiously stepping toward the wall to my left, where the shelves stretch from top to bottom.

"No way…" I whisper.

The entire wall is packed with all sorts of guns and ammunition. It's like I'm suddenly in an action movie, everything neatly arranged as if he works for the fucking military or something.

Shock and disbelief hit me all at once as I try to make sense of what I'm seeing. I can't seem to pull my eyes away from the sheer number of weapons lined up, glinting under the dim light of the closet.

"What the fuck?"

What is Cal doing? Why does he have so many weapons? Why does he have even one weapon, for that matter?

My belly twists as I realize I've been wrong all along about him. Everything seems to be clearer now. I should have trusted my instincts. I shouldn't have fallen for his charms. Are those for protection–or something else?

Could Cal be the one people need protection from?

I look through the doorway of the closet into the sprawling, impossibly expensive penthouse apartment. I think of his car, his fancy clothes, his life of luxury… as the owner of a dingy bar.

I suddenly realize there's no way he's just a bar owner. He's up to something. Something bad.

3 1

CONFRONTING HIM

IT'S PAST 9:00 P.M. AND THE SKY IS FULLY DARK OUTSIDE BY THE TIME Cal returns home. After finding his closet packed with guns, there was nothing else I could do other than sit on his couch and wait for him to return to ask what the fuck he's got all those weapons for.

I pondered the situation for so long, my brain working overtime, convincing myself that I should give him the benefit of the doubt. I can't believe that he would do anything to harm me. Even if that meant keeping things like this from me.

The entire afternoon, I tried to think of reasons why he would need to have guns inside his home. He's a businessman after all. He might have... unruly patrons at the bar? But no matter how hard I tried, I couldn't come up with an explanation as to why he would need an entire wall of weapons that look like something out of a gangster movie.

That's why I'm still here when he returns. In the morning, my original plan was to surprise him, to have a romantic dinner prepared for when he got home, and then we could have a movie night like he mentioned earlier today. But now, all I can think about is confronting him.

"Hey, you're still here," Cal muses as soon as he opens the door and finds me planted on the couch–in the same spot I've been for the last couple of hours. He looks tired, but the way his face lights up when he sees me has my heart jumping in my chest, betraying my mind. I need to focus so I can ask him the questions I need to know the answers to.

"I wanted to ask you about something, but even after pondering it for the whole day, I'm still not sure I want to hear the answer," I start coldly, looking away from him. My eyes are now focused on the wall in front of me, my arms folded across my chest.

"Sure, what is it? Did something happen?" he asks, his tone curious but also concerned.

"Yes, something happened," I say through gritted teeth, finally turning back to look at him. It's clear that he has picked up from my serious expression and my cold voice that I'm mad.

Cal straightens up, removing his jacket and hanging it on the back of a chair. "What is it, Heidi?" he presses, his tone lowering.

"I didn't mean to pry. I hope you know that. I was trying to find something to wear…" I explain, and a glimpse of darkness crosses his gaze as he stares back at me.

He knows I saw it.

By the way his jaw is clenching, his fist tightening beside him, he knows.

"Why the fuck do you have so many guns in your apartment?" I finally blurt out, my voice so distant and cold that I don't even recognize it myself.

He flinches at my accusation, but it's so quick that I wonder if I have imagined it.

"Why would you even need *one?*" I press, desperation getting the best of me.

Who did I get myself involved with? Who even is this man in front of me?

"I can explain all that," is the only thing that comes out of his mouth.

He sounds calm and firm, although I can see there's a spark of anxiety in his eyes. But Cal doesn't budge. He doesn't lose control of his emotions like I have. He's as composed as a person can be. I imagine that must come with the job. Whatever it is that he does.

"Go ahead then. Just don't try to lie to me or make a fool out of me because I won't fall for that, Cal," I warn him firmly. "I might be young and innocent, but I'm not stupid."

"I never thought you were," he tells me, taking a step toward me.

"Stay where you are," I grunt, holding my hand in front of me so he knows I mean it.

I can't have him coming near me now. No matter how mad and confused I am, having him near me won't do me any good. I'm sure he will be able to convince me of anything he says if I get a whiff of his intoxicating scent or feel his warmth near me.

"I own a bar in Manhattan," Cal begins, stating the obvious. I fight the urge to roll my eyes. "Things can get dirty sometimes when you run a business like that."

I frown, narrowing my eyes at him. "How dirty? Wouldn't just one gun solve whatever problems you're referring to? Do you need a whole arsenal?" I bite back.

"I'm responsible for the lives of everyone that works for me. My men need to protect themselves as well, not to mention their families," he proceeds to explain. "We don't use them as frequently as you might think, Heidi. In fact, if you think about it, I have them all up here, hidden, in case we someday need them. We're not walking around, carrying them with us every day."

It makes sense, but something still doesn't sit well with me. "It's a lot of weapons, Cal," I note. "Do you expect me to believe you need all of that for protection? What are you guys protecting yourselves from? The army?"

He swallows hard, looking away from me and runs a hand through his hair. For a minute, it feels like he's losing the grip on his patience and self-control. But when he looks at me again, he has the same stoic expression on his face. "I know it's hard for you to believe me, but can you trust me on this?" he pleads, his eyes turning softer as he walks toward me.

It's like he's casting spells on me, his gaze keeping me trapped on the couch. A chill runs down my spine as his cologne hits me, as strong as when he left this morning. My brain is clouded, making it hard for me to think clearly. What was it that I was arguing with him about? Why did it feel like I needed to confront him in the first place?

Ah… the guns!

"How can I trust you when you have all those weapons inside your closet, and you never once mentioned them to me? I don't know what to believe, Cal. What do you expect me to do?" I ask. "I don't know who you are."

He looks offended for a second, which almost makes me regret my words. "I'm the same guy you've been hanging out with for days," he replies calmly, his voice suddenly softer and kinder. "The same guy who you spent New Year's Eve with. The same guy who you went on a date with, who helped you during a hard time. The same guy who held you when you fell asleep last night. I'm that guy, Heidi. Isn't that enough?"

Is it?

It should be.

Cal has done nothing but make me think he's a good guy. I should trust him. He never did anything to make me believe otherwise. Sure, the guns are suspicious as hell. But I also know how hard it is to run a business in New York. Especially a bar like his. He must have all sorts of shady clients. So, is it too absurd to think he might need to protect himself every once in a while?

And he's right—he is responsible for everyone that works for him.

Also, the way he's looking at me right now is making it hard for me to think of reasons why I should leave his apartment and never return.

Cal approaches me, his eyes lowering to my exposed thighs, and then his gaze shifts to something more feral, hungry. "Is that my shirt?" he asks, his voice now low and hoarse, his eyes narrowing on my thighs.

"Yes. I was trying to find something clean to wear after my shower," I explain, still a bit sour. "Like I said, I didn't mean to pry."

"I know you didn't," Call admits, his fingers slowly tracing a trail up my legs.

Butterflies flutter in my stomach as I realize how close he is to making me forget about everything we just discussed.

An alarm goes off inside my head, but I can't find it in me to pay attention to it right now.

"You have no idea how happy I was when I found you here after returning home from a hard day of work," he muses to me, his voice enveloping me as if I'm a snake being hypnotized by a flute.

"Don't change the subject, Cal," I warn him in what I hope is a forceful tone. "You won't make me forget about it by using your charm. It won't work on me."

What an unbelievable lie, Heidi!

I don't even believe it myself. Of course, Cal will pick up on that. If the way he's smirking at me, his lips dangerously reaching the nape of my neck, is any indication, he already knows I don't mean it.

"I'd never try to do that," he says, so close to my ear that my entire body shivers.

Shit...

"You can ask me whatever you want," he continues, placing soft, hot kisses on my neck.

I close my eyes, begging my brain to focus, but it's so hard when he's provoking me like this.

"I..." I trail off, clenching my fists beside me when I feel his fingers caressing my leg. Cal knows damn well what he's doing, and if I could see his face now, I'm sure I'd find that stupid grin still splattered on his face. I hate that he has me in a chokehold like this. Why can't I react when he's so close to me? I should push him away and demand he tell me the truth. I can partially believe what he told me, but something within me tells me he's not sharing everything.

But do I really want to know the truth? What will it do to us? Am I ready to give up on what we have? I have mixed feelings, but none of those emotions answer my questions. Right now, I can't find the strength to shove him away and leave his apartment.

"Are you going to finish that sentence, or can I change the subject again by saying I never thought I'd be so turned on by finding you wearing my shirt, on my couch, looking as beautiful as ever, just waiting for me?" Cal whispers in my ear, and I need to clench my legs to order my body to behave and not fall for his plan.

He's trying to distract me, and he's damn near succeeding.

"This is not fair," I complain in a murmur, my eyes still closed.

"Do you want me to stop?" he asks, his hand teasing me by trailing up my leg and reaching close to where I shouldn't want him to touch me at the moment. I should press for more answers. But everything seems so irrelevant now.

How can I refuse this when he is so close to giving me what I so desperately want?

32

A LITTLE WHITE LIE

Cal

Coming home to find Heidi waiting for me was an unexpected, but very welcome, surprise. After the day I had at the bar, dealing with countless business deals that went wrong—not to mention getting nowhere with the threat of the cartel looming over our heads—I planned on coming home and drowning myself in whiskey until I passed out and forgot this day ever happened.

But as soon as I spotted Heidi on my couch, wearing nothing but my Knicks shirt, her toned legs exposed, my brain short-circuited, making me momentarily forget about my bad day. Taking a more thorough look at her though, I could tell she was pissed off.

'*Why?*' was the first question that came to mind. When I left this morning, we seemed fine. *She* seemed fine. She never mentioned the '*I love you*' thing again, and I figured the best move was to pretend it didn't happen. Maybe she regretted it. Maybe she wanted me to pretend I hadn't heard. Was that a bad move on my part? Was that why she was pissed off about? But as soon as she mentioned the fact she wasn't prying, I knew it.

I knew she had seen the guns.

I should have fucking locked my closet when I left. I never expected she would stick around long enough to see what was in there, but damn, that was a stupid–not to mention amateur–mistake on my part.

I didn't want to lie to her, but it was the only thing I could come up with on the top of my head. I'm not ready to share the truth with her. It's in her best interest to stay in the dark. If this is how she reacted when she found out about the guns, imagine what she'd do if she discovered what I actually do for a living.

She would break things off with me in the blink of an eye. That's not even the worst of it…. Her knowing this side of my life would open up a whole new world of danger. She's already in a precarious position being watched by my enemies. One wrong move, one slip of her lips, and she could be taken from me.

I can't let that happen.

That's why I had to act quickly and hopefully make her forget about it. With any luck, she'll believe the lie I just told her. Which, in my defense, is not exactly a lie. It's part of the truth.

The guns *are* for protection.

They're also used for other purposes.

"Don't change the subject, Cal," she warns me. She's acting all serious, but she couldn't look cuter. "You won't make me forget about it by using your charms. It won't work on me."

"I'd never try to do that. You can ask me whatever you want," I tell her, kissing the soft skin of her neck. She smells so delicious, I really hope she drops this whole argument so we can enjoy each other. I miss her, even though it's been less than a day since we've been together.

"I…" She's losing the battle against her self control. I can tell by the way her body is reacting to my touch.

"Are you going to finish that sentence, or can I change the subject again by saying I never thought I'd be so turned on by finding you wearing my shirt, on my couch, looking as beautiful as ever, just waiting for me?" I whisper in her ear.

Heidi squirms in her seat, pressing her legs together.

A smirk spreads on my lips, but I don't pull away from her. My plan is working, and I can't risk failure right now.

"This is not fair," she whines, her voice low and breathless.

"Do you want me to stop?" I ask, but instead of pulling away, my fingers trail up her leg, getting close to her panties.

Heidi doesn't answer, but if her erratic breathing and her thumping heart are any indication of what she wants, stopping doesn't seem like an option for us now.

I don't want her to think I'm trying to shut her up with sex, so as much as it pains me, I pull away from her, finding her eyes widening, an expression of disbelief on her face. "What are you doing?" she blurts, her eyebrows raising.

"You didn't answer me. I'm not moving forward unless you tell me to," I reply.

My body curses me at this very moment, but I can't do it. Heidi doesn't deserve this, and although I'm not ready to share the entire truth with her, I'm also not going to do something that goes against everything I believe in.

If she doesn't want this, I'm definitely not forcing it. I can think of a plan B.

Heidi's shocked face would be laughable if I weren't so turned on right now. Every part of me is struggling to survive this proximity and the pent up energy building, so I need to focus.

"I'm… going to take a shower," I grunt when she doesn't answer.

"Wait!" she exclaims when I get to my feet. Heidi stands, too, stepping up on the couch so her height matches mine. "I didn't tell you to stop," she tells me matter-of-factly.

I raise my brows at her. "Yes. But you also didn't say you wanted me to continue," I point out.

"Isn't the fact that I didn't tell you to stop enough?" she counters. She looks so fucking hot when she's mad.

"You should probably be more clear when it comes to something so important, Heidi," I mutter, the bulge in my pants annoying me immensely. I wish she would just give me the green light so I can undress her and claim her right here and now.

Her cheeks flush aggressively, and I can tell she's struggling to say what she wants. It's endearing. "Fine," she huffs, rolling her eyes. She reaches for my neck, her hands locking behind me, keeping her trapped against my chest.

I smirk, studying her beautiful face. "Fine?" I repeat. "What exactly does that mean, huh?" I tease, knowing I'm getting on her nerves by making her say exactly what she needs.

"Are you going to make me beg or what? I'm not that desperate," she warns me, and although her entire body says otherwise, I'm not willing to take the chance of her stepping away from me.

I reach for her waist, gripping at her flesh possessively.

"I told you to be clearer," I grunt in a low voice, my eyes darting to her pink, juicy lips.

"And I said I'm not desperate to beg. Also, I'm mad at you for keeping things from me, so shouldn't you be the one trying to get on my good side again?" Her eyes have a different spark now, and by the amusing tone in her voice, I can tell she's no longer mad at me. At least not as much as she was before.

She's provoking me, and God, she knows how to do that. Heidi is determined to make me fight for it, even though her arms are still locked around my neck, but she doesn't budge. She doesn't make a single move while she stares at me, waiting to see my reaction.

"What should I do to get on your good side then?" I try, watching her lick her lower lip in slow motion.

"Beg," she murmurs, a grin spreading on her face.

I'm getting tired of this little game. With a swift movement, I pull her flush against me, making her feel how desperate I am. And she might be saying she isn't, but if the moan that just escaped her lips means anything, I'd say she's just as eager to get to the next step as I am.

I swallow her moan with my mouth, kissing her passionately. Our tongues dance together, and my hands roam over her body before reaching for her ass and lifting her off the couch, her legs instantly hooking around my waist.

"How do you feel about a hot shower now?" I ask against her lips.

"I've already showered," she replies, her voice cracking slightly.

"Would you be against another one?" I grin at her, pulling her tighter against me, her core brushing against my hardness.

"Oh…" Her eyes widen with surprise. "I would not," Heidi answers, chuckling as she realizes what I was referring to.

"Good."

Blindly, I guide us toward the bathroom and turn on the shower, the steam fogging up the mirror in a few seconds. Heidi's hands move fast but accurately as she removes my jacket and shirt then proceeds to unbuckle my belt and remove my pants and boxers.

I, on the other hand, only need a swift movement to get her completely naked.

"I must admit it breaks my heart a little to have to take this shirt out of you," I tell her, my eyes devouring her. "But it's worth it."

Heidi laughs, and I waste no time getting her back into my arms and walking us both inside the shower. The hot water feels like a balsam of relaxation for my stiffened muscles, but it also adds to the fire burning inside of me. I press Heidi against the wall, and she arches her back in surprise.

"Shit, the wall is cold," she explains, a chuckle escaping her throat.

"Sorry," I murmur, claiming her mouth again.

I find the back of her thigh and pull her up, granting me more access to her. I'd love to lavish her with attention and worship her, but right now, I really need some release. I can work her up later, make her pass out from exhaustion, but I just need to forget about my problems for a minute.

I entice her a little, my tip grazing her slick folds, and I watch as Heidi leans her head back on the wall, her eyes closed while she enjoys it. I play with her a little, making her beg me to enter her, and when I finally do, I slide inside her easily.

Her hands find support on my shoulders, her nails sinking into my flesh as she tries to steady herself. I thrust in and out of her, finding the nape of her neck with my nose. I kiss and lick her skin while she rocks her hips in time with mine, taking my time until we're both on the edge of release, and when she comes, I grunt, releasing myself inside of her.

3 3

SAGE ADVICE

CAL

EVENTUALLY, WE MANAGE TO FINISH OUR SHOWERS WITH HEIDI HELPING me scrub my back and massage my stiffened muscles. Her tiny, smooth hands feel so good as they glide over my soaped skin that I almost give up on letting her tend to me and move us into round two.

I watch as Heidi washes her hair, complaining that she already did that earlier today and wasn't planning on doing it again. She's so cute when she pouts. Then we dry ourselves, heading for the bed right after.

I'm so drained and exhausted today that my brain feels like it's melting inside my head. I have no strength to take Heidi out to eat or even to go down to the kitchen and cook something for us.

Lying under the sheets, our legs entangled, the air conditioner on full blast, and our bodies embracing each other is helping me recharge somehow.

This feeling is so unusual to me, but I find myself more and more addicted to it, and it scares me how much I think about these moments when I'm not with her.

Heidi's stomach growls as if on cue in the silence of the room, and she hides her face in my chest with embarrassment.

"I'm guessing you didn't have anything to eat, am I right?" I tease her.

"I was going to cook dinner for us, but then I found the guns and got pissed off. I…" She sighs, looking up at me with pleading eyes. "I'm starving now and craving fast food."

"Just pick what you want, and I'll have it delivered here," I encourage her, handing her my phone.

"What are you in the mood for?" she asks, scrolling through the food app.

"You," I tease, pinching her below her rib cage.

"I'm serious." She squirms, laughing.

"Me too," I reply. "But, whatever you want, I'm good with it. I'm just so tired, I could pass out without eating anything."

"Why are you so tired today? Did something happen?"

I know what's eating me up, and it has nothing to do with my job. Or the deals that went wrong. Or even the cartel being on our trail. Truth is, I couldn't get Heidi's confession out of my head the entire day. And the fact I didn't say anything back is eating at me as well. Because my heart knows the truth. But, there's no use for me to keep running from it when I know for a fact that I love her, too. There's never been a woman like Heidi in my life, and even though she is much more than I deserve, I can't give her up. I can't stand the thought of letting her go.

I considered doing just that today, and the fact that she confronted me about the guns tells me that we're fated to fail. She will leave me as soon as she learns about my secret life, and I don't know what to do about it. For the first time in my life, I am screwed beyond repair. I'm unable to come up with a plan to keep her by my side.

Heidi props herself on her elbow to face me. "Cal?" she says, worried. "Did something happen?" Her brows are creased as she studies me, clearly concerned about my silence.

I shake my head, trying to reassure her. But I know she needs more than that. And honestly, the words are stuck in my throat, threatening to choke me if I don't let them out.

That's why, without thinking, I let all my feelings out, not caring about the consequences.

"I've been thinking about what you said to me last night," I start, noticing her eyes widening in shock and realization at what I'm referring to.

Her mouth opens and closes, but no word comes out as she stares at me in disbelief. I don't think she was expecting me to bring this up now. Or ever.

"I wasn't sure if you meant it or if it was just… you know… something that you said without thinking, but…"

"It was," she confirms, her expression serious and determined. Her voice is also firm, not cracking the slightest. It's like a new, confident Heidi just stepped up, letting the insecure one go. "I didn't want to scare you or anything, I should have kept it to myself. I just–"

"I'm glad you didn't," I tell her softly, removing a strand of hair from her cheek. "You know… I've gotten used to being alone, Heidi. I never thought I would care for someone like I care about you. I never imagined myself experiencing what I have with you now."

She swallows hard, her eyes barely blinking as she listens.

"And I don't think I deserve you, I really don't," I emphasize when I notice her wanting to disagree. "You're way more than I could ever wish for, but now that I have you, selfishly, I don't want to let go of you. I want more and more of you every day."

"Cal…" she whispers.

"Because I have fallen in love with you, too. Deeply. And even though it scares the shit out of me, I can't think of moving forward without you in my life," I confess, noticing tears swelling at the corner of her eyes.

Her beautiful, hypnotizing, dreamy blue eyes.

Every time I stare at them, it feels like I'm on my way to heaven, being forgiven of all of my sins.

A sob escapes her, but before I can continue with my confession, Heidi jumps on me, kissing me deeply. It's a different kiss this time, though. Even though the passion and the fire is still there, there's so much emotion in it, so much depth, that it disorients me for a moment.

"I love you too," she murmurs against my mouth, pulling away from me just enough for us to be able to look each other in the eyes. "You've always been so kind and thoughtful to me. You always make me feel seen, heard, and cared for. And even though I've had people looking out for me my entire life, it just feels different with you. I feel safe. I feel… alive."

The word *safe* rings a bell inside my brain, but I ignore it.

She has no idea how wrong she is about that. Because she's not safe with me. My life is anything but safe. But there is no going back now. I've already opened my heart to her. All I can do now is make sure I do everything in my power to make it as safe as possible for her to be with me.

I'll put myself at risk any time, any day, if that means I can make her as happy as she makes me.

I cup her face and slowly pull her toward me again. Our lips collide once more, and my tongue asks for permission to explore her mouth. She grants it, and in less than a second, we're acting like we haven't just had sex less than an hour ago.

The good thing is we didn't put on any clothes after our shower, so there's nothing in the way this time to slow the process. Heidi is on my lap in a blink of an eye, her legs straddling me. I slip on a condom from the drawer next to the bed and then guide her hips as she adjusts herself before sliding herself down on me.

I grunt, my grip on her waist tightening as she begins to ride me. A couple of minutes is all it takes for us to reach climax again, Heidi collapsing on top of me as she tries to catch her breath.

Heidi is no longer in bed by the time I open my eyes. The sun is already up, and I look around trying to find her .I don't even know when or how I fell asleep.

Before I freak out, Heidi steps out of the bathroom wrapped in a towel, her long hair wet and splayed around her shoulders.

"Good morning," she says cheerfully with a big smile on her face.

"I hate to have to leave you in bed like this, but I promised Grandma I'd visit them this week."

"Do you want me to take you there?" I offer, sitting on the bed.

Heidi shakes her head, reaching for her dress. I should really get her some clothes to leave here at the apartment for whenever she wants to spend the night.

"I'll head home and get changed, then I'll call an Uber. We can see each other tomorrow. I've kept you busy a lot lately, so you can take this opportunity to catch up on work–or whatever."

I feel like disagreeing with her, but she's right. I need some time to myself, to think of my next steps. Having her here every night is great, but it stops me from making reasonable decisions.

I need to figure out what to do. I hate to let her leave by herself, but I can't guard her 24/7. She wouldn't let me anyway. And I don't want to freak her out, so I end up agreeing, even though it kills me to know I won't see her beautiful face again until tomorrow.

As soon as Heidi is out of the door, I grab my phone, texting Tony. 'Meet me at the bar as soon as you can.'

Heidi leaves, and I drag myself to the shower before getting dressed and heading to work.

My office door opens as the clock hits 6:00 that evening, and Tony walks inside, looking as sharp and elegant as ever. He looks a bit tired, but I guess that's what a life being a dad, a husband, and a mafia boss does to you.

"Having trouble with the woman already?" he asks in a teasing tone as he closes the door behind him and flops onto the couch.

I raise my brows at him. "How do you know I called you to talk about women?"

He shrugs, gesturing for the whiskey. "I doubt you have news on the cartel or you'd demand I come here as soon as possible. Also, I know you. I can see that look in your eyes, like you're in too deep, which is a weird ass look on you."

I curse him, pouring both of us a glass. I hand one to him and sit in the chair across from him. "Things are getting serious between us. And I hate lying to her. But I don't know what to do. She found my guns at the apartment and confronted me about them. I can't tell what she'll do if she finds out the truth," I admit, taking a deep breath and sipping my drink.

"Do you think she won't stick around if you come clean?" Tony pries. "She confronted you about the guns, but she didn't leave, did she?"

I shake my head. "No, but I'm not sure I was able to convince her. I came up with a pretty shitty lie."

"Still, she stayed. Any other woman would have run out of the apartment when she saw something like that. You need to give it to her straight. She seems very brave, if you ask me."

Because she is, I realize.

Maybe Heidi will understand where I'm coming from. Maybe she knows who I really am and will accept everything about me, even the shittiest parts.

"She might not want to be involved with someone like me, though," I note. "Having guns to protect yourself is one thing, but being the head of a mafia gang is another thing completely."

Tony gulps down his whiskey, staring at me over the glass. "You won't know until you tell her, man. There's no other way to do it. You'll have to come clean sooner or later. It's best if you do it while you're not in that deep."

Fuck that. I already am.

So deeply in love with her that I can't imagine a life without her in it.

34

WHO HE IS

Heidi

Visiting Grandma and Grandpa at the nursing home feels somewhat bittersweet. I've missed them a lot, and I wish I could spend more time with them like I used to. But they have a new routine now, and it's not like I can come by every day to check on them and spend time here. I need to get back on my feet, to get on with my life. I need to get my job back.

On the cab back home, I look out the window, contemplating the past few weeks and how much my life has changed ever since. Everything revolves around Cal. He told me he loved me last night. He shared his heart, and the things he said about me and how he thought he wasn't worthy of me, it was all so sweet that my heart still skips a beat whenever I replay it in my head.

Is this what I want my entire life to be like? Sharing it with Cal, no matter what?

I still have my doubts about what I found in his closet, it's true, but I'm sure Cal will tell me the truth about everything one day. Despite what I said to him, and how I feel about him, our relationship is still new. I can't blame him for not telling me everything. I can't force him to share his entire life with me either. We haven't even labeled whatever we have between us yet. How can I demand that he tells me all the details about his life?

Sure, I have the right to decide I don't want to be with him anymore because he wasn't honest with me about something that could potentially cause me harm. But so far, nothing he's done has put me in danger. We can cross that bridge when we come to it. Until then, I'll enjoy the happiness Cal provides me. Because I *am* happy when I'm with him.

A little voice in the back of my mind reminds me of the fire in my bookstore and losing everything because of something *related* to Cal. I still haven't figured out what really happened. He never denied being responsible for it, even if indirectly, so that should serve as an example of why things might be more concerning than what Cal is letting on. But how can I worry about anything when in his arms I feel the safest? No matter how hard I try, I can't imagine my life without him in it anymore.

As soon as I arrive at the apartment, I start cleaning it up, deciding to take the day to give my new home some attention. Staying at Cal's lately has made me neglect this place a bit. I also need to go grocery shopping because everything I bought in the first week here is already gone. It's a long busy day of chores and errands, and eventually, I tucker out and make my way to bed.

It feels weird to lie on the mattress alone–without Cal by my side–but it's good to take some time for me as well. I need to have a clear mind so I can make decisions, and being in his apartment with him won't help me do that.

Grandma told me the insurance money will probably be in our hands by this time next week, so I need to rush to find a place to set up my new bookstore. I'd still prefer to rent the space I saw in Greenwich Village, but I need to make an offer first because I can't afford the price they are asking for now. I know Cal offered to get it for me, but if I can get it myself, that'd be ideal. I don't want to depend on him for everything, even if we're together.

My phone rings on my nightstand, and I reach for it, finding a text message from Cal.

'Sleeping already?'

I smile to myself, typing an answer right away.

'Not quite yet. I'm in bed, but my mind is completely awake.'

I stare at the ceiling while waiting for him to reply.

Calling would probably be faster, but maybe he's busy at the bar. It's late for me, but for someone like him, who works at night time, it's still considered early. Also, Cal has been missing work at night since he's been staying with me, so he probably has a lot to do.

Another message from him dings on my phone. 'I'll miss you in my bed tonight. But we'll see each other tomorrow, right?'

'Sure. Want to come over tomorrow night? I have to go to Greenwich Village in the morning, but other than that, my schedule is pretty free,' I text back.

'Sounds like a plan to me. I'll bring the wine.'

I text him a heart emoji as a reply, and before I know it, I'm fast asleep.

The next morning, I get up and take a shower, getting dressed to go to the shop in Greenwich Village to see if I can make an offer to the owner. I put on my best suit, trying to look presentable and professional, hoping my appearance will help me with my goal.

The day is sunny and the weather isn't as cold as yesterday, but I still need to wear gloves as I call for a cab on the sidewalk. While I wait, my eyes catch something that makes my stomach churn.

I instantly get a bad feeling. Call it instinct, a sixth sense, or whatever, but I just know something is wrong. I'm not one to be suspicious of everything and everyone, nor am I someone who thinks I'm being watched or followed, but this black car on the other side of the street gives me the creeps.

I shake my head, telling myself that I'm probably overthinking. Maybe the guns at Cal's place have made an impression, and my subconscious is starting to play tricks on me. I go on about my business, hopping in a taxi and traveling across town.

But when I get home from my failed meeting at Greenwich

Village, and the car is still there, I panic. Not just because of the car but because of whoever is driving it. I can't see his face clearly because of the tinted window, but I know he's following me with his eyes, barely blinking as he watches me walk inside my building. My heart starts thumping in my chest, and I clench my fingers around my purse, considering what to do. I might be freaking out for nothing. I might be imagining things.

If I call someone, what will I say? Will I say I'm being followed? How would I prove it? Or worse…what if I accuse an innocent person of something that my brain is probably making up?

I swallow hard and grab my phone from my purse, not waiting to see if the car will leave. I head upstairs, hoping to get out of their sight as quickly as possible. If they really are following me, they know I live here by now, so there's no use trying to mislead them.

Cal's face appears in my mind's eye, and I know I need to call him. He'll be really pissed at me if I don't and then something happens. I don't want to scare him or anything, but at this point, I'm so nervous that my hands are shaking as I try to find my keys inside my bag.

As soon as I'm safe inside my apartment, the door behind me locked, I dial his number.

"Hey, sweetheart," he greets me, his voice a bit distant and muffled by chattering around him. He must be at the bar, but I don't bother to ask.

"Hi," I reply weakly. "Listen, I don't mean to scare you, but I think there's someone watching me outside my building.

"Where are you?" Cal asks right away through clenched teeth.

"I'm safe. I'm at home," I tell him.

"Stay right there. I'm on my way."

It takes him less than five minutes to arrive, and considering this is New York City–even though I live close to his bar–it's still impressive.

He knocks on my door, making sure to call my name so I know it's him. I pull the door open, and he barges inside, crossing half the living room with a couple of long strides. His eyes roam around, taking in every inch of my small apartment. His jaw is tense, his brows creased, and his fists are clenched beside him. His shoulders are so stiff that I wonder how he's even able to move his neck from side to side so fast like that.

"Cal, it's fine. No one followed me inside," I reassure him, not sure if this is what he wants to hear. By the look of it, he's not even listening to me. I've never seen him like this before. It seems a bit overdramatic to me, if I'm being honest. His behavior is frantic and erratic; it's nothing like the composed, confident man I know.

"What did you see?" he asks, turning to face me now that he's certain no one is inside my apartment, hiding to jump out at us any minute.

"I-It…" I stammer a little, caught off guard for a second. "It was just a feeling. It could be nothing. I might have overreact–"

"What did you see, Heidi?" he presses, coming close to me.

"I went out to run errands this morning, and there was a black car on the other side of the street. At first it felt like I was just imagining things, but when I got back, the car was still here, and the man inside was following me with his eyes," I explain, trying not to be intimidated by his expression.

"What did he look like?" Cal asks, his eyes scanning every inch of my face.

"I couldn't see him clearly. The windows were tinted," I answer. "I didn't even see the plate because I sort of panicked, but it was a black car that looked pretty expensive."

"Fuck," he mutters to himself, his hands darting to his hair in frustration. He tugs at it, and I widen my eyes, watching his odd reaction.

"Cal… What is it? What are you not telling me? Do you know who it was?" I press, the panic within me threatening to crawl back.

He doesn't answer me, grabbing his phone from his pocket instead, and typing something quickly.

"Cal!" I urge, my voice raising a pitch. He looks up at me, his eyes darkened. "Tell me now what you're hiding from me. First the fire, then the guns, and now this. There's clearly something going on that you're not divulging, so you'd better start telling me the truth. Now."

He closes his eyes, taking a deep breath, and that's enough confirmation for me to know something is very wrong.

Everything starts making sense. It's like the puzzle is finally coming together. Like I stepped out into the light. I was ignoring it. All along, everything about Cal screamed danger to me, but I chose not to pay attention because of my feelings for him. But now, judging by his reaction to a simple suspicion of mine, I can't be wrong about this.

"What is it?" I insist, my tone softer and calmer now. It might be a better approach if I want him to give me an answer.

Cal looks at me with pain in his eyes, and I'm pretty sure whatever comes out of his mouth next will crush me.

"I'm the boss of the Irish Kings."

3 5

SHATTERED

I BLINK ONCE, TWICE, MY BRAIN STRUGGLING TO MAKE SENSE OF THE words that just came out of Cal's mouth.

Irish Kings?

What the fuck is that?

Why do I recognize this name from somewhere?

But where…?

Then it occurs to me, like a meteor hitting me straight in the face.

Irish Kings…

That's the name of the Irish mafia gang in New York. I have no idea why or where I remember it from, but I might have read about them at some point in the past, or heard about them on TV or in the news.

"The Irish Kings…as in, the mafia?" I ask, hoping that saying it out loud will convince me that that isn't what he meant because that would be utterly ridiculous.

The whole idea is stupid. Even repeating the name sounds idiotic to me. There's no way I fell in love with a mafia boss. Is there? This is not a fucking movie. This is real life.

I remember joking about it once with him in the car right after we met. He slammed on the brakes so hard that we were almost rear ended. I had no idea how close to home I'd hit back then, but now, his reaction makes so much sense to me.

Cal's looking at me with a painful expression, as if he'd rather be hit by a bus than be here with me having this conversation. "It wasn't something you needed to know. I didn't think we'd get close like this. I didn't want you involved in that part of my life because it's not safe." His eyes darken with unsaid words. Words I desperately wish he would say because this is insane. "When we got serious, I wasn't sure how to broach the subject."

I huff, crossing my arms. "Telling me the truth would have been a good start." I hate being rude like this, but I feel so betrayed and stupid right now that I don't know how else to deal with this.

"You'd still be mad at me if I had, wouldn't you? I didn't want to lose you, Heidi. I didn't want to lose what we have," he explains.

I feel so overwhelmed right now that I don't even know what to think. Cal is a mafia boss. I got involved with someone who runs illegal businesses. I don't even know what he does. I don't know this man, and yet, my heart is shattered as if I just lost the love of my life.

Because that's what he is, isn't he?

I was beginning to think Cal was the kind of guy I read about in the books I love, the man I would eventually marry. I was beginning to believe the stars had aligned and that we would one day get married and have a little family, with kids running around the house. Just thinking about it used to put a huge smile on my face. But now, it feels like my entire world is collapsing. I don't know what to believe in anymore.

"You lied to me," I remind him. "You hid who you were from me this entire time–and what you do for a living."

Cal inhales sharply, not taking his eyes away from me. "I had to."

"Right..." I roll my eyes.

"Do you realize what could happen to you if the wrong people found out about us? Just being seen with me makes you a mark. I left you in the dark to keep you safe!"

"You LIED. You lied about the guns to my face. You had a chance to tell me the truth–"

"I didn't have a choice!"

"So, what now?" I ask, edging toward him. "What do you actually do, then? Go around killing people, dealing drugs–"

"It's more complicated than that."

I narrow my eyes at him. "I've seen the movies, Cal."

"Then you have a wild imagination." He narrows his eyes at me.

"So you have killed people?"

He doesn't answer me. He simply stares into my eyes.

I gasp in disbelief. "You have," I murmur more to myself than to him. Realizing Cal has blood on his hands makes it all seem more real, more believable.

And that seems to be the final nail in my coffin. The end of our relationship.

Cal takes a step forward, moving closer to me, but I raise my hand so fast that my shoulder cracks.

"Don't. Don't come near me," I tell him in a warning, firm tone. And this time I really mean it. He won't be able to persuade me about this. I won't fall for his charms anymore, even if the dark look in his eyes is making my body betray my mind.

"Heidi…"

"I don't know what I'm more upset about," I continue, a bitter taste in my mouth. My eyes sting from unshed tears, but I shake them away. I won't cry. "The fact that you lied to me about all of this or that you're involved with the fucking mafia. I mean, not *involved*. You run a fucking syndicate. That's what you do."

A cocky smile tugs at the corners of his lips but otherwise falls flat. "I do. Here, and back in Ireland."

"And you're proud of that?"

"It's who I am."

I wait for him to say something else, to grovel at my feet and beg me to stay, but he stands firm, his feet braced for a fight.

"That car you saw? That was because of me. They know about you Heidi, which is why you needed to stay ignorant. You're never been part of the live. You've seen the movies and read the books, sure, but this is real life, and you're in danger–"

I shake my head before he finishes his sentence. "I don't want to hear another word from you." I clench my jaw and point at the door. "I want you to leave."

I barely recognize my voice. I'm doing my best not to cry before Cal is out of my apartment. I won't let him see how he's shattered me. I won't allow him to see my disgrace.

"Is that really what you want?" he whispers, remaining in the same spot on the other side of the room, not attempting to get close to me again.

"Don't," I snap back. "I can't trust anything you say to me anymore. I want you to leave, Cal," I rasp, hot tears threatening to flow down my cheeks. "I should–I should call the police, shouldn't I? Since I have a murderer in my apartment!"

Another ghost of that cocky smile has my body begging to just run to him, and my heart and mind are at odds. He's not sorry. He's the opposite of sorry. This is who Cal really is, and I'm just collateral.

"My friends on the force would love to meet you," he smirks, shaking his head.

My heart thuds. Of course, he has cops in his back pocket. It suddenly strikes me how real this is. I got involved with a mob boss. I need him to go. I just need him out so I can… so I can think.

He exhales deeply, running his fingers through his hair before dragging his hand down his face. With a slightly bored sigh, he says, "I'll have some guys keeping an eye on you. Just to make sure you're not being followed–"

"I don't need your protection. My life was safe, normal, before I met you. If I need protection now it's because I met you." The words taste like venom in my mouth. Tears are rolling down my cheeks now, and it feels like my heart is being ripped out of my chest. The pain is so physical and intense that it makes me feel like I'm out of breath.

"I need you to understand that you're being hunted," he grinds out with obvious frustration.

"Like I said, I don't need your protection," I cut him off once more. "Now, go!" I order, a sob coming out of my throat.

Cal takes me in for another second before ducking his head and turning to leave. I watch as the door opens and closes behind him, and that's when I let it all out, not even caring if I'm loud enough for the neighbors to hear me.

How stupid was I to let myself fall for him? What did I get myself into? Everything we had seems like a complete lie now. I don't know what to believe in. He said he loved me, but how can I believe it when all this time he's kept so much from me? Important things...things... that involve my safety. My grandparents' safety. How can I know if our relationship so far has been truthful or if I was just being misled by the illusion of who Cal made me believe he was?

I don't know what to think anymore, and it feels like I'm dying.

It hurts so much...

3 6

A CLUE AT LAST

CAL

"FUCK!" I HISS, PUNCHING THE WALL NEXT TO THE ELEVATOR OUTSIDE Heidi's apartment. Thankfully, there's no one with me as I head downstairs after being told to leave her home, so I'm left alone with my anger and frustration.

I should've seen this coming. It was bound to happen from the beginning. Of course, she would find out. How did I ever think I could keep it hidden from her forever?

I could've treaded more carefully, but as soon as I heard her saying over the phone that she thought she was being followed, I saw red. I rushed to her apartment, not even trying to control my feelings and emotions. I was all over the place, all sorts of scenarios running through my mind until I could make sure that she was all right.

She immediately picked up that I was hiding something from her. Once I decided to come clean with her, everything just poured out of me, and everything I'd been struggling to keep from her was completely exposed.

As soon as I get to the building exit, I hesitate, halting in my steps.

215

I shouldn't leave her alone.

Then I remember the reason I came here in the first place. After our argument, it completely slipped out of my mind that she had called me because she thought she was being followed.

In my rush to see her, I completely ignored my surroundings. I didn't search for someone lurking on the street or around the building.

When she told me she had seen a black vehicle, I instantly knew what she was referring to. It's the same car that has been following me lately, the same one who attacked my bar on Christmas Eve.

The cartel is on our tail, and now I'm sure they know about Heidi and where she lives. They know I'm with her. They are closing the circle on us, and I still have no idea how to stop them from doing so.

My head snaps from side to side as I try to find the vehicle or anything that will make my skin crawl. I can feel they are still here. Now that I'm paying attention, my instincts are telling me to watch out. The street is somewhat empty for an evening in New York, but I still take my time to study the surroundings.

That's when I spot the vehicle parked at the corner, somewhat hidden under a thick tree. The tinted windows prevent me from seeing inside, and the engine is turned off, but I know it's the cartel. Maybe they moved from where they were parked before because Heidi saw them earlier.

But they still didn't fucking leave. What the hell are these mother-fuckers planning?

An anger so strong creeps up on me, and red is all I can see. With strong and determined strides, I head in the direction of the car. I clench my jaw so hard that I can even hear my teeth gritting against each other.

With a swift movement, I pull the driver's door open, finding a man in probably his forties looking at me with wide eyes, slightly surprised. If I could guess, I'd say I caught him off guard. His eyes are red, which tells me he was probably taking a nap.

I grab him by the collar, lowering myself to his level. I take him in, and my hatred boils up when I realize I don't recognize him. "Who the fuck sent you?" I snarl in his face, making sure I keep my voice low in case someone passes by.

"No one," the man chokes out. He sounds a bit too scared for someone who works for the cartel, and for a split second, I consider the idea of having made a mistake.

But I didn't. He's probably just a very good liar.

I land a punch square in his face, and a grunt escapes him. His nose is bleeding when he looks at me again, but I don't let go of his collar. Instead, my grip tightens around his shirt. "I'm not against killing you right here, so you might want to give me a fucking answer," I threaten. "Are you from the De La Cruz cartel?"

The mention of the cartel's name makes his eyes pop as he stares at me. A grin forms on my lips before I punch him again–and again. When I feel his body go limp in my hand, I realize I knocked him unconscious.

With my brain working at its full capacity, I look around to make sure no one is coming and then I pull him out of the car, throwing him over my shoulder. I kick his door closed before heading for my car that's parked a few spaces away.

A couple of old ladies pass by us and look at me with suspicious, frightened eyes, but I only offer them a kind smile and a nod while continuing on my way.

As soon as I get to my car, I open the trunk, tossing the man's inside. I zip tie his hands behind his back and put tape on his mouth before closing the trunk.

I disappear from the site as quickly as possible, making sure no one else saw me. It'd be a bother to have to deal with the police right now, not to mention it'd take me a lot of time to deal with bureaucracies, and time is something I can't afford to lose at the moment.

Sam is the first person I call when I make sure I'm not being followed by someone from the cartel. I take a detour, utilizing the alleyways, even though I was already very close to the bar. I want to make sure no one is after me.

"Yes, Boss?" Sam answers on the first ring.

"I'm bringing someone to the bar for interrogation," I inform him.

"He was lurking around Heidi's apartment." I add the location of the car, telling him to have it towed to a car lot we own.

"Roger that. I'll prepare the room for your arrival," he says. "Do you need anything else?"

"Put some men on the streets. The cartel might want retaliation when they realize one of theirs was taken," I order, while a major headache threatens to take away my focus. But I can't allow that to happen. The night will be long if I have to interrogate this guy, and I can't let anything distract me. "And place a team outside of Heidi's building immediately. I don't want to risk anyone coming for her."

"Consider it done."

I hang up and immediately dial Tony. If the cartel is hunting in our city, he also needs to know. He takes longer than my man to answer, which puts me a bit on edge. I hope no one from the cartel went after him as well. Since we have no fucking clue what they're planning, we're both being cautious when it comes to their next steps, but anything can happen.

When I'm about to give up, he finally answers the call. "Shit, lad. What took you so long?" I grumble.

"We've got some problems out here in Staten," he explains, growling under his breath. "Is everything okay out there?"

"No, it's not. I have a man knocked unconscious in my trunk, and I'm taking him to the bar. He was fucking following Heidi outside of her apartment."

"Fuck," Tony hisses. "Cartel?"

I nod even though he can't see me. "I can deal with him by myself. I will let you know if I get something out of him, though. Just be careful. We don't know what they're planning."

"*You* be careful," Tony retorts. "Tell me right away if you need me, and I'll be there in a second. We've had them sniffing around Staten Island again."

"I appreciate it. I'll keep you posted." I hang up and finally reach the back of the bar, noticing Sam and Hunter already waiting for me by the door. Hunter leans against the wall, a dark look on his face. I'm sure he's eager for some action, and I can't blame him.

A few punches to this guy's face wasn't enough to satisfy me. If anything, it only got me hungrier for some answers. I am beyond fucking frustrated with all of this, and I can't wait to finally put my hands on someone from the cartel and find out what the hell they want with me.

I climb out of the car, gesturing with my head toward the trunk. Sam and Hunter are on the move immediately, removing the guy from my car. I shove my hands inside my pockets, watching the alley as my guys take him inside.

Today was supposed to be a fucking good day. I planned to take Heidi out for dinner, enjoy my time with her, but everything went completely opposite to what I had pictured in my head.

She found out I'm a mafia boss, broke up with me, and as a bonus, I discovered someone from the cartel watching her. Everything is a fucking mess in my life right now, and I hate not knowing what to do. It was never like this before. I was always one step ahead of my enemies.

I underestimated the De La Cruz cartel. I never thought they would come after me. I still don't know why they're so eager to come for me and not Tony, since he was the one with a problem with Mateo.

The fact that I helped him shouldn't put a moving target on my back, but apparently, I was completely wrong. Maybe they're coming for me first before heading for Tony. Maybe they think the Irish Kings are a weaker, easier target before moving for the Saints.

But they couldn't be more wrong.

If they want me to show them what we're capable of, I'll be pleased to do so. I'll make them regret coming for me.

I'll make them regret targeting Heidi, too. Because now I understand the fear of losing someone I love. Now, I have something to fight for. Now, I have someone to protect.

And I will keep my promise to her.

I won't allow anything to happen to her. Even if I have to put my life at risk to keep that promise.

37

HANDS TIED

Heidi

As soon as Cal's out the door, I'm left desolated, as if I'm drifting. My mind is numb, and I'm momentarily frozen in place, unsure of what to do. Nothing makes sense and, for a moment, I think I might be dreaming that all of this is just a weird fantasy, some sort of illusion I created in my head. How can Cal–this sweet, sexy, and kind human being–be a criminal? It's absurd…

Lifting up from the floor where I've been static for a couple of minutes, I walk toward the window, eager for some fresh air. I pull it open, breathing in the cold evening air. It feels like a wakeup call, the wind brushing against my face, drying up the tears streaming down my cheeks.

The night is so beautiful, the moon shining so bright up in the sky. It contrasts sharply with the chaos and the destruction that I feel within my heart. I've never felt this broken before in my life.

Maybe when my parents died, yes, but I was too young to remember exactly what it felt like. But now that I'm mature enough, I can tell for a fact that having your heart broken hurts like hell.

I had so many plans for the both of us. I really thought we could build something together in this crazy world, where love feels like an unrealistic goal. Cal made me feel like it was possible to be loved. To find someone to share everything with. To want to go through everything for the person I love.

I should accept him for what he is then, shouldn't I? If what I feel for him really is love, shouldn't I accept what he does for a living? Shouldn't I embrace him completely, the good and the bad parts?

So, why can't I make myself do that?

Why can't I accept that reality is ugly and not what I had dreamed of?

Looking down at the street below me, I watch as the cars come and go, each person heading for their homes or their businesses, none of them aware of what I'm going through.

And it's not like I can talk about this with anyone–firstly, because I don't have any friends. Secondly, because my grandparents are the only people I can talk to, and they would never in a million years understand–or accept–what I'm going through right now. I wouldn't put this burden on them either.

My eyes roam through the streets, noticing some people walking with their dogs, others coming from the supermarket with bags in their arms, some on their phones, talking excitedly with whoever is on the other end...

Life is moving forward outside, and here I am, sulking in my own misery.

I hate acting like a victim, but I don't have the strength tonight to put this behind me. Not yet, anyway.

Something odd happening on the corner catches my attention, and I squint my eyes to see it better.

There's a guy punching someone inside a car.

How come no one is seeing it? Why isn't anyone doing anything?

One more close look and I gasp in horror, realizing who it is I'm looking at.

"Cal?" I whisper, my voice cracking with disbelief. What is he doing?

The guy is inside a black SUV, and then realization hits me. This was the vehicle I saw parked in front of my building, and Cal is probably hitting the man who was watching me earlier.

No one seems to be noticing the commotion happening in the middle of the street. Sure, this isn't the busiest street in New York, but still… it's New York City.

Cal throws a few more punches at the guy's face, and he seems to lose consciousness.

"Oh, my God…" I mumble to myself. Then Cal tosses the man over his shoulder and takes him to his car, throwing the guy in his trunk. "What are you doing?" I ask, anxiety and fear getting the best of me. Where is he taking the man? Is he… tying his hands? I consider going there and confronting him again, asking what he's going to do with the guy. But I realize I don't want to know.

Now that I am aware of who he is and what he does, I feel like the answer won't be something I'd like to hear. I hope Cal doesn't kill the man. I don't know who he is or why he's been following me, but with surprise I realize I'm not scared for the man.

Or myself.

I'm scared for Cal.

I don't want anything to happen to him. And even though he seems to be in control right now, I fear what can happen afterward. What if someone retaliates? What if he loses his leverage or the guy wakes up while he is driving, and they get into an accident?

Lots of horrible scenarios run through my mind. I'm frozen in place, watching the scene unfold before my eyes, unable to force myself to do anything.

I widen my eyes while Cal drives away, leaving no trace of anything even happening behind. The only evidence is the black SUV that is still parked in the same spot. I hope no one comes after it. What will happen when the guy's allies discover that he was taken? Will they go after Cal? Will they come after me?

Rushing to the apartment door, I make sure it's locked before returning to the couch. I flop myself down, sinking my head in my hands.

I consider calling Cal. I don't know why I'm not freaking out about being abducted after seeing what I saw. Instead, I'm losing my mind over the mere idea of Cal being in danger.

This is not the type of feeling I was expecting after I discovered he's part of the mafia. I thought I'd be scared for my life–which I partially am, because I know I'm a target because of him–but still, I wasn't counting on being this worried sick about him.

Is this what it's going to be like if I decide to stay with him? Why am I even considering it since I told him to leave?

Isn't our relationship over?

"Get your shit together, Heidi. You can't be with him," I tell myself in a determined voice.

I take a deep breath, propping myself up on the couch. I can't spiral like this. I need to move forward, focus on myself and my grandparents. I need to get back on track, return to my normal life. Meeting Cal has done nothing to me other than pull me off track in regard to my goals and dreams. My thoughts are consumed by him because I have a lot of free time. I'm not occupying myself with anything, therefore I am focusing too hard on him and our relationship.

But no more.

From tomorrow onward, I'll make sure I have tasks to focus on. I'll get a new storefront, work on having my bookstore reopened, and eventually, I'll forget Cal ever existed, that he was ever a part of my life and my heart.

Maybe, if I work hard, I can one day buy a house for my grandparents and get them out of the retirement home. I could have them near me again while I can, while God continues to allow them time on this earth. Then, when they're no longer here, I'll be by myself, but I have to believe I will eventually fall out of love with Cal and find someone who can give me the life I want.

Out of danger. Away from any harm. A life filled with love and attention. And if not, I'll have to learn to live by myself. Lots of people do it. It shouldn't be that hard. I've been on my own besides my grandparents for years anyway. I can do it again.

Yeah... right. As if you believe that, Heidi.

My stomach growls as if on cue, to remind me that I haven't eaten anything yet. But right now, I can't think of putting food in my mouth. I feel sick and nauseated, not to mention my head is killing me.

I force my legs to take me to the bathroom and start removing my clothes. I stare at myself in the mirror. I don't like what I see. My eyes are red and swollen, my cheeks puffy from all the crying. The sparkle I was starting to get used to seeing in my eyes ever since meeting Cal is gone now. I feel empty. Hollow.

Stepping into the shower, I let the hot water cascade over my hair, down my back. I close my eyes and take a deep breath, steadying myself.

I'll think about what to do tomorrow. Tonight, I'll just crawl into bed and forget this day ever happened. Maybe, for a few hours, I can pretend I'm still living that fairytale life I had with Cal when I was unaware of all the shit he's involved in.

And when I wake up in the morning, I'll figure out what to do.

38

COMFORTING TALK

Heidi

Despite my hopes that I would drop into a deep slumber and not wake at all during the night, my dreams were haunted by faceless men following Cal and I around town. Inevitably, one or the both of us got shot in each of my nightmares. In one of those dreams, these men get to my grandparents. That's when I wake up sweating and unable to fall asleep again.

I get up from bed and make some coffee before the sun is even up. After that, I grab my laptop and start searching for shops to buy again since my meeting with the owner of the Greenwich Village store yesterday wasn't successful. The guy wasn't willing to budge on lowering the price, and since I don't even have the insurance money yet, I couldn't commit to something I couldn't afford.

I spend the entire morning on real estate websites. However, none of them really stick out to me. I don't particularly love anything I see, and by the time the clock strikes eleven in the morning, I'm tired of looking at the computer screen, my eyes stinging from the effort. I get up from my couch, heading for the kitchen to pour myself another cup of coffee. I check my phone a couple of times, secretly hoping to see a text from Cal. But that doesn't happen.

Bored and suffocated inside my apartment, I decide to head out and grab something for lunch. Maybe afterward, I can pay my grandparents a visit again. They will probably be confused as to why I'm visiting them so frequently, but I can't stay in this apartment by myself anymore.

As soon as I step outside the apartment, anxiety courses through my veins, but I force it away. I can't allow myself to be scared. I need to live my life. I can't stay at home, afraid that someone will be following me around town every time I step out of my building. Cal took the guy who was watching me yesterday, so I can only hope no one was sent to take his place overnight.

When I reach the sidewalk, I notice that the black SUV is not there anymore. Someone might have come to remove it, or maybe it was towed. I don't know. And I don't want to overthink this.

I signal for a cab and tell the driver the address to a restaurant near the retirement home. This way, after I eat, I can walk to meet my grandparents.

Needless to say, Grandma is surprised when she sees me. She's alone, reading a book in her armchair by the window, the sunlight creeping through the glass and illuminating her face and her white hair. "What are you doing here again so soon, dear?" she asks in a cheerful voice. She moves to stand up but I raise my hand in the air to prevent her from doing so. Then I walk over and place a kiss on her forehead.

"Hi, Granny. I was just in the neighborhood and decided to pay you a visit again," I lie.

She narrows her eyes at me, clearly not buying what I said. "You know I love you, sweetie, but you've always been a terrible liar. Plus, you look exhausted. Did something happen?" she carefully pries.

I swallow hard, feeling the urge to cry all of a sudden. I look around to prevent her from seeing the tears swelling in my eyes and pretend to be searching for something. Which in a way, I am.

"Where's Grandpa?" I ask, ignoring her previous question.

"He went to play pickleball. It's his thing lately," she answers, putting her book aside. "He should be back in a few minutes, though."

I make myself comfortable, sitting in the chair opposite from her. "So, what you've been up to?" I try making small talk.

"You were just here, honey. Not much has happened since then," Grandma replies in a teasing tone. "You should be the one with news, don't you think?"

I shrug. "Not really. Your life has always been busier than mine." I offer her a smile. If only she knew how excited my life has become in a matter of days, she'd be shocked. And not in a good way

The doorknob clicks, and Grandpa walks inside wearing a polo shirt and shorts. "Oh, Heidi, dear. I didn't know you'd be here today," he says, a huge smile spreading across his face.

I get to my feet, widening my arms and welcoming him in a hug. "It was a last minute decision. I hope that's okay."

"Of course that's okay. More than okay actually. You're welcome to come whenever you want," he tells me, placing a kiss on my Grandma's cheek. "Is everything all right?" he adds, turning to look at me again.

"That's what I've been trying to discover. She looks so tired, doesn't she?" my grandmother asks him, her eyes still on me.

"Well, thanks, Granny," I grumble.

"Your grandmother is right. Is this about the bookstore?" Grandpa pries, studying me while pulling another chair over to sit close to us.

Now I have both my grandparents staring at me as if I'm in an interrogation room. What did I get myself into?

"Partially, yes. I need to figure out what to do, but I can't find a nice place to buy or rent. Everything is so expensive in New York," I explain with a huff. "I loved this one place in Greenwich Village, but the guy doesn't want to lower his price. We can't afford that."

"I'm sure we can figure it out somehow. In fact, I was about to call you later. I just received a call from the insurance company, and the money was transferred to my account this morning," Grandpa starts, surprising both me and my grandmother. "And it's all yours."

"Oh, thank God," Granny muses.

"Grandpa, that's great! But I can't accept all the money you guys received. I will accept *some* help since I promised you I would, but you both worked so hard for your entire lives," I protest kindly. "I won't be comfortable if you give me all of it."

"Sweetie, you're already living in this new apartment God knows how. It's okay to accept help. Also, it would give us some peace of mind to know you're taken care of. We only have you, and we don't need this money. I still have some saved for this." He waves a hand around their tidy apartment.

My grandfather's words leave me even more unsure of what to do. I feel bad for accepting their money, but I also understand where they are coming from. If the situation was the other way around, I'd have done the same for them. I can't blame them for wanting to take care of me.

"Fine," I finally concede, receiving a smile back from both of them.

"As for the shop at Greenwich Village, see if you can make a better offer. Maybe they just want to see you fight for it a bit," Grandma chimes in. "Real estate brokers can be a tough nut to crack, but they are not that unbending if they need money."

"Okay, I will think of what I can do," I promise them.

Cal's offer rings in my ear. He had offered to buy the place for me before. I'm glad I didn't accept it. I would be regretting it so hard right now if I had.

"Now, will you tell me who made you cry?" my grandmother's gaze hardens.

I almost choke on my saliva. "Who said I was crying?" I retort, clearing my throat.

They both chuckle at the same time.

"As if I wasn't the one who raised you," she replies, a little offended. "I know you better than you know yourself."

I roll my eyes, knowing there is no way out of this conversation. I consider what to tell them, what to share about what happened with Cal.

"I was seeing this guy, but it's over now," I say, not bothering to give too much information.

"Why?" Grandpa is the one who addresses me this time.

"He wasn't who I thought he was. He kept things from me. I know it was for my protection, but still, I…" I trail off, knowing I can't go into details with them. The less they know about this, the better.

"Do you love him?" he asks, surprising me.

I was not expecting this question. The mere mention of it is enough to make all the tears I've been keeping inside since last night, when I promised myself I wouldn't cry anymore, to bubble to the surface.

Grandma immediately stands and comes to me, patting me gently on the back. "Oh, honey. Don't be like that," she comforts me. "Love is hard, but I'm sure you will figure this out."

"I-I can't, it's…over," I stammer between sobs.

"If this is real love," Grandpa adds, "you will work it out eventually."

I sniff, looking up at him.

"You know," he continues. "If life has taught me anything, it's that things hardly happen according to plan. It might not be how you imagined it would be, but there's always a way to get around anything–except for death and taxes."

"Your grandfather is right," my grandmother says, still holding me close to her. "You need to follow your heart. Now, I don't know what happened, but if you love him, and he loves you, too, which I'm assuming he does, there's probably a good reason for him to have kept things from you. Am I right?"

I nod. I hate that Cal had to lie to me about all of this, but thinking clearly, I can understand why he did it. I believed him when he said he did it to protect me, even if I hate to admit it.

"Communication is essential in any relationship. I'm sure if you guys talk, you can make it work," my grandfather encourages. "And if not, well, as much as it hurts, no one ever died from a broken heart before. You'll get over it one day. And we'll be here to help you."

"Thank you." I wipe my nose with the back of my hand and chuckle. "I really love you guys. And I miss having you in my life every day."

"I know," Grandma agrees. "We miss you, too. But we're here. We always will be, no matter how far away we are."

With just that sentence, everything instantly feels better. Maybe that was all I needed to be able to see the light at the end of the tunnel. I might be lonely, but I'm not alone. I still have my family with me. And even though I can't see them every day, I know they will always be there for me, no matter what.

That's all I need to know to carry on.

39

MAKE ME FORGET

"Are you sure you don't need me to come with you to talk to this guy?" my grandfather offers for the millionth time in the past hour. "I'm positive I can convince him to sell me the shop at half the price he's demanding."

I chuckle, shaking my head.

"I'm good, Grandpa. If he doesn't accept my offer, I'm sure I can find another great place somewhere else. As much as I love this one, I'm not willing to pay more than it is worth."

Grandpa nods, finally conceding.

"Well, I have to get going," I say, getting up from the chair. "You guys have to get ready for dinner, and I stayed for too long already. I don't want them to forbid me to come visit you next time."

"They wouldn't dare," Grandma murmurs, standing and pulling me into a tight hug. It instantly makes me feel like I can fight the entire world. Her embrace charges my battery, and I feel renewed. Determined. Ready for whatever the world throws my way.

"Thanks, Granny. I love you," I tell her. Then I pull away from her to hug my grandfather. "I can't thank you enough for everything you've done for me."

He scoffs. "Who else would we do it for? You're all we have. So, please, take care of yourself, okay?"

I nod. "I promise I will. I'll be back soon."

I walk out of the retirement home and onto the street, considering what to do next. I call a cab, and when the driver asks me where I'm going, I open my mouth to guide him, but I have no answer for him.

I don't want to go home.

There's something nagging at my heart, and before I know it, before I have the chance to make sense of what I'm saying, I'm giving the driver the address to Cal's bar.

It's like something has possessed me, and I have no control of my choices anymore. But the truth is, the conversation with my grandparents made me realize that I can handle this. Even if we don't agree, even if all of this goes against my moral values, I can't give up on Cal like that. I'm sure we can work something out.

I decide to give him a chance to really talk. I didn't let him speak last night, but I can at least hear what he has to say.

A few minutes later, the driver stops in front of the bar, which is still closed, but I know the door is unlocked, so I waltz inside, finding a pair of surprised eyes staring back at me from behind the counter.

"Good afternoon, Ian." I greet the bartender, not bothering to stop moving. I carry on, walking toward the stairs that lead to Cal's office.

Ian replies to me, but I'm already gone when he does. He doesn't try to stop me, which I'm grateful for. I haven't considered a scenario where Cal's men forbid me to come inside.

Luckily, I don't run into any more of them on the way to his office. The door is closed, and I don't bother to knock before busting it open.

Cal is at his desk as usual, his head sunk into his hands. He's clearly not happy. But then he looks up to see who has just knocked his door in, and his eyes meet mine. His expression changes from distraught to shocked in the blink of an eye. "Heidi?" he asks, obviously confused.

I close the door behind me, but other than that, I don't make a move. My heart is beating incredibly fast now that I see him, and I realize I don't know what to do.

I came here to talk to him, but seeing him look this sad, so helpless, does something to me that I can't control. I want to comfort him, to hold him in my arms and reassure him that everything will be okay. There's something going on here that he hasn't told me yet, and it must be something bad if it's leaving Cal in this state.

"I–" My voice disappears before I can even start to speak. What do I even want to say anyway?

"What are you doing here?" he asks, standing. This time, he doesn't try to come near me. He doesn't even attempt to take a step forward, remaining in the same spot behind his desk as he waits for my response.

"I don't know," I reply honestly. "I came here to talk, but…"

"But?" Cal presses, his brows raising slightly.

"I don't feel like talking all of a sudden."

Which is true.

My heart and my body yearns for him. I don't think I'm in the right state of mind for us to have a serious conversation. I thought I was, but I was wrong. Looking at Cal now, all I want to do is toss myself at him and forget for a moment that this is the shitty reality we find ourselves in right now.

"Heidi, I—"

"Shut up," I cut him off, but my voice is so quiet that I barely hear it myself.

"What?" His distraught expression returns, and I'm taken over by an emotion that is stronger than me.

"I said," I walk toward him with long strides, "shut up." I reach him, wrapping my arms around his neck and pulling him toward me. Our lips collide, and it's like fireworks explode around–and within–me. His hands dart to my hips, and he pulls me against him, making me moan against his mouth. His tongue asks for permission, and I happily grant it, opening wide to let him inside. The feeling is so familiar, yet every time I kiss him, it's like the very first time. I wonder how long this will last. It's an inebriating and addictive sensation that I can't seem to get enough of.

Cal's hand moves down to my ass, and his fingers grip my flesh possessively. I gasp, feeling him hard against my core. But then his movements stop out of the blue, his body stiffening instantly.

"What?" I manage to get out.

He pulls away to face me, his brows creased and his jaw clenched. "I... I thought you wanted to talk. Are you su–"

"I told you to shut up," I repeat, pulling him into a kiss again.

That seems to be enough for him to understand I don't want to talk anymore. I just want to feel him, to have him claim me as his own and make me forget about how my life turned upside down so quickly. I don't want to remind myself that this could be the last time I have Cal. I need him to just fuck me into oblivion so I can pretend I'm still his, and he's still mine.

"What do you want me to do?" he asks in a murmur against my lips.

My core throbs with need. "You already know what I want," I answer, my voice hoarse with desire.

Darkness clouds his eyes, and then his hands are roaming all over me, removing all of my clothing. He first tosses my coat on the floor, then my sweater and my pants, leaving me only in my green panties.

Cal scans me, and I see his Adam's apple bob up and down as he slowly removes his blazer. He's wearing a suit today which makes him look hotter than ever.

I press my legs together while I watch him slowly approach me, his eyes never leaving me.

I reach for his tie and pull him forward, removing it and tossing it over his shoulder. He doesn't let me take off his shirt because he's in such a rush. He tears it off, leaving his toned abs exposed for me to drool over.

No words are necessary between us now. In fact, they would feel like a bucket of icy water dumped over my head, so I'm glad he's not saying romantic or even dirty things to me this time. Our eyes and gestures are enough to deliver a silent message, and this is all I need today.

Cal takes a step in my direction, with his pants still on, and tosses me on his couch. My back hits the cold leather, contrasting with the heat radiating from my body. I lean back, watching as he kneels before me and spreads my legs apart with his large hands. I squirm with anticipation.

He finds the hem of my panties, and slowly, he slides them down my thighs and calves. Then, he swiftly grabs my ass and scoots me forward, adjusting himself between my legs.

I bite my lip, preparing myself for the wave of pleasure he's about to provide me. My head drops backward against the couch as soon as I feel his tongue touching me.

Cal takes his time, not as hungry and eager as the other times we had sex. He makes sure to shower me with affection while he savors me. It's almost too much for me to bear.

My eyes roll to the back of my head when he adds a little pressure, and I swallow down a moan.

This is what I was talking about.

This is what I need to forget about everything.

And damn if it's not working.

4 0

SEX AND DOUBTS

CAL

I SPENT MOST OF THE NIGHT AND THE MORNING TRYING TO GET something out of the cartel's man I found lurking outside Heidi's building. Anything useful at all that will help me put an end to all of this nonsense.

The interrogation took several hours, and I was so fucking mad that I didn't let any of my men deal with him even though I was exhausted. It was ugly, to say the least, and I split my knuckles multiple times as I tried to force some words out of his mouth. But in the end, I didn't get much.

The guy eventually murmured some addresses to me, but so far, my men only hit dead ends with the investigation on the De La Cruz cartel.

At some point during the night, Tony showed up and helped me a little bit with the interrogation, and then he left, saying he would ask his men to start investigating as well.

So far, I haven't heard from him.

The sun was rising in the sky by the time I came to my office. I sat

239

down in my chair to clear my mind, hoping I could think about what I heard and make my brain work for me for a change. Staying awake the whole night didn't help my case. I stayed still for hours, barely moving from my chair, but I couldn't come up with a new plan. And I also couldn't get any work done.

Seeing Heidi burst into my office a few hours later wasn't something I was expecting to happen today. At first, it felt like a dream, as if she was a fragment of my imagination.

I hadn't talked to her ever since she kicked me out of her apartment–rightfully so–and I was trying to give her some space to think about everything. I didn't blame her for wanting to stay out of my life, to put some distance between us. I have nothing good to offer her. My love is not enough.

She came in saying she wanted to talk but changed her mind faster than a bullet, and I was so fucking confused when she jumped on me, kissing me like she missed me as much as I missed her. I loved how bossy she was when she told me to shut up. It was a side of her I had never seen before.

I still can't believe she's here, offering herself to me as if she still belongs to me.

Her moan pulls me back to reality. I've been working her up on my office's couch, savoring her as if she is the most mouthwatering meal on this planet.

"Oh, God. Yes! That's it," she hisses while I slide my tongue over her folds. She tastes fucking delicious.

I love the way she squirms under my touch. My entire body aches for her. My brain is obsessed with her moans, and my dick is fucking hard against my pants. I need some release, but seeing how she's enjoying what I'm doing, I can't find the courage to pull away from her.

Not yet anyway.

I have no idea what this means for us, but if this is the last time I get to have Heidi to myself, I'll make the best of it. And I'll make sure she never forgets me, no matter how hard she tries or how many men she uses to get over me.

The mere thought of another man touching her is enough to make me go feral, but I shove the idea away from my mind immediately. I need to focus on her right now.

Heidi writhes under my touch when I insert two fingers inside of her. She's so wet and ready for me that I grunt with anticipation, desperate to thrust myself into her. But I'll get to it in a minute.

I move my fingers against her walls, feeling them throb around me as she reaches her orgasm. Heidi tightens her fists, leaning back on the couch, her eyes closed.

I don't want to say anything to her and risk her coming back to her senses and giving up on what we're doing now.

When I'm certain she's done, I pull my fingers out of her and stare at her, waiting to see what she's going to do. My dick is so hard right now that it's physically painful, but if she wants to stop, I'll abide by her wishes, no matter how much that would kill me.

She opens her eyes and looks at me, her cheeks flushed, her forehead slightly sweaty. "Come here," she orders in a murmur, pulling me on top of her.

My lips find her neck while my hands roam over her body. The heat radiating from the both of us makes this room feel like a stove. I barely have time to grab a condom from my pocket.

I lay Heidi on her back while climbing on top of her. She struggles with my belt, trying to unzip my pants and remove my boxers. I help her with one hand while the other adjusts her legs around me, spreading them apart so I can fit between them.

It's a bit uncomfortable doing this on the couch, and I have to be careful so as not to hurt her or topple off myself, but I don't care. As long as I can feel Heidi one last time, I'm up for anything.

She pulls my pants and boxers down to the middle of my thighs, and once I'm free from every layer of clothing and have the condom on, I slide myself into her. She's so wet; I start thrusting in and out of her, inhaling her sweet scent, allowing it to intoxicate all of my senses.

Heidi moans against my ear, her nails sinking into the flesh of my shoulders. "Cal..." she whimpers breathlessly, her voice coming out hoarse and low.

"You feel so good," I say, not able to hold myself back any longer.

She opens her mouth to reply, but I press myself further into her, and another loud moan escapes her throat. "Shit, I'm close," she informs me, her eyes rolling up again as she rocks her hips faster to meet my rhythm.

"Whenever you're ready, baby," I encourage her, grabbing the back of her knee and pulling it up so I can hit her deeper.

Heidi bites her lower lip as her pleasure reaches its peak, and it doesn't take me much longer to follow her, my body stiffening as I release myself, too. My heart pounds hard against my ribs, and my arms are slightly numb from holding myself up so I don't crush her completely with my weight.

I collapse beside her on the couch, and since we don't have much space for the both of us to fit, I wrap my arm around her waist and pull her backward against me. Her hair brushes against my nose, and I take a deep breath, taking in her delicious fragrance.

We stay in silence for a few minutes, our heavy breathing and the muffled music from the bar upstairs the only sound. I hesitate to be the first one to say something. I have so many questions, so many doubts, but I know as soon as I open my mouth, Heidi will close up again and probably push me away and tell me this was a huge mistake.

I don't want this moment to end, so as much as it pains me and frustrates me to not know what to expect, I remain quiet, holding her against me while I can.

I can also sense she wants to say something but is hesitating, too.

Both of us are walking on eggshells with each other right now.

When five minutes pass, and she doesn't speak, I start getting anxious. I hate this feeling. It's fucking irritating to stay here and not be able to be myself with her, afraid that she might run away from me the minute I utter a word. However, I can't stand this anymore.

If she was the one who came after me first, wanting to talk, maybe I should insist a little more. "Heidi?" I try, my voice as low as possible.

"Hm?" she murmurs, not moving from my arms.

"Can we talk?" I ask, finally gathering the courage to address the elephant in the room.

It takes her a few seconds to reply or even signal that she heard me. Then she turns to face me, and when our eyes meet, I wrap my arm around her waist again, cuddling into her, keeping her trapped against me.

"Okay…" she finally agrees.

I nod sharply, breathing in while holding my gaze on her. "What does this mean?" I want to know. "What did you come here to talk to me about?"

41

HONEST CONFESSIONS

"What does this mean?" I want to know. I *need* to know. "What did you come here to talk to me about?"

Heidi stares at me for a bit until she inhales sharply and turns her gaze to the ceiling. She is clearly uncomfortable with my questions, but I can't move on not knowing what's going through her mind.

Does the fact that she came here to have sex with me in my office mean that she forgives me? That she's willing to put everything behind us and start anew? That she belongs to me completely, no questions asked?

Knowing her, I doubt that's what it means.

But I need to hear her say it. I need to understand what she's thinking. Otherwise, I might misinterpret all of it and ruin every-thing–again.

"Heidi?" I call softly when she doesn't answer me.

She looks at me again, her beautiful, big eyes watching me intently. I push her hair out of her face, and lean forward to kiss her lips. It's a soft kiss, but I try to convey all of my feelings for her through it.

"I don't know what this means," she finally answers. Her voice is firm, and I note her honesty in it. "I'm not familiar with this situation. All of this is new to me. I don't know what to think or do."

I nod slightly, not moving my eyes from her, but I don't say anything. Now that she's finally talking, I decide to let her vent all her anger and to say everything she wants to say to me.

"I'm not comfortable with it, but mostly, I'm hurt that you lied to me and kept this from me. I know you don't owe me anything, but I thought we were building something together," she tells me. "You misled me into falling for you."

I swallow hard, cursing myself for being responsible for the sadness crossing her face right now.

"I hate myself for doing so, trust me," I confess. "It was never my intention to hurt you. What I said to you before was true. I wasn't expecting to fall for you. None of this has ever happened to me before, Heidi. Normally, I end things before they get too deep. I knew the moment I told you the truth, it would be over between us. I was selfish for not wanting it to happen."

Heidi's eyes fill with tears, but she doesn't let them fall. "Can you imagine how I am feeling right now? How confused I am?" she asks in a soft voice.

"I do," I reply firmly. "I really do. I don't blame you for how you dealt with it. I don't think I'd have been this patient if I were in your shoes," I admit, strengthening my grip on her waist and pulling her toward me. "But I love you."

Heidi stares into my eyes until she drops the only question I wasn't ready to hear. "Is that enough, though?" Her eyes fall to my hand on her hip, and she notices my knuckles split, dried blood covering each one of them. She swallows hard and looks up at me again, her expression more serious this time. "How am I supposed to accept that this is what being part of the mafia means? Do you truly expect me to be okay with seeing you get hurt all the time, risking your life because of what…?"

I see her point. I hate that she's right.

"We've barely started seeing each other, and I already have someone following me, waiting outside of my building, and watching my every move. And I have no idea why!" she exclaims, starting to get worked up again. However, she doesn't signal wanting to leave my arms, which I'm glad for because I'm not ready to let go of her yet.

I know the moment I release her, everything will fall apart, and we'll go back to being two strangers.

"Why do you do it, Cal? Why be part of the mafia when you're so smart and have so many abilities?" Heidi questions, catching me completely off guard.

I would never expect her to ask something like that. In the past, I asked myself the same questions but never found the answers I was looking for. I just happened to fall into this world, and I never managed to get out. Eventually, I just accepted that this was my fate and learned to turn it into my favor. "I don't think I have an answer for you," I tell her honestly. "It's just been a part of me for so long that I can't even remember what my life was like before this. It's everything I know. It's the only family I have."

Heidi contorts her face into a grim expression, and I'm not sure how to interpret it.

"Seriously? A family? A gang is your family?" Her tone is a bit accusatory, if not offensive, but I know it comes from a good place in her heart. She is hurt, and like she said, this is unknown territory for her. She'd never understand what the Irish Kings mean to me.

"They have been all I have ever since I was really young and came to America," I explain matter-of-factly. "I earned my place within the family, which eventually led me to lead it. We take care of each other, Heidi. Not everyone has the luxury of having a real family to provide and care for us."

She flinches, and I realize what I said was wrong. I didn't mean to hurt her. I wasn't even referring to her. I was just thinking back to everything I suffered when I was young–with an alcoholic father who beat my mom and was good for nothing, who constantly told me that

I would get nowhere. That I was useless. That I would never manage to build a life for myself.

It was a pity that he died before I got the chance to show him the empire that I built in one of the biggest cities in the world. He got what he deserved, though.

"I didn't mean it like that," I murmur apologetically. "It's just that… life was hard, Heidi. And I had no one to watch over me. The Irish Kings were the ones who took me in and helped me survive this crazy world." I caress her cheek, my finger tracing her scar softly. She doesn't pull away, which I assume is a good sign, but her jaw is clenched, and her eyes are still narrowed at me.

"I can understand that," she admits in a whisper. "And I would never hold it against you for wanting to survive. I get that. But I'm not sure I can be a part of it, Cal."

My stomach twists at her words, but I remain stoic.

"Can I ask you something?" she continues.

"Of course," I reply with a nod. "Anything you want."

Heidi takes a deep breath as her blue eyes roam over my face. I get lost in the freckles covering her nose and cheeks, and my heart shrinks at the thought of never being able to see them up close like this again. I can sense that whatever she is about to ask me will dictate our future—whether we'll be together or apart.

"Would you ever consider leaving the mafia?"

It's like a bucket of pure ice water is dumped over my head.

I had seen it coming, but now that she's asked it out loud, I feel cornered. Betrayed. Insufficient.

And what I hate the most is not the fact that she isn't willing to accept this part of me but the fact that I have the answer for her even before she finishes her question. I grit my teeth, calmly releasing my grip on her waist. "Sorry, Heidi. But I don't think I can do that."

Darkness clouds her expression, her features instantly turning cold and distant. It's like I have just built a large wall between us.

Quietly, Heidi stands from the couch and starts looking for her clothes spread over the office floor. I sit up, putting my boxers and pants on while watching her. The only sound in the room is the rustling of our clothes. The silence is overwhelming.

Once she's fully dressed, she turns to me, although her eyes are on the floor. She fidgets with her fingers, clearly nervous. If I could guess, I'd say she's about to cry, but her pride is enough not to allow her to do so in front of me now.

"I have to go," she murmurs, her voice so quiet that I barely hear it.

I open my mouth to convince her not to, to tell her that we can find another way, that our love should be enough, but no words come out.

Heidi hesitates for a split second as if waiting for me to stop her. But when I don't, she takes a deep breath and lifts her chin, walking toward the door with confidence.

Then she is out of the office, the door slamming behind her sounding like the lid dropping on my coffin.

"Fuck!" I yell, tossing the first thing I find, a vase of the table, against the wall behind my desk. Glass shatters as I drop my head into my hands. I can't fathom leaving the Irish Kings, but I know in my heart I've made a huge mistake.

4 2

LIGHT AT THE END OF THE TUNNEL

Cᴀʟ

I ᴄᴏɴsɪᴅᴇʀ ɢᴏɪɴɢ ᴀғᴛᴇʀ Hᴇɪᴅɪ. Fᴏʟʟᴏᴡɪɴɢ ʜᴇʀ ᴜᴘsᴛᴀɪʀs, ɢʀᴀʙʙɪɴɢ her by the arm, turning her to me and crashing my lips into hers, hoping she can feel how much I love her and how much I'm willing to fight for us.

But that'd be a lie.

And also unfair to her.

Because if I truly was willing to do *anything* for her, I'd accept turning my back on the mafia and the Irish Kings without a question. I wouldn't hesitate. I wouldn't consider anything other than having her by my side.

But I can't.

I can't give her what she wants. I can't promise her something I'm not ready to do. Therefore, I'd rather she hates me now, while she still has any feelings for me, then watch her fall out of love with me while we are together. That'd hurt me more than anything.

Realization begins to sink in. We're truly over now. There's no turning back, no saving this relationship that's barely even started. I try to convince myself that this is for the best. Heidi will finally be safe away from me. She can return to her life. She will be happier that way.

But that doesn't seem to be enough to make me relax. If anything, it only makes me more anxious and frustrated. Being the boss of the Irish Kings was never an issue for me before, but now, it seems to be the only thing preventing me from being with the woman I love.

Why do I have to choose, though? Why can't I have both? Is that too greedy on my part?

Apparently it is.

I pour myself a glass of whiskey and walk toward my desk, flopping into the chair with a sigh.

This day is proving to be one of the worst of my life.

I sit frozen in my seat for some time after Heidi leaves the office.. The only thing that pulls me back to reality is a knock on my door. I close my eyes, considering telling whoever is on the other side to just fuck off and leave me alone. But it could be something important, and I can't be neglecting my bar and my businesses anymore.

"Come in," I order grumpily.

Sam's head pops through the door, and he eyes me with hesitation. "Hey, Boss. Is everything okay? I just saw, er, Miss Heidi storming out of the bar," he begins cautiously, coming inside and closing the door behind him.

I grunt, leaning back in my chair. "No, it's definitely not okay, but there's nothing I can do about it, so…"

"Do you need me to do anything?" he offers. I'm really grateful to have Sam with me during all this time. He's been so loyal and a great friend throughout the years. I wouldn't have come this far without him.

"Destroying the fucking cartel and finding out who is after us would be a great start," I reply with a sarcastic tone.

"You didn't have any success with the guy?" he asks, referring to the cartel member I have cuffed in my basement.

I had momentarily forgotten about him. Heidi clouded my brain when she came in, but now that I am thinking more clearly, I need to figure out what to do with him. My frustration is so out of control at the moment that I consider going there and releasing all of it on him. Again. But he's been beaten pretty badly already, and truth be told, I'm fucking exhausted for spending so much time with him already.

"He didn't say anything other than what you heard," I tell him. "I don't think he'll tell us anything else, no matter how much we torture him," I confess.

"It's fucking annoying that he won't give us a name–or anything." Sam grumbles, a frown forming on his lips. "We don't even know who's running the cartel now."

I grunt in response, my head pounding. "Do we have any news on the addresses he mentioned?"

Sam shakes his head. "Hunter went there with the guys, but it was empty. It seemed like they cleaned it in a hurry, but we didn't find anything useful that would lead us to their boss."

I sigh. "And no one came after that bastard?" I figured whoever is running the cartel would send someone after their guy when they realized he had been taken, but so far, there's been no movement on their end. And that fucking leaves me on edge.

"No. But you need to get a fucking rest. Otherwise, you won't be able to fight if anyone does show up to try to spring him," Sam advises me.

"I know. But how am I supposed to sleep? I'm fucking tense all the time. I need our men in strategic places so we're not caught off guard. We can't afford another surprise attack."

Sam nods sharply. "Consider it done. And about this bastard? What should I do with him?"

I close my eyes again, pondering what to do. Releasing him is not an option. Killing him won't be beneficial for me, but I can't keep him in my basement forever. I don't think he'll tell me anything else. Using him as a bargaining chip doesn't sound good to me either. I doubt whoever his boss might be now is worried about him or what he might tell us. If that was the case, they would be at my door already, bringing hell to us for taking someone important to them.

"Fuck," I hiss, running my hands down my face and through my hair with frustration. "I can't fucking think right now. Give me some time, and I'll figure out what to do with him."

"Gotcha," Sam agrees, turning to leave.

I remain in my chair, urging my brain to function properly. I can't afford the luxury of taking some time off. I need to fucking do something. Otherwise, I'll be dead soon. The De La Cruz cartel is not playing around, that much I know.

They also aren't aware that Heidi and I are no longer together. So they could still be on her tail.. I have some of my men guarding and watching over her, but that still doesn't keep me satisfied.

Frustration bursts inside me, and I get to my feet, striding toward the door. I need to vent my anger on something—or someone. Otherwise, I'll go insane inside this office. I'm already feeling suffocated within these walls.

But before I get to the door, I hear my phone buzzing on top of my desk. I consider ignoring it, letting it go to voicemail. Whoever it is can wait. However, a little voice inside my head tells me that it could be important. It could be Heidi, although I doubt she would call me for anything really.

But what if she's in danger? What if someone got a hold of her?

Because of that, I rush back to my desk and grab the phone, seeing Tony's name flash on the screen. I'm relieved to know it's not Heidi, but if he's calling me, it's probably something important too.

"Yeah?" I answer hastily.

"Guess what?" he asks, his voice sounding a bit too lively for my taste at the moment.

"What is it, Tony?".

"My guys had an altercation with the cartel when they got to that address in New Jersey," he informs me. "We captured a couple of them. They seem to be higher in the hierarchy than the guy in the basement. Wanna take them in for an interrogation?"

Anticipation boils within me at the idea of getting closer to whoever is turning my life into a living hell. I can't wait for this all to be over. It's been dragging on for way too long already. "Where are they now?" I ask, sitting down in my chair.

"One is in my trunk. The other is with Armando," Tony replies. He sounds just as excited as I am to finally have something to go on.

"Great. Bring them over," I reply, hanging up and cracking my split knuckles in preparation for some action. Damn my exhaustion. I'll only be able to sleep when all of this is over. At last I'm seeing a glimpse of light at the end of the tunnel.

43

___

GETTING ANSWERS

CAL

TONY TAKES A LITTLE LONGER THAN I'D LIKE WITH THE CARTEL bastards the Saints captured. By the time his men haul in two guys who are, I'd say, unrecognizable, I'm basically digging a hole in the floor with all my anticipation and agitation, having spent the last hour pacing.

The guy I cuffed in the basement looks up from his spot in the corner, and his eyes widen when he sees two more of his people have also been taken by us. He doesn't have any strength in him to say anything, but he's been pretty quiet anyway compared to some of the smart-mouthed assholes I've beaten the shit out before.

"Hey," Tony greets me, walking behind his guys who are now restraining the newly kidnapped men to chairs, away from the first one. "Brought you a little present."

I grunt. "After the day I just had, you have no idea how glad I am to see them," I tell him, darting a deathly glance to the newcomers and cracking my knuckles.

257

"I owe you already. I'm glad I could return the favor for once," Tony says, smirking at me.

I shake my head, not the slightest interested in going back to that conversation. I've already told him several times that he owes me nothing. Everything I did to help him and Chloe was because he's a good friend of mine, and that's all.

I never expected him to do the same for me, but I do appreciate it. I know he feels partially, if not completely, responsible for the cartel coming after me, but this is just how things work in our world.

I don't hold it against him.

"Did they say anything?" I ask, pulling away from everyone else so we can have a one-on-one conversation.

"Not much," he answers simply. "They seemed to be in control of one of the bars in New Jersey, but considering the documents we had access to, they are close to the new cartel boss. Funneling drugs into the states through Miami, up the eastern seaboard. We just don't know who's in charge yet. We didn't really have much time to interrogate them before the police arrived, so we can continue here."

I nod, considering what to do next. "Great, I need to vent some of my anger. That'll be a good workout," I murmur through gritted teeth.

"You look like shit, man."

I narrow my eyes at him, silently threatening him to stay quiet if he doesn't want me to take my frustration on him, too.

"Sorry," Tony adds, tucking his hands in his pockets in surrender. "It's the truth, though. Now, let's get this over with so you can get back to your lady and fix whatever it is that went wrong between you two."

"How do you know something went wrong?" I frown.

"Come on! It's written all over your face. Plus, a little bird told me someone stormed out of the bar a while ago, so I guessed you guys had an argument or something."

I grunt, turning my back to him. "Let's fucking deal with them, shall we?"

My footsteps echo through the room as I approach the new guys who are now tied to two metal chairs in the middle of the room. Their old friend in the corner is still quiet, watching the scene unfolding before his battered eyes with great attention. He looks slightly scared, and I'd say he was probably expecting someone to come rescue him, instead of two more of them to be taken for interrogation.

This gets me a little more excited than earlier. At least we're getting somewhere, and apparently, the enemy was not expecting it.

"Now, who wants to go first?" I ask threateningly.

No one around me makes a sound. They just watch as I get closer to the guy on my left. He looks more terrified than his friend. His eyes are swollen, there's a huge bruise on his cheek, and his lip is split. Dried blood covers his mouth and chin, and there are stains on the collar of his shirt. His shoulders are shaking slightly, and even though he has his hands tied behind his back, I can also tell they are trembling.

"You look like you have something to tell me," I continue, lowering my voice and leaning forward to look him in the eye. His pupils are dilated, and he smells like cheap liquor and weed, which makes me nauseated. I throw a punch in his stomach, making him groan and bend over in pain.

I give him a second to compose himself and think about what he'll do next.

When he looks up at me again, I grin at him.

"Just to let you know, I can stay here all day. Not to mention I had a fucking terrible day, so I'm looking for someone to vent my anger on. That someone could be you or your friend here." I point to the guy on his side. "It's up to you." I take a deep breath and crack my neck before addressing him once more. "Now, I want to know who the fuck is ordering you to follow me around and attack me," I demand in a snarl. "Give me a name, and I might consider letting you walk out of here alive."

"I-I don't know what you're talking abo–" he chokes out, and my fist meets his jaw before he has the chance to finish the last word.

"Don't fucking play that game with me, or I swear to God, I'll tear you to pieces and feed them to the dogs," I threaten, my patience wearing thin. "I'm not in the mood for games, so you better tell me something useful, or you're as good as dead."

He spits a mouthful of blood close to my feet, and I sneer, rolling my eyes at him before punching him again, this time making sure he's left unconscious. I can go back to him once he wakes up.

I look to my right and head for the second bastard. I could stay here all day beating them up, but I'm already tired of all of this. So, with that thought in mind, I grab the gun from the holster in my belt and point it at his forehead, watching his eyes widen in fear, and maybe a little surprise.

"I won't repeat my question. And I won't play nice anymore," I inform him darkly. "If you don't fucking tell me who your boss is, I'll shoot you right now."

He swallows hard and nods at me, signaling he will cooperate. "His name is Milo Moralez," he finally spills. "He's Mateo's younger brother."

I bite my cheek so hard that the taste of copper fills my mouth. Everything is starting to make much more sense now.

"Mateo doesn't have a brother," Tony chimes in from behind me, clearly as angry and annoyed as I am. "We investigated everything about him and the cartel a while ago."

The asshole in front of me scoffs, and I press my gun harder against his forehead, reminding him that I still have the power here. "Milo wasn't active in the cartel until his brother died. Or, more accurately, was murdered." He glares at Tony. "Then he had to take over and get revenge for his brother."

"Revenge my ass," Tony snarls, and I hear a commotion behind me that I assume is caused by his men trying to hold him back. "He fucking tried to kidnap my wife and daughter."

"Where the hell is Milo now?" I cut in, hoping to end this argument that will get us nowhere. Tony has every right to be angry, but I can't let him ruin this now that we're finally getting some clarifying answers.

"I don't know. He changes places every day," the guy replies. "I swear!" he yells when I cock the gun in front of his face. "I really don't know, I'm not that close to him."

"Why me? Why is he coming for me if Mateo had a problem with the Saints?"

I don't mean to throw Tony under the bus or anything, but this is a question that's been bugging the both of us for a while now. I don't think Tony will mind me asking.

"He knows you were helping the Saints and thought it would be easier to get your family first," he explains, and it doesn't sit well with me to hear the De La Cruz cartel thinks the Irish Kings are easy. I'll show him *'easy.'* "Then he'd go after the Saints and get revenge on the group directly responsible for his brother's death."

"He should have known better than to come unprepared because now he's got a fucking war coming his way." Tony grunts behind me.

Before I have the chance to tell him to chill so I can carry on with my questions, a loud ruckus starts upstairs, causing all of us to turn our heads toward the closed door. Even behind thick walls and a metal door, the noises in the bar are so loud that it seems like it's happening right inside the basement.

"What the fuck is that?" Sam asks, looking around as if to make sure all of the enemies we kidnapped are still here.

But I know what this means.

Milo and his cartel have finally come to rescue his men.

The animal within me snarls as I prepare for battle.

This is it.

This is the moment I have been waiting for.

"They're here," I inform everyone around me. "Let's get this fucking over with."

4 4

FORGET ABOUT HIM

Going after Cal was a mistake. I knew it would be, but I still did it anyway.

What was I thinking? What was I even expecting to happen? That if I came and asked him to drop his entire life and career for me and he'd do it?

Ha! What a joke.

Even if I mean as much to him as he says I do, giving up something you've been building your whole life is hard. I should know better than that. I wouldn't give up on *my* life and dreams either if he asked me to. So, why am I feeling so heartbroken? Why do I feel so sad, so left out?

I storm out of his office with tears blurring my vision. His scent is all over me, and my lips are still tingling from our kisses. No matter how much I want to turn back and run into his arms, I know I can't do it.

This is it. This was the last straw, the confirmation I needed that we're indeed over.

For good.

"Miss Heidi, is everything okay?" someone asked from behind me as I walked out of the bar.

It was rude on my part to ignore whoever it was, but I couldn't stop to talk to anyone at the moment. I needed to get as far away as possible from that place. And from Cal.

The cold wind slaps my face as I walk down the sidewalk, my gaze falling on what used to be my bookstore and my apartment not more than a month ago on the other side of the street. My life has changed so much in such a short amount of time that it scares me. Sadness overwhelms me, and for a second, I don't know what to do.

I have no one to talk to.

And even if I did, it's not like I could just come and say that I'm breaking up with the guy I love because I just found out he is the head of a mafia syndicate, and his life is constantly spent in danger, consequentially putting me and my grandparents in danger, too.

I decide to walk home, taking the time to distract myself and my wandering mind. On the way, I watch people passing by me, too occupied with their own lives to worry about a girl bawling her eyes out, mascara running down her cheeks in the middle of the street. My heart feels like it's shrinking inside my chest. How has someone I met less than two months ago become such an important part of my life so quickly? How could I allow Cal to take such a huge place in my heart like that?

I should have been more careful.

I should have known he was trouble.

I should have trusted my instincts.

I reach my building a few minutes later, and the doorman, an older gentleman with gray hair and the kindest face I've ever seen, widens his eyes as he takes in my state. "Miss Sullivan, are you okay? Did something happen?" he asks, standing from his usual seat and coming to check on me.

I nod, offering him a soft smile. "I'm all right, Mr. Thompson. Just life hitting me in the face, I guess." I chuckle.

His eyes soften as he pats me on the shoulder. "It can be hard sometimes, yes. Just keep on moving. It will eventually get better, I'm sure of it." His words comfort me a little. It feels nice to feel cared for. Mr. Thompson has been thoughtful and polite to me ever since I moved into the building, and I could tell from the first day that he is a man with a golden heart.

"Thank you. I'm hopeful it will."

He nods at me, encouraging me to continue on my way. "I'll be here if you need anything. Have a great rest of your day, Miss Sullivan."

I thank him and continue on my way. As soon as I get inside my apartment, I realize I can't live here anymore. This place is being paid by Cal, and even though I told him I'd pay him back once I am back on my feet, I don't want to owe him anything. Now, besides looking for a place to reopen the bookstore, I also need to look for a new apartment that I can afford.

In New York City, that will be easy peasy.

As if...

"Oh, God," I lament, grabbing my laptop from the coffee table and flopping on the couch. The rays of sunlight beam through the windows, and I instantly feel its warmth on my skin. I hadn't realized how nice this place is until now. Now that I have to let it go. I suddenly don't feel ready to get out of here.

Opening my laptop, I find the real estate websites I was looking at before and start a new search with different filters. Even though I was ready to finally get the bookstore back on track, finding a new apartment is my priority now.

I check the boxes where I can get results for small apartments, close to the neighborhood I'm already in, and preferably one that doesn't cost me an arm and a leg each month.

Nothing nice shows up. Not unless I want to live in an alley where I know for a fact I'll be kidnapped or murdered.

Thirty minutes pass, and I still haven't gotten anywhere. I get up and head to the kitchen, pouring myself a cup of coffee to stay awake. This will take me the whole night, and after crying so hard and getting a headache as a result, I'll probably fall asleep on top of my computer.

Returning to it, an intrusive thought suddenly crosses my mind, and my fingers hesitate on the keyboard. Before I know it, I'm typing the word 'mafia' into the Google search bar. Nothing nice comes up, of course. I scroll down the first page, but nothing I see catches my attention or gives me the answers I'm looking for.

Cal told me he was the leader of the Irish Kings. That'd probably narrow down my research, so I type the term on the bar and press enter. A couple of articles from New York papers appear on the top of the list, both addressing rumors of a cargo ship being tracked and opened by the FBI last year containing drugs and slot machines. Sources linked the Irish mob to it, but nothing was proved, nor was anyone arrested. Eventually, the issue was dropped and forgotten.

I huff, still not satisfied. I type 'Cal Duncan' next but hesitate to press search this time, afraid of what I might find. With a deep breath, I close my eyes and do it, slowly opening them back to see the list of results.

The name of his bar is the first thing that appears. There's a social media page, where it only addresses him as the owner, but other than that, no other information is provided.

I go back to the Google page and scroll down, but just like the previous terms I searched, I don't see anything important or anything that links him to the mafia or the syndicate he mentioned. They must be really careful—as every crime family should be—so as not to let any information leak. It frustrates me, but I guess not being traceable might be a good thing. For him, that is.

Leaning back on the couch, I let out a tired sigh, staring at the ceiling while my brain works at its full capacity on everything that's happened in the last forty-eight hours.

Giving up on looking for places, I push the laptop aside and head for my bathroom, ready to spoil myself with a hot shower. I need to release the tension in my muscles and get rid of Cal's scent that's still all over my skin. It is not helping me focus at all.

As much as it kills me to know this might be the last time I get to smell his cologne, I need to force myself to move on with my life. To get over him and all the craziness we experienced together and focus on myself and my career–which right now is pretty much non-existent. I'm not a very ambitious person, so I don't have big dreams when it comes to my professional life. I guess living in a busy, crazy city like New York has made me want to go the opposite way of everyone else. I want the simplest things life can offer me–a cozy home, a satisfying job, and to be surrounded by the people I love–people who love me in return.

At the moment, I don't have any of it.

My home is not mine. I have no idea when I might be able to get back to work, and the people I love are either living far away from me or leading a criminal enterprise I don't want to be a part of.

This has to change–and soon.

I won't allow myself to fall into a black hole of depression. I'll get back on my feet and forget Cal Duncan ever walked into my life and turned it upside down.

One way or another.

4 5

GOING STRAIGHT TO HELL

CAL

LEAVING THE BASEMENT AND MAKING SURE AT LEAST ONE OF MY MEN stays behind to watch the cartel assholes we have tied inside, I rush upstairs with Tony, Sam, and Hunter with the rest of my men on my tail.

Even though the noises upstairs are muffed by closed doors and thick walls, I don't like what I hear as I approach the bar. Frantic screams and intermittent gunfire can never be a good thing.

"Fuck," I hiss to myself. "They seem to be heavily armed," I inform my men over my shoulder. "Are you guys loaded?"

"I have a couple of guns with me. Armando is outside with my men," Tony informs me.

I don't want to think about the possible scenarios we're about to encounter. The rest of my men are also upstairs, but if they were caught off guard–even though I had them keeping a close eye out for any strange movement–things might be ugly.

"I'll grab a shotgun from the safe," Hunter tells me. "Do you need me to get you anything, Boss?"

269

"No, I have my pistol on me," I reply through gritted teeth.

I hate being trapped like this, taken off guard for the second time. But the only good news I can think of right now is that they arrived after Heidi left. It gives me immense relief to know she's out of harm's way. At least for now.

"Gotcha," Hunter murmurs before disappearing to our right to get to the deposit.

Pulling my gun out of its holster, I prepare myself to open the door that leads to the main salon of the bar. I cock the pistol, hearing the others do the same behind me, I give myself a split second to take a deep breath, I pull the door open and rush outside.

The bar is in complete chaos. Tables are turned, chairs tossed to the side, walls covered with bullet holes, and several men are engaged in battle.

I drop behind a broken chair, noticing Tony and Sam heading the other way. Then I turn my attention back to what's happening around me, trying to make sense of what's going on without putting myself in the line of fire.

Within a few seconds, I notice that most of my men are inside the bar, hidden behind the counter or anything they could find to protect themselves, and the cartel men are at the entrance, protecting themselves behind the door.

Some managed to get inside, but they are now lying on the floor, motionless.

I hope they are dead.

Anger rises within me, and my vision turns red. I clench my jaw so hard it cracks. I get on my knees, and pop my head around the chair, aiming for the first guy I see that I don't recognize. He's definitely not one of mine, so I shoot him, watching him fall to the ground. The noises around me are so loud that my ears are ringing, making it hard for me to orient myself.

"On your left, Boss!" someone yells, and I only have the time to snap my head to the side and dart out of the way of a bullet that passes so close to my ear that I can feel a rush of wind. The guy who shot at me is dead before I have the chance to react.

Bodies begin to clog the doorway, and I start aiming at whoever I can spot within this small enclosure. I hate feeling cornered like a fucking rat.

MORE MEN MANAGE TO COME INSIDE, AND NOW THE CARTEL IS CLOSING the circle on us, keeping the entrance blocked so none of us can leave. We could all escape through the back door, but to hell with it if they think we're such cowards. I will leave here either dead or with their boss's head in a duffel bag.

If he's even brave enough to be here, that is. So far, I haven't spotted anyone that closely resembles Mateo or that carries himself with the aura of a leader.

I decide to move from my hiding place. I'm too exposed now. I also realize I haven't put on a bulletproof vest. When there's a break in gunfire, I jump to the side, rolling on the floor until I get behind the counter.

Several of my men are here already, using it as a barricade. They rise to their feet in sync, quick enough to shoot at our enemies then squat to protect themselves again.

The entire situation has me fucking pissed. They shouldn't have been able to attack us in our own business. For weeks, I've had my men on the lookout, watching our street and surroundings 24/7 to make sure we couldn't be taken by surprise again. What the hell went wrong? What did we miss? How did they manage to get here without being noticed?

Maybe I underestimated Milo and his leadership. Until an hour ago, I thought the cartel was running wild, aimless without a new leader. But I was fucking wrong.

Someone screams loudly close to me, and I snap my head in their direction. Ian is on the floor, one hand holding a gun and the other applying pressure on a wound in his upper arm. It doesn't seem to be something grave, but I hate the fact that he is hurt at all.

"Are you all right?" I yell to him over the noise.

He nods sharply in response, allowing Sam to rip a sleeve off his own shirt and wrap it around his arm to stop the bleeding. Then, he's back on his feet, checking his gun to see if it's still loaded.

I'm getting tired of this fucking nonsense.

Moving to the side, I find a blind spot. I can see the enemies through a small gap, but they can't really see me from their current positions. I place the muzzle of my gun in the gap between the bar and a fallen table and aim for an exposed leg.

The bastard screams in pain and falls to the floor, holding his shin and letting go of his weapon. Another shot and I knock him out completely, watching his body go limp and lifeless.

That's when something else—or better yet, someone else—catches my attention. The man is hiding in the shadows, but just a glimpse of his outfit, and I just know who he is.

He clearly has poor taste in fashion, that much I can say.

"Milo is right behind that column, at ten o'clock," I inform Hunter, who is squatting beside me.

His eyes dart in the direction I pointed, and he nods sharply at me, understanding the silent message I'm conveying.

"Cover me," I request, and in the blink of an eye, I move out from behind the counter, my gun pointing straight at Milo's face.

He seems genuinely surprised, seeing me walking toward him. I have a shit-ton of comments I'd like to shout at him, but right now, nothing seems to be enough. All I need is to put a bullet in his head. That will be the only thing that will satisfy me.

Everything happens so fast that it takes my brain a moment to understand.

One minute, I'm pulling the trigger, watching Milo's eyes widen with terror. Then, I'm on the floor, a sharp pain in my abdomen threatening to knock me unconscious. My vision darkens, and I gasp for air.

"The boss was hit!" someone yells from a distance.

Footsteps around me feel like needles piercing my brain, but I can't move or make them stop.

"I got him. Follow them and make sure to end them," another voice orders, this time closer to me.

Someone grabs me, trying to pull me from the floor, and even though I know it would probably be best for me to cooperate at this point, I can't force my body or my brain to obey me.

All I can think about is that, if I die, I'll never see Heidi again.

I'll die right here, and she won't even come to my funeral because we fucking broke up.

She might not even know I'm dead. For all I know, she left my office with the idea of never wanting to see or hear about me again.

I pass out, going in and out of consciousness, between dreams and nightmares. In all of them, I get to see Heidi's face, and that's the only reason why I don't seem to care about what is happening to me.

I feel nauseated. It's like I'm being transported somewhere, but I can't force my eyes to open and see what's going on. For all I care, God can take me now.

That would be so much easier.

Not that I'm looking forward to going to Hell, which is probably where I'm headed. I was never religious, so right now, I'm starting to wonder if it wouldn't have been better to have some sort of faith. Maybe God would allow me to beg for forgiveness.

A familiar voice is talking to someone beside me, and even in my state, I know that it's Tony. The lad has been so loyal, such a good friend to me. I never told him how grateful I am for everything he's done for me and my syndicate.

"Make sure he really died," he tells someone. His tone is angry and demanding, exactly what the head of the Saints should sound like. "We can't afford a fucking mistake this time. I want this over with for good."

Who is he talking about?

Why isn't my brain cooperating with me anymore?

I black out again, and the next time I come back to my senses–sort of–Tony is still speaking, but this time his voice is lower and softer.

"There's been a fight, and Cal was shot," he's saying. "I need you not to panic. We're taking him to a doctor at a safe house. Hopefully, he'll make it." Silence follows his statement, and for a second, I wonder if I've died. But then he continues. "I can't make you that promise, but we'll do our best to save him," he informs whoever it is he is talking to.

I try to open my mouth so I can communicate with him and tell him that I'm okay, but the pain in my stomach comes back so strong that I pass out immediately.

If this is what death feels like, it fucking sucks.

4 6

THE CALL THAT CHANGES
EVERYTHING

I step out of the shower and put on a set of comfortable sweats. The weather in New York City has been merciless lately, and even inside the apartment, I can still feel the cold wind blowing against the windows outside, seeping through cracks in the apartment I can't see.

I blow dry my hair in an attempt to warm myself, and that's why I don't hear my phone ringing the first two times. It's only when I decide to order something to eat since I don't feel like cooking anything that I notice I missed two calls.

Before I grab the phone to check who it is that called me, I can't stop myself from hoping it was Cal. But when I spot the unknown number, I roll my eyes. Of course he wouldn't call me. I ended that. He made it pretty clear that he doesn't intend to change his lifestyle, and since I'm not willing to give up on my principles either, I won't hear from him again. I should make peace with that instead of keeping my hopes up.

I'm about to put my phone down again, not really interested in

275

knowing who it is that called me, when it rings again, surprising me.

"Hello?" I answer cautiously, my brows creased with confusion. I have no idea who it could be.

An idea that something might have happened to my grandparents crosses my mind, but I immediately shove it away. If something had happened to them, the nursing home would have called me using one of their main lines, and I have all of them saved on my contact list.

"Is this Heidi Sullivan?" a man asks on the other end. He sounds like someone important, his voice cold and firm.

"Who is this?" I ask, not comfortable giving away personal information to someone I don't know.

"I'm Tony, a friend of Cal's," he replies. There seems to be a commotion happening around him, which makes it hard for me to hear him clearly. "There's been a… *fight,* and Cal was… shot," he informs me slowly. "I need you not to panic. We're taking him to a doctor at a safe house. Hopefully, he'll make it."

I blink once, twice, completely paralyzed. What did he just say? *Shot?* As in… with a gun? A real gun?

Of course it was a real gun. You saw the arsenal he had at home. Why wouldn't it be a real gun, Heidi?

I'm trying to rationalize with myself, not wanting to interpret what these words could mean. What is a safe house? Why aren't they taking him to a real hospital?

"Heidi?" Tony calls, his voice sounding distant and edged with urgency

"Is he going to die?" I finally manage to ask. I don't recognize my own voice. My heart feels like it has left my chest, sinking to my stomach and staying there.

"I can't make you any promises," Cal says—not what I wanted to hear. "But we'll do our best to save him."

I can't believe what I'm hearing. Tears begin to fall down my cheeks as I ask, "H-how is he now?"

"It's hard to say. The doctor's not here yet, and he's passed out," Tony explains. "But he's a tough guy, and I've seen him go through worse."

He seems to be trying to convince himself of that fact, but at this point, I will hold onto whatever hope and positive thoughts I can. I wonder why he decided to call me to inform me of this. Is he one of the men who works at the bar? He might be. I haven't met all of them, and the ones I did, I don't know their names.

As if hearing my thoughts, he continues, "I thought you'd like to know, though. It might be your… last chance to see him."

Last.

Chance.

These are the only words I hear for the next few moments, being repeated inside my head over and over like a mantra, until I forget I'm still on the phone.

"How can I come and see him?" I blurt. For all I know, people who aren't members of the mafia aren't allowed in such places. I'm not *that* familiar with how the mafia works, but I've seen movies before, and I'm guessing these are universal rules between them.

"I can make it happen. I'll send someone to pick you up," Tony explains. "We can't risk having anyone follow you. I hope you understand that."

I nod sharply even though he can't see me. "Yes, of course. I understand."

I shouldn't want to go. I should want to keep my distance and take this as an example of why I should stay away from Cal–and his lifestyle. I made up my mind an hour ago, so why am I changing it now?

"I'm sending a car to pick you up. Make sure to check the plate before getting inside," Tony instructs me.

My stomach twists with apprehension. There's so much cautiousness involved in this situation that it leaves me on edge. But it's for a good reason. I need to make sure Cal survives. This can't be the end of him. This can't be the end of us. None of my previous reasons to leave him seem to make sense now, no matter how hard I try to force them to.

"I'll text you the plate and the name of the driver," Tony concludes.

I take a deep breath. My hands are shaking, my heart is pounding like crazy, and my mouth is dry. I'm so scared that I can't even think about what I'll find once I get to this safe house. I just need to see Cal and make sure he is okay. He can't die!

"Save him! Please?" I beg, tears continuing to stream down my face.

Tony inhales sharply before answering me. "Like I said before, I can't promise you anything, but we're doing everything we can. I know that's not what you want to hear right now, but I won't give you false hope."

I swallow a sob, forcing myself to appear tough on the outside. I can't be weak and unsteady if I want to be with someone like Cal. I have no idea if I'm ready to give up on all of my beliefs yet. The only thing I can think of right now is that I can't lose him. He is the only man who has ever mattered to me, no matter how many times I repeat to myself that I will find happiness again with someone else.

I don't believe it for a second.

"I understand that, too," I finally say.

"I know you guys aren't on the best terms, but he needs you to be strong for him right now," Tony encourages me.

"I will be. I'm heading downstairs now," I inform him, not bothering to take anything with me other than the apartment's key and the phone in my hand. I slip on a pair of shoes I left by the door. Then, I head for the door and take the elevator. My heart is beating a mile a minute, all sorts of thoughts running through my head while I wait. I'm struggling to control my tears and my emotions.

I said so many things to Cal that I regret now. He probably thinks I hate him. He probably thinks I don't give a damn about whether he lives or dies. It kills me to even consider the idea of him leaving this world without knowing how I feel about him.

I told him that his love was not enough for me… How could I be so cold? How could I reject his love like that? Now, all I want is to hear him say he loves me one more time. But there's no guarantee that will happen. None of this is in my control now. It's all up to fate now.

A car pulls up to the sidewalk, and I take a step back inside the building. The windows are so tinted that it matches the black color of the car. It looks similar to the vehicle that have been following me, but it's from a different make and model, and honestly, it looks more expensive, too, now that I'm paying more attention.

I check the plate twice, looking at the text Tony just sent, and only get inside the car when the driver lowers the passenger's window and gives me his name. It's the same guy Tony told me would come for me, so when I'm certain he isn't someone who will kidnap me, I climb inside, praying that Cal is alive by the time we arrive.

"Is Cal okay?" I ask the driver after a few minutes of silence.

He's driving through the streets of New York, speeding in and out of traffic as if he is in a Formula 1 race. It leaves me slightly anxious, but to be honest, I'm in just as much of a hurry to get to Cal as he is—more even. Also, he seems to be pretty skilled, so that makes me feel a bit more secure.

"I can't really say, miss," he answers, his eyes focused on the road ahead. "If you want to hear the truth, though, he didn't look so good the last time I saw him."

My heart shrinks, and I feel short of breath. Not being able to see and check on Cal for myself makes it all so much worse. Being in the dark is excruciating.

"How long until we get there?" I press, not wanting to give too much space to the intrusive thoughts in my head. It's counterproductive, and I need to be in my best state when I arrive. I need to be strong for Cal, like Tony told me, and I can't do that if I freak out and cry when I see him—whatever state he's in.

The driver checks the clock on the panel and shrugs slightly. "I'd say fifteen more minutes, if I can get out of this fucking traffic."

I lean back in the seat, closing my eyes and inhaling sharply. Fifteen minutes feel like an eternity, but soon, we are entering through heavy, metal gates that are protected by men with guns, big ones. The driver comes to a stop in front of a mansion. Then he steps out of the car and I fly out of the passenger side of the car, barely waiting for him to tell me where to go.

"First door to your left!"

THE GOOD AND THE BAD

CAL

MY EARS PICK UP MURMURS AROUND ME, BUT I CAN'T FORCE MYSELF TO open my eyes. My entire body is sore, and the pain in my abdomen feels like someone is pressing and squeezing all of my organs together. It's hard to breathe, but I force my lungs to receive as much air as I can inhale.

My back hurts, so I try to adjust myself on what feels like a bed, or maybe a couch, but the smallest movement makes me grunt with pain.

"Easy there, boss. You have a hole in your stomach," someone warns, their voice distant but somewhat playful.

I groan again, frustrated at not being able to move. My eyelids seem to weigh a ton, but I need to see what's happening around me. I need to know where I am and why. Images of the confrontation in my bar come back to me in snippets. I don't remember the details about what happened, especially how I got shot, but I do remember seeing Milo. I have no idea how much time has passed, and I also don't know the outcome of the fight, so I need to make sure my men are okay and that Heidi is safe.

"Are you feeling all right?" the same voice asks again, this time closer to me.

I try to open my eyes, but the brightness that hits me makes me close them again in a hurry. I try again, blinking slowly to adjust to the room's illumination. I find myself staring at a white ceiling. Then my gaze roams over a bedroom that I don't recognize. There are two open doors on the wall opposite me that lead to a closet and a bathroom. There's a table on one side of the room and a desk on the other side. I'm lying on what looks like a king size bed. It's a nice room, but I have no fucking idea whose house this is.

When I turn my head to the side, I spot Tony staring down at me, a small grin spread on his face. "Glad to see you're alive," he says.

"Am I though?" I retort, my voice hoarse. "Why does it feel like I died then? Everything fucking hurts."

"Ah, always in a great mood," Tony remarks with a smile, pulling a chair to sit beside my bed. I now realize the room is only dimly lit by a lamp on the nightstand, even though it seemed like the sun itself was in here a minute ago. I take him in; his shirt is stained with blood, his right eyebrow is covered by a small bandage, and his hair is disheveled and slightly wet from what I assume is sweat. "You look like shit," I note.

"Thanks. You too," he replies, leaning back in the chair. "How are you feeling?"

I shrug, making sure I don't move my torso too much. "Like I've been shot."

"Hm, and pretty bad I'd say. The doctor barely managed to pull the bullet out of you without taking you to the hospital. Thankfully, it didn't hit any vital organs. You're not out of the woods yet, though, so make sure to stay put and keep your ass on this bed."

I should be a bit more concerned about my well-being and my health, but right now none of that seems important. "What happened? Is everyone okay? Did anyone die?" I ask, dreading his answer.

Tony shakes his head, his expression calming me immediately.

"Not on our end. Ian was shot in the shoulder, but he's fine. I can't say the same about Milo, though," he tells me. "You killed him."

My brows shoot up in surprise. "*I* killed him?" I repeat, making sure I heard him right.

"Yeah. It was just like an old western. You two pulled the trigger at the same time, but thankfully, your aim was better. He still managed to shoot you in the stomach, but well, you're here and he's not, and that's all that matters."

I close my eyes and take a deep breath. *It's over.* The boss of the De La Cruz cartel is dead, and we don't have to worry about them anymore.

"They won't come after us now," Tony reassures me as if I am struggling to put two and two together. "I made sure of it."

I nod, staring at him. "Thanks. I realize I never got to say how grateful I am for your friendship. It really means a lot," I tell him honestly.

Tony grimaces, but a small smile curls his lips. "Ugh, did the bullet turn you into a fucking baby? Shut up, man. I hope you're feeling well enough for visitors because you've got one on the way."

My heart rate increases at the mention of a visitor. My delusional brain can only think of one person I want to see, but I must be out of my mind to even consider that Heidi would want to come here, especially after what happened at the bar.

"What are you talking about?" I ask, suspiciously.

Tony gets up from the chair and puts it back against the wall. "Your lady is coming."

As if on cue, I hear footsteps approaching in the hallway, and even though the bedroom door is closed, I can already sense it's her.

Tony gives me one last smile and turns toward the exit, making sure to leave the door open behind him. Not a second later, Heidi appears, and I'm left speechless. She looks like an angel.

Sure, she's wearing sweats, her hair is tied up in a messy bun, strands falling around her face, her cheeks are flushed from the cold weather, and her eyes are watery, but she's never looked prettier.

"Cal?" she calls softly, so quietly that I barely hear her.

But it's more than enough for me. This is exactly what I needed to hear. Now I know I'm alive, though it's hard to believe I'm not dreaming.

She takes a few cautious steps inside the room, her eyes glued on me. I know I must look like shit, but I can't find it in me to care. I wish I could move so I could get out of this bed, take her in my arms, and make sure she never leaves again. But, unfortunately, that's not going to happen right now.

Heidi strides across the room, and within a second, she's by my side, her fingers tracing over my cheek, gently, while she studies my face and body.

"What happened to you? Are you okay?"

"I am now," I tell her.

She chokes on a sob and covers her mouth with her hand. The tears pooling in her eyes before are now sliding down her cheeks, and I reach up to wipe away.

"It's all right. I'm okay now." I try to reassure her. Tony said I'm not exactly out of danger, but the simple fact that I'm alive is enough for me.

"You don't look fine. I was told you were shot, and that they couldn't promise anything, and—" she cries, finally allowing herself to break down.

I remain silent, caressing her hair and patting her shoulder to comfort her. It's the only thing I can do from this bed, in this position. I'm just so thankful that she's here.

Once Heidi composes herself, she pulls over a chair, sitting down with a sigh. Her gaze is hard on my face, her eyes and nose red from all the crying. It's endearing, just like everything else about her.

"How did you even get here?" I ask curiously.

"Your friend Tony called me," she explains. "He thought you'd want to see me when you woke up, and that I might want to see you one last time too, in case—"

She starts crying again, and I shush her, trying to comfort her once more.

"I'm so relieved you're okay," she carries on. "I was really scared.

I…I thought I'd never be able to see you again, and all I could think about was how I left your office like that… I—"

"It's okay, sweetheart. I know, and I'm truly sorry for putting you through this," I reply, grabbing her hand and squeezing it in mine. "But it's over now. They won't come after us again."

She seems to consider what to say next, but then she shakes her head as if whatever it was is not worth mentioning.

Heidi takes a deep breath and clears her throat. "Look, I thought a lot about our argument and everything I said to you. It wasn't fair of me to ask you to give up something you've fought for your entire life. I know you won't leave this life behind, no matter how much I ask you to or how much it pains me to see you like this," she says, her eyes never leaving mine. "But I also realized after all that's happened I can't live without you. I love you, Cal. And if that means accepting you completely, the good and the bad, so be it."

4 8

IRISH QUEEN

Hearing those words from Heidi makes me wonder if I have truly died. Maybe all of this is a figment of my imagination. Maybe God is allowing me to live one last happy moment before I get to suffer for eternity in Hell.

But there's no way this perfect woman in front of me is an illusion. She looks so real. Her eyes—her beautiful eyes that I love so much—are staring at me so intently and expectantly that I couldn't look away even if I wanted to.

And she *loves* me.

She's willing to turn her back on everything she believes in to be with me. This is much more than I deserve. So much more.

I realize I don't want a day to go by that I don't get to hear those words come out of her mouth. I want to spend every day telling her how much I love her, too. I don't deserve her, but it will become my life's mission to make sure she doesn't regret her choice, that I shower her with love and attention, and that she knows how much she means to me. I am far from perfect, but I'll try my best to be for her.

So, instead of replying to her, instead of saying anything to all, I push myself from the bed, hissing in pain. Heidi widens her eyes, trying to prevent me from moving, but I force myself to a sitting position, leaning back on my elbows. The pain is almost enough to make me faint again, but I fight it, taking deep breaths to stay aware.

This moment could wait, but I can't.

"What are you doing?" Heidi exclaims in shock. "You can't sit up! You're going to open your wound again!" she warns, but I ignore her.

I look up at her, certain I look pathetic, sweat pouring from my forehead because of the effort, my torso completely covered with bandages. But when I realize what I'm about to do, the adrenaline kicks in, making me completely forget about the pain as I manage to take her hand in mine. "Heidi, I know my lifestyle is not ideal and nothing you'd ever choose for yourself. I also know I'm far from what you deserve, but I promise you I'll make you the happiest woman on this planet if you agree to stay by my side," I begin.

Her eyes are filled with tears again as if she is anticipating what I'm about to ask.

"I wish I could do this the right way, exactly like you deserve, but I'll spend the rest of my life making it up to you. I'll do whatever I can to give you everything you need and anything you want."

"Cal," she whispers between sobs.

I chuckle, shaking my head. "I know I don't have a ring with me right now, but I'll get you one as soon as I'm out of here. Will you marry me, Heidi Sullivan? Be my wife, my partner, my guardian angel," I propose. "You're the best thing that's ever happened to me, and I can't bear the thought of not having you beside me every day until the day that I die."

Her tears stream down her face as she looks at me. I can tell she's slightly stunned at my sudden proposal. So much has happened in the past couple of days, I'm sure she wasn't expecting anything like this to happen.

I wasn't either, but given the circumstances, I have no doubt this is the right decision.

"Can you please lie back down?" she finally asks, ignoring my question.

She didn't say yes–but she also didn't say no. I frown, wondering what this means exactly.

"Please, Cal," she insists, taking me gently by the shoulder and helping me lie back on the bed. The adrenaline is washing away, and the pain is coming back at full force, so I do as I'm told, but my eyes never leave her face.

Once I'm tucked under the blanket, Heidi leans down and places a kiss on my lips. It's a tender kiss, but filled with emotion. Her wet cheeks brush against mine, and I feel how cold her skin is.

Then she pulls away, her blue eyes taking me in. "Nothing would make me happier than marrying you, Cal Duncan," she finally tells me. She walks around to the other side of the bed where there's more room, pulls the sheet up, and lies beside me. "We'll–we'll talk about it again when you have had time to recover from almost dying, okay?"

I wrap my arms around her immediately, afraid that she'll vanish if I don't. She doesn't seem to want to go anywhere other than here. This is where she belongs. With me.

"You won't be able to go back on your word, hear me?" I warn her in a joking tone, squeezing her slightly.

"You're out of your mind, Cal."

Just having her here causes me to suddenly feel a hundred times better. She's the only medicine I need. Nothing hurts anymore now that I have Heidi close to me. It makes me want to laugh when I realize how head over heels I am for her. I never once considered myself lucky enough to be able to find someone to share my life with. Then Heidi appeared, and everything I thought I knew changed.

"I don't want to go back on it," she states firmly.

"Good," I murmur, leaning forward to claim her lips.

Our tongues dance together, slowly at first, but then the room seems to heat up. My hand is on Heidi's ass before I know it, pressing her against my side, since I can't turn to face her. Her right leg is on top of me, her knee brushing against my hardness. It's excruciating not to be able to move more, but I'll have enough time to enjoy her for the rest of our lives. For now, I'll take what I can get from her.

Heidi moans against my lips, scooting closer to me as if she wants to close the little space left between us.

"I can't believe you're here," I whisper against her mouth.

"Me neither. I was firm on my decision to leave you," she informs me with a mischievous smile on her face.

I squeeze her ass tighter.

"And I'll make sure to punish you for it," I reply.

"Yeah?" She raises her brows at me. "How will you punish me?"

I sneer, pecking her lips again. "You'll see."

"Hmm." She looks up at the ceiling in contemplation. "I wonder how a mafia boss punishes people who go against his wishes."

I tilt my head to the side, cursing myself for being shot in the stomach. I wish I could show her right here and now exactly what I meant by that. "Don't tease me, sweetheart. I might have been shot, but I'm not dead," I tell her in a playful tone. "I also have a very good memory, so I won't forget the torture you're putting me through now."

"Is that so?" She finds my crotch and grips my hard length through my pants, making me hiss and curse. She starts stroking me up and down. My eyes roll to the back of my head, and I lean back on the pillow, just enjoying how great she makes me feel. I make a mental note to make sure I pay her back for this.

We don't get to finish what we started because of my condition and also because my stupid stomach starts hurting again, but I keep Heidi beside me, enjoying the time we have to ourselves before the doctor comes back to check on me.

I try to order her to go back home so she can rest properly, but she tells me to shut up, affirming she won't leave my side until I'm clear to return to the city myself.

We start discussing all of our plans for the future–where we want to live, what the wedding is going to be like, when we'll hold the ceremony, and who we're going to invite. Her eyes sparkle every time she shares her dreams and plans, telling me she's had it all figured out ever since she was a teenager.

"You can do whatever you want, my Irish Queen," I promise her, placing a kiss on her forehead.

Heidi narrows her eyes, confused with her new nickname. "Irish Queen?" she repeats, sounding genuinely curious.

I shrug. "Well, you're the queen of the Irish Kings now. I used to call you Bookgirl before, so… I guess you've been promoted."

Heidi laughs. "It does sound like a promotion… Irish Queen." She rolls the words on her tongue as if evaluating how they sound and how she feels about it. "You know, I kind of like it. It's powerful and sexy."

"Exactly like you," I state, pulling her into a hug. "I love you."

49

———

ROUTINE

Two months later...

Cal's recovery wasn't fast, but he did heal faster than the doctor thought he would. A couple of days after he was shot, he was allowed to be moved back to his apartment, which made it easier for me to take care of him. His place is close to everything, and I could come and go to grab groceries and also visit my grandparents every once in a while.

Eventually, I had to tell them about Cal and that we were not only in love, but getting married, and they made me promise I'd take Cal to visit them. But Cal offered something else instead, and we all ended up going on a small trip so they could get to know each other.

Needless to say, Grandma and Grandpa love him. They couldn't stop smiling and were elated that I finally had someone to share my life with. I guess this is what they wanted the most for me.

Adjusting to Cal's apartment was also a struggle at first. I had few things to take with me since I didn't buy a lot after the fire, but he basically forced me to buy new stuff, so I spent two days going to the mall to find a new wardrobe and also get things for the house to add a woman's touch. He told me to make it my own, but I honestly loved it as it was, so I only bought a plant and a couple of items I needed to begin the library he said he'd build for me in one of the spare rooms.

Some other things also changed. Despite being hesitant at first, I demanded to know everything about his businesses and what it actually meant to be a part of the mafia. Surprisingly, I had to admit that it made me somewhat excited. Not the part where he had to deal with guns and enemies invading his bars and shooting everyone for a living, but the part where he had to make sure no one from the cartel ever decided to come back looking for revenge again.

Organically, I found myself becoming more and more familiar with the syndicate to the point I offered to help him turn a few of his establishments into legal businesses where we could try to earn more revenue since we wouldn't be losing a lot of money on shitty deals. So, I'd stop at his office every once in a while to take a look at what I could do and how I could help to make sure we were protected from enemy cartels. It also became a way for me to be closer to him and keep an eye on him while he recovered completely.

Now, he's almost fully recovered. There's only a few small conditions the doctor is still requesting from him, but Cal has proven to be an easy patient, despite all my fears.

In his office, I'm checking some contracts he had with this "firm" in Miami when the door opens. I look up from the leather chair behind his desk, my feet casually crossed on top of it.

Cal walks in, slamming the door behind him. He's wearing a black suit today because of an important meeting he had to attend, and I'm equally dressed up since I asked to join him to learn more about the business. He takes me in from the head to my heels, spending a little longer on my cleavage, which is not as on display as he'd like, but even I have to admit this dress makes me look sexy, showing enough of my collarbones and pushing up my breasts.

"Have I mentioned how fucking hot you look today?" he murmurs, crossing the room in two strides.

I raise my brows and smirk at him. "Twice, if I don't count this last one," I reply.

"When I asked you to marry me, I never thought you'd also become this bossy queen, full of ambition," he points out, sitting on the edge of the desk and looking down at me.

I shrug. "Well, I just want to make sure we're not bothered by those assholes again. And if I can help you make some of our money legal, so I can spend it without fear, why not?" I joke, tossing the papers I'm holding on the desk and standing.

Cal pulls me to him, spreading his legs so I can fit between them, and I wrap my arms around his neck. "So, what did you think of the meeting this morning?" he asks, his eyes momentarily darting to my lips.

I grin at him, leaning forward to kiss him. "It was amazing," I reply against his mouth, then I deepen our kiss, tightening my arms around him.

His grip on my waist strengthens, too, and he pulls me closer to him. This has become a routine for us. I guess it's also one of the perks of coming to his office so often. I get to have a piece of the mafia boss all to myself.

At home, Cal is my man, but here, he's a lot more than that. These men will do whatever he says at the drop of a pin. And that makes him… hotter. Sexier. He's *the Boss*.

Cal stands and pushes me backward until my back hits the wall. He doesn't break our kiss while his hand reaches for the zipper of my dress. I gasp against his mouth, anticipating what he's about to do.

He gets it off effortlessly, not even bothering to look. His hand finds the hem of my panties, sliding beneath the lace and finding me wet and desperate for him.

"Shit," he whispers while he slides his fingers up and down my slick folds. I groan, rolling my eyes as he touches me.

Slowly, I start rocking my hips back and forth as he pleasures me. A moan escapes when he inserts two fingers inside me, thrusting them in and out until I begin to see stars. My walls throb around him as I reach climax, and my hands grip his shoulders, looking for some sort of support. My legs are wobbly and threatening to give out, so I grab onto him so I don't fall.

"You're so fucking hot, sweetheart," he murmurs against my ear, his fingers still working inside me.

I don't bother to answer, allowing myself to fully enjoy this moment. Cal waits for me to compose myself, my breathing becoming more regular, before taking his fingers out and licking them clean. It's so fucking sexy that it's all I can do not to undress him right here, right now. But we still have work to do.

"I actually came here to give you a gift," he tells me suddenly.

I reach down and grab my dress off the floor, slipping it back on, and he zips it for me.

"Wasn't that the gift?" I joke, pecking his lips in appreciation.

"Not really, but if you want to give me points for it, I won't refuse," he replies with a smile. But when he pulls a little box out of his pocket, I frown with confusion.

"You already bought me a ring," I remind him, raising my hand in front of his face to show the huge diamond ring he got me a week after he proposed to me.

Cal chuckles, shaking his head. "This is not a ring."

He hands me the little box and waits for me to open it.

I don't know what it can be, so I have no idea why my heart is beating so fast. I pull the lid off the small box and find a key inside. "What is this for?" I ask, looking up at him. I already have the keys to his apartment–that is now ours–so I have no clue what this could be for.

Cal doesn't answer me, instead taking me by the hand and walking out of the office. "Why don't we go find out?" he suggests. His tone is full of amusement, and it's clear that he's enjoying this way too much. I hate surprises, but he always seems to be able to impress me–in a good way--so I can't complain.

"Come on, Cal," I press as he guides me out of the bar and toward his car, which is parked in the alley. "Can't you give me at least a hint? This isn't fair," I whine.

But he shakes his head, circling the car to the passenger's door. He pulls it open for me, gesturing for me to get inside in an extravagant gentleman pose. "Miss…" he muses with a huge smile on his lips.

I smirk, rolling my eyes and feigning annoyance. "No more '*my queen*'?" I tease.

"You're all of that to me, sweetheart," he replies, kissing me again. "I promise, you'll love it," he adds, and I finally climb inside the car.

5 0

───────

UNTIL THE END OF TIME

Heidi

Cal drives us through the city, but I don't recognize the path he's taking until he stops in front of the exact same store in Greenwich Village that I had my eyes on for weeks when I was searching for a place to rebuild Sullivan's Bookstore. At first, I frown, wondering what we're doing here. It's a tease, honestly. My heart beats fast when I look at the front window and realize it is no longer for sale. I don't want to assume anything, so I turn to look at Cal, who has the biggest grin on his face. "What is this?" I ask, just to make sure I'm not crazy.

After Cal was shot, I kind of set the idea of having a new bookstore aside. I focused on helping him recover, then having my things moved to his apartment, and after all of that was settled, I turned my attention to learning his businesses instead of going back to my own profession. I was frustrated and disappointed at everything failing in that department, so I simply ignored it.

Until now.

Seeing this store brings back all those thrilling, yet devastating, emotions. The idea of having my grandparents' shop up and running again has me excited for the future and the possibilities of what I can create with it this time, adding my own touch to it. But I've been hampered by the difficulties of finding a new storefront. New York City real estate is cut throat.

"Isn't this the store you loved?" Cal raises his brows at me.

I nod, not sure I can speak.

"Well, it is all yours now," he tells me, and he's just as excited as I am. I love him for it. Knowing he has my back and supports all of my dreams means everything to me.

"Are you for real?" I blurt, excitement coursing through me.

Cal nods in confirmation, and I let out a squeal, rushing to open the door.

I hear him following, but I'm so focused on gripping the key he gave me that I don't bother to look back and make sure he's coming, too. "Oh, my God, oh, my God, oh, my God!" I repeat as I insert the key in the lock and hear it click, revealing the inside of the shop.

Everything inside has changed. So much so that I barely recognize it. It used to be a boutique before, but now all the shelves and furniture are gone, leaving it completely empty for me to fill it with whatever I want.

I'm already thinking about the design. I wander around the place, staring at the walls that I'm definitely going to cover with a new wallpaper. I also know where I want the shelves to be, the small lounge for people to read and spend some time in–maybe with a coffee bar– and the check-out counter.

"You really bought this for me?" I turn to look at Cal, who is standing behind me with a proud expression on his face.

"Yes, I did," he replies. "You told me you loved it but couldn't afford it, so..."

"I couldn't afford it," I emphasize. "I still can't. And you shouldn't be spending your money on me like this."

"*Our* money," he corrects me, taking a step forward. He wraps his hands around my waist and gently pulls me toward him. "Everything that I own belongs to you as well, Heidi. You're my family, there's no such thing as 'my money'. Hear me?"

I nod, still a bit uncomfortable with all of this. I know Cal doesn't care about money as much as one might think he does, and I understand where he's coming from because I wouldn't want him to think anything I have isn't his. But still, I feel like I'm taking advantage of him for some reason, and even though this is something I need to work on, I'm still not there yet.

"So that you don't feel completely dependent on me, you can use the insurance money to furnish the space and purchase your inventory," he continues. "And if you find yourself short of money to finish it, I'm happy to help however I can."

"Thank you," I tell him honestly. "Really, I'm so happy you managed to get this place. I was so in love with it the moment I saw it. I can't believe it's going to be my new bookstore soon!" I exclaim, stepping away from his embrace and returning to my inspection. I have so many ideas running through my mind that I can't wait to start working on. I can't wait to see it done and open to the public.

"I'm happy to be the one to help you fulfill that dream," he says behind me.

I turn to Cal again, wrapping my hands around his neck this time and pulling him in for a kiss.

"I love you," I say against his mouth. "And I can't wait to start the rest of my life with you."

His grip on me tightens as he kisses me again. "Speaking of which, the wedding is approaching, and you still have a lot of things to decide," he reminds me.

We decided to wait until fall to get married. I have a lot of ideas, but I still have a ton to do, including picking out my wedding dress. "Ugh, I know…" I murmur, rolling my eyes.

"Did you really just roll your eyes at the mention of our wedding?" he asks, but his tone is teasing and playful.

"It's just that now I can't think of anything else other than opening the bookstore," I explain. "You should have waited until the wedding to tell me you bought it. So, technically, it's your fault."

"Ha," Cal scoffs. "I can take the key back and give it to you in… what, eight months? Maybe nine? This way the wedding will be over by then, and you can focus on the store."

I narrow my eyes at him. I know he's teasing me, but I can't even imagine returning to my normal life knowing that I have an entire store to build and decorate. "You wouldn't dare. And I can take care of both things," I say, determined. "You won't be seeing as much of me in the office, though."

He smirks. "That will be torture but will also keep me anxious to get home sooner so I can see you. Besides, the guys will be relieved to know you won't be visiting as often."

"What?" I squeak, surprised. "What do you mean? They don't like it when I show up?" My jaw drops in shock. I never once thought they didn't like me being around.

"It's not like that." Cal shrugs, and clears his throat to try and explain. "It's just that, you know men… they like to be assholes sometimes without being judged, and with you there, it feels like they're just naughty kids who are being watched by their mother."

"Oh, my God! You never told me that before. I feel so stupid now for invading their space," I retort, bitter. And a little mad, as well.

"Come on," Cal muses, pulling me against him. "You're not *always* there, anyway. Not to mention, I'm the boss, so my opinion is the only one that counts. I'm just saying they will be delighted to know they don't have to watch their language anymore. I, on the other hand, am not as happy. I will miss having you beside me, acting all sexy and bossy during the day."

"Really? You're not just saying it to please me?"

The power he has to make me melt with everything he says still astonishes me. I'm putty in his hands so much that it scares me sometimes.

"Of course," Cal agrees, a mischievous grin appearing on his face. I feel his hard length against my core and widen my eyes at him.

"We're in the middle of the store!" I scold.

"So?" He shrugs, walking me backward toward the spare room to our left. "This is the best way to celebrate your new ownership, isn't it?"

"How can you be so horny all the time?" I ask him, but truth be told, I'm trying my best to feign indifference and act hard to get because the idea of having sex on the floor of my new shop is somewhat enticing.

"How can I not be? Have you seen my woman?" he teases, kissing my neck. "She's fucking hot."

Desire pools at my core, and I strengthen my hold on his neck, supporting myself as he guides me backward. "You're helpless," I note, finally surrendering to his touch.

"And you're perfect. And I love you. And I can't wait to see you walking down the aisle. I can't wait to have a bunch of mini yous running around the house. I can't wait to wake up next to you every day for the rest of our lives," Cal whispers, kissing me in different places every time he adds a new wish to his infinite list.

I chuckle, a joy bubbling up within me so foreign I hardly recognize myself. It's overwhelming, but in a good way. Meeting Cal was the best thing that has ever happened to me. Sometimes, I can't even believe he's mine. Life has changed so much for me, and if someone told me this is how it was going to be, I wouldn't have believed them.

But now that I have him, I can't imagine it being any other way.

Being the Irish Queen will be difficult at times, but with Cal at my side, I know we can do anything.

51

AN IRISH GOODBYE

Cal

The Basilica of St. Patrick's Old Cathedral hums with excitement. Murmurs from the intimate crowd waiting in the pews whisper through the air, rising to the impressive ceilings as sunlight fans through the stained glass.

I'm sweating balls in the tuxedo Tony insisted I wear. It fits like a glove–perfectly tailored–which Tony said was because his tailor is Italian, and they always know best.

In fact, Tony's wife, Chloe, and her mob wife minions put this wedding together for us down to the smallest detail. I don't know half of the gathered crowd, but judging by the cheetah print and hair gel, most of these people are Saints in some way.

The Irish Kings stand out, however, because they're lining every exit–armed to the teeth.

Tony stalks over to where I'm standing near the altar waiting for the ceremony to begin. He glances around, leaning in to say, "I've got guys outside."

"Thanks," I grumble, tugging at my tie.

He looks toward the crowd. I know he feels the same way I do about this very public spectacle. Not only are we prime targets for other crime families, but the feds are probably stationed nearby, waiting for any one of us to do something worthy of an arrest.

I check my watch for the thousandth time. Tony is the only one standing beside me. Heidi keeps her circle small, and while she's made friends with some of the Irish Kings' wives and girlfriends over the past few months, she decided to ditch the notion of bridesmaids.

She's not a fanfare type of woman. We nearly eloped, actually, and in retrospect, that may have been a better idea than having a church wedding in the center of Manhattan with a reception at the Ritz to follow, but here I am regardless, waiting on my bride, praying shots don't start firing the second she starts walking down the aisle.

I lean into Tony, whispering, "Any news about the Russian problem?"

"The Triads made it sound worse than it was," Tony grumbles. "Whoever this Oleg character is, his faction within the Russian mob is closed off. He's moving in secret and not disturbing my territory by any means. It sounds like his issues are completely internal."

My brows raise. "Nothin' like a little infighting to keep things interesting, I guess."

Tony chuckles at the same moment organ music starts to wail, cutting through the whispered conversations taking place in the pews.

Tony hops down from the platform and moves toward his family, standing beside his wife and children in the front row.

The doors swing open, revealing a vision in white lace, escorted toward me with her grandparents on either side.

Heidi looks like something out of my wildest dreams. I feel almost giddy, unable to stop the delirious smile spreading from cheek to cheek as she beams at me, tears in her lovely eyes. Her dress is stunning—a true work of art—but it's not what I expected her to wear by any means. I imagined her in silk, something simple that highlighted her curves. Better yet, something I could easily get my hands beneath on the ride home from the reception after an evening spent dying to touch her, to taste her, to hold my *wife*.

This dress screams the Italian wives got ahold of her and dragged her to their seamstress of choice.

She looks like a princess.

I smile, shaking my head as she nears, her veil trailing behind her as the women in the crowd ooh and awe.

"You take care of her, you hear?" her grandpa says, shaking my hand before kissing Heidi's cheek, tears gleaming in his eyes.

Her granny is too beside herself to even function and is led back to the pews without saying much other than that she loves Heidi, and me, of course. I've become a family favorite, the sweet Irish boy who flirts with the old ladies at their retirement community in exchange for hard candy and cookies, much to Heidi's annoyance and everyone else's amusement.

Her family doesn't know what I really do, and we mean to keep it that way. I bought us a brownstone, preparing to welcome in the next phase of my life as a husband and father. Our kids might figure out where the money comes from one day, but today…

"Look at you," I whisper against her veil, ignoring the fact we have a crowd of people and a priest watching us. Heidi blushes, trying to look unfazed. "What're you wearing under all those layers of lace?"

"You told me you'd be on your best behavior today, Cal," she whispers, trying and failing to shoot daggers up at me.

"You look beautiful," I tell her, pressing a kiss to her temple.

"So do you," she echoes as the priest begins to ramble to the crowd.

I steal a glance over my shoulder, wondering how many steps it'll take me to get from the altar to the door with Heidi and her giant dress in my arms.

"Want to get out of here? I know a place."

"Oh, yeah?" she says, her voice hushed.

"It's this seedy little Irish bar. No frills. Your shoes might stick to the carpet, and the bartender's missing some teeth, but it has the best pours of Guinness this side of the Atlantic."

"Do you take all the girls there?" she teases.

"Just one." I look into her eyes. "Just my wife."

She squeezes my hand, turning her head toward the priest.

Hours later, full of champagne, I pick my way through the crowded, upscale ballroom in search of my bride. Music blares as the reception shifts from quiet elegance to an all-out party, with the Saints and Kings dancing and mingling like we haven't been at war against each other as much as we've been allies.

I spot Heidi teetering in her heels as she mingles. She senses my presence and looks up, locking eyes, and smiles.

It was a beautiful wedding; money well spent.

Now, I'm ready for an Irish Goodbye.

"No one will even know we've left," I whisper against her temple while carrying her out to a car parked around the corner from the hotel. People walking in the street stop to look at us–a bride and groom making their grand escape–and shout congratulations or cheer.

I ignore them, throwing the back door open and shoving her and her dress inside. The driver turns his head, asking where we'd like to go.

"Home," Heidi and I say at the same time, and he rolls up the partition.

"I love you," she says breathlessly as I slide in beside her, slamming the door.

"I love you–"

"Please, for the love of God, help me get out of this dress."

THE END

ALSO BY BELLA MOONDRAGON

The Alpha King's Breeder series:
Bought by the Alpha: The Alpha King's Breeder Book 1
Loved by the Alpha: The Alpha King's Breeder Book 2
Lost by the Alpha: The Alpha King's Breeder Book 3
Luna of the Alpha: The Alpha King's Breeder Book 4
Legacy of the Alpha: The Alpha Kings's Breeder Book 5
Daughter of the Alpha: The Alpha King's Breeder Book 6
Descendants of the Alpha: The Alpha King's Breeder Book 7
Shadow of the Alpha: The Alpha King's Breeder Book 8
Son of the Alpha: The Alpha King's Breeder Book 9
Spare of the Alpha: The Alpha King's Breeder Book 10
Claimed by the Alpha: The Alpha King's Breeder Book 11
Atonement for the Alpha King: The Alpha King's Breeder Book 12
Rejected by the Alpha: The Alpha King's Breeder Book 13
Abducted by the Alpha: The Alpha King's Breeder Book 14
Wolf Shifter Fairy Tale Retellings series
Beauty and the Alpha Beast
Sleeping Beasty
Tangling With the Alpha
The Luna's Vampire Prince series:
The Culling
The Kingdom
The Conquered
Pregnant With Four Alphas' Babies
Chosen As the Breeder

Mated to Four Alphas

Threats Against the Breeder

At War for the Breeder

The Stolen Breeder

Four Alphas, Four Babies

Becoming the Luna Queen

Descendants of the Breeder

Desired by the Devil series

Whispers of the Devil

Banter of the Devil

Murmurs of the Devil

The Mafia Kings series

Indebted to the Mafia King

<u>Loved by the Mafia King</u>

Claimed by the Mafia King

Secrets of the Mafia King

Burned by the Mafia King

Kidnapped by the Mafia King (coming soon!)

Dark Stalker Romance series

Tempted by Sin

Fated to Sin

Secret Billionaires series

Finding the Secret Billionaire by Olivia Bhelle Kildare

Falling for My Secret Billionaire by Bella Moondragon

Driven by the Secret Billionaire by ID Johnson

Wolf Shifter Alpha Kings series

Ravens and Ruins

Sundrops and Shadows

Snowflakes and Sabotage

The Vampire King's Feeder series

Claiming the Alpha's Daughter

Loving the Alpha's Daughter

Finding the Alpha's Daughter

Bewitching the Alpha's Son (coming soon!)

Writing as B. Moon

The Boy Who Died

Sign up for Bella's newsletter here.

Or get a free novella from The Alpha King's Breeder series when you sign up here:
The Beta and the Maid

Follow Bella on Facebook here.

Follow Bella on Bookbub here.